"COULD I . . .
WHAT ABOUT A KISS FOR LUCH

When George stared at her, she explaine[...] the sort of thing your Benedetti cousin might say.

"Well. For the sake of getting into the role, then." In a second, he had dropped his evening gloves on the floor, crossed the room, and taken her face in his hands.

As she caught her breath, he lowered his head and pressed his lips to hers.

It was a sweet brush, a slow savor of mouth upon mouth. She shut her eyes and tried to think of nothing else in the world, to sink into the sensation and wrap herself in its boldness.

It was not so easy to turn off her thoughts.

What did she hope would happen? Would the world shift? Would he drop to one knee again and offer her a ring under his own name? Would his heart pass into her keeping? Would hers become his?

Books by Theresa Romain

Season for Temptation

Season for Surrender

Season for Scandal

Season for Desire

Fortune Favors the Wicked

Passion Favors the Bold

Lady Rogue

Lady Notorious

Published by Kensington Publishing Corporation

LADY NOTORIOUS

THERESA ROMAIN

ZEBRA BOOKS
KENSINGTON PUBLISHING CORP.
www.kensingtonbooks.com

ZEBRA BOOKS are published by

Kensington Publishing Corp.
119 West 40th Street
New York, NY 10018

All Kensington titles, imprints, and distributed lines are available at special quantity discounts for bulk purchases for sales promotion, premiums, fund-raising, educational, or institutional use.

Special book excerpts or customized printings can also be created to fit specific needs. For details, write or phone the office of the Kensington Sales Manager: Attn.: Sales Department. Kensington Publishing Corp., 119 West 40th Street, New York, NY 10018. Phone: 1-800-221-2647.

Zebra and the Z logo Reg. U.S. Pat. & TM Off.

First Printing: March 2019
ISBN-13: 978-1-4201-4545-8
ISBN-10: 1-4201-4545-2

ISBN-13: 978-1-4201-4546-5 (eBook)
ISBN-10: 1-4201-4546-0 (eBook)

10 9 8 7 6 5 4 3 2 1

Printed in the United States of America

Chapter One

On night watch, this was the hour when anything seemed possible but nothing seemed likely to happen.

The longcase clock in the study had just struck one in the morning. Cassandra Benton heard it through the closed door, mere feet away from where she hid in the shadows beside the main staircase of Deverell Place.

This watch was a nightly ritual, one she'd adopted along with the guise of housemaid when she'd been hired a week ago under false pretenses. What with keeping up the daily duties of a maid and shadowing Lord Deverell each night until he went up to bed, she'd hardly slept since then.

Ah, well. One couldn't expect infiltrating a Mayfair household to be effortless.

One could, however, wish something would happen to break up three to four hours staring at a shut door. Her twin brother, Charles, always got the more interesting parts of a job. Placed as a footman due to his height, he could move around anywhere in the house. Their employer had asked Charles to keep an eye on the safety of the ladies of the family: his lordship's two half-grown daughters, plus her ladyship. In theory, this meant dignified vigilance.

In practice, Cass kept up the dignified vigilance in her maid's garb, and Charles disappeared for long afternoons alone with pretty Lady Deverell, the earl's much younger second wife.

She'd no idea where her fool of a brother was now, but finally, her own nighttime vigils had begun to yield results. The most interesting had been two nights before, when Lord Deverell, wearing worry like a mask on his dissipated features, had welcomed an associate to drink with him at midnight. Cass hadn't recognized the caller, but from her hiding spot, she'd memorized his features before the two men closed themselves into the study. She'd risked listening at the door after that, catching only one word out of every few. But she had caught the hush, the worry, the change in mood as they'd mentioned the special term: *tontine*.

That was why Cass was here, and Charles, too. George, Lord Northbrook—son and heir of the Duke of Ardmore— had hired the Bentons privately to learn more about this tontine, a wager placed decades before. And to make certain nobody died as a result of it.

Privately, Cass thought it was likely to be no more dangerous than any of the wagers noblemen were constantly placing. But for the exorbitant fee of five pounds a week, she'd hold her tongue and keep her eyes and ears open for Lord Northbrook.

So far tonight, the darkness pressed heavy, and the silence in the house was a weight. There was nothing to see but the faint outline of the study door, traced by the light of the candles within, and the great snaking spiral of the staircase stretching up overhead. Nothing much to hear, either, save for the crystalline clink she knew to be decanter against glass, decanter against glass. The earl liked his spirits strong and plentiful. Though for a while now, there had been no sound at all. Perhaps his lordship had gone to sleep, the lucky old dog.

She shifted against the wall, easing creaks and pops out of her spine. Being a housemaid wasn't a good cover identity. It was far more labor than investigating, and she didn't even perform the work all that well. If she did, her nose wouldn't be tickled with dust right now. But who had time to wipe down every baluster and newel post and bit of trim on the handrail—especially when there was an earl who needed to be observed?

She settled more deeply into the shadows, pinching at her nose to hold back a sneeze.

Then the screaming began.

Cass tipped her head. "That's odd," she murmured.

Screaming at one o'clock in the morning was always odd, but in this case, it was particularly so. The screaming was not coming from the study in which his lordship had sequestered himself, unaware of possible threats to his life. It was coming from upstairs.

And it was hardly the slurred baritone of a drunken lord faced with a pistol or stiletto. This scream was that of a woman, probably Lady Deverell from the timbre of it.

As Cass strained to hear, the scream changed from wordless panic into a call for help. *He's fallen,* it sounded like the voice was shrieking. *He's fallen!*

Oh. That meant the scream wasn't odd at all. Cass blew out a breath, relaxing back against the wall.

All that had happened was that Charles had fallen out the window. Again.

She was certain of this not because of a miraculous connection between the minds of twins, but because of past experience. Her brother, sometime Bow Street Runner and incorrigible flirt, was notorious for conducting affairs in an impractical way. He fancied himself a Robin Hood, or Romeo, or some other disastrous creature starting with an R who pursued women he ought not and climbed about on the outside of buildings. Charles found it romantic—another disastrous R—to climb up and down ivy or trellises when conducting an assignation, instead of using stairs like a normal adulterer.

Lady Deverell's calls for help hadn't yet shut off, which meant that not only had Charles fallen and startled her, but he had probably hurt himself when he fell.

Hell.

By now footsteps were thumping as the servants were roused and ventured forth from their attic or basement rooms. A door opened at a distance, spilling anxious voices out, and then slammed shut again. The household jerked awake in startled fits.

Cass sidled along the wall, looking up into the dim nighttime heights of the first-floor landing, then back at the still-shut study door. His lordship was foxed, as usual—too foxed to respond to the panicked cries of his wife. This was good, since he wouldn't call Charles out in a duel. Though if a threat on Lord Deverell's life materialized, as Northbrook seemed certain it would, the old fellow wouldn't be able to do much about it except offer brandy to his would-be killer.

Another step sideways as Cass craned her neck to look up the sweeping staircase. Who was passing on the floor above? Was that the butler running toward her ladyship? If she could just get to a better vantage point—

With her next step, she smacked into a person, tall and unyielding.

An intruder! Reflex took over. She pressed her lips together, cutting off a scream, and drove her fist forward hard.

A muffled curse. "Cass," came a whisper. "It's me. George. Northbrook."

Lord Northbrook. She drew back, squinting, as if that would help lighten the shadows. Why had no one lit candles, if they insisted on thundering about the house at night?

"Sorry about that," she apologized. "You caught me by surprise." Her hands were unsteady, and she hid her fists behind her back.

She ought to have expected the presence of the young marquess. Every night near this time, he tried to meet her at this spot beside the stairs so she could share what she'd learned. She always unlocked the front door for him when she took up her post, then secured it again before she went off to bed. It was a process that left her vulnerable, but she carried a pistol and was, as her employer had just learned, effective with her fists.

"I let myself in when I heard screaming," he replied. "After a crash."

"You heard it from outside?"

"The crash was outside. The screams I heard through an open window."

Cass smothered a sigh. "I believe the window is Lady Deverell's, and the crash was my brother, Charles."

"Charles's what?"

"Charles himself. His person."

"What? Was he climbing to her ladyship's window? But why?"

Cass waited a moment while Northbrook's realization sank in.

"Oh. He—*oh*. Well done, Charles," murmured the lord.

The study door remained stubbornly shut, but candle-light now spilled down the stairs along with a clamor of voices. Backlit though Northbrook was by the dim light, Cass could pick out his familiar form. Like her, he was dressed in black, and his face was all hollows and shadows and grim planes. He was scented of citrus, another characteristic she ought to have recognized at once. Whether it was his soap or whether he was uncommonly fond of oranges, she'd no idea. But it was not unpleasant.

Footsteps sounded on the main staircase—close and coming closer. Quicker than thought, Cass grabbed the front of Northbrook's shirt and yanked him into the corner where the staircase met the back of the entrance hall.

Pressed beside her, he whispered into her ear, "How forceful you are, Miss Benton. If you wanted to catch me alone in the dark, you had only to say so."

She hissed back, "Next time I'll be more direct. I'll bash you on the head and drag you off to my lair." Then she covered his mouth with her palm. Double hell! Her hands were bare. Why hadn't she covered her hair and worn gloves? In this darkness, a redhead with pale skin might as well be carrying a lantern about.

Blessed relief; the footsteps halted. "No, he's still in the study," said a woman. "I can see the door. He hasn't even opened it." Cass recognized the voice of the housekeeper, Mrs. Chutley. The elderly woman's knees pained her, and she wheezed slightly when she took stairs.

An indistinct reply followed in a male voice.

"You ought to go on back to bed, Jackson," answered the housekeeper. "He won't need you tonight. Time enough in the morning to tell him—whatever her ladyship wants to tell him."

Mrs. Chutley chuckled, and the man to whom she'd spoken—Lord Deverell's valet—laughed as well. The panic was over, the servants now more annoyed at broken sleep than worried about their mistress. Charles, Cass guessed, was not Lady Deverell's first lover.

A week ago, Cass would have thought it strange that the servants saw to their master using the main stairs instead of the back staircase, which had a door letting directly into the study. Now she knew that the earl's study was sacrosanct. When the door was shut, no one was to enter or even speak to him, on pain of dismissal.

As the housekeeper retreated up the stairs, grunting at the effort of each step, a hot tongue stroked the center of Cass's palm. *Northbrook.* She hissed and drew her hand back, wiping it on her skirts. "My lord! I haven't washed that hand since I cleaned the grates."

Northbrook clapped a hand over his own mouth, gagging.

"Only kidding," Cass whispered back. "I didn't clean the grates today." She really was a terrible housemaid. "But don't *do* things like that. I'm trying to keep you *quiet,* and you'll be no help to either of us if you start licking me."

He smothered a laugh.

"See? You're no help at all." Her palm felt strange, though she'd wiped it. Northbrook had put his tongue to it, hot and sudden, and now it didn't feel like her own hand anymore.

The marquess was silent then, seeming to catch the urgency in her whispers, and held still at her side. She counted the moments off, her back tense against the wall, and waited for whatever would come next. Someone else passing on the stairs? Lord Deverell bursting forth from the study? Charles limping in through the front door, apologizing for causing such a rumpus?

None of those things happened. The candlelight spilling down the stairs was snuffed, the voices dimmed. All that remained was a gold-outlined study door, with silence behind.

No one was going to check on Charles? It seemed not. And no one was going to check on Lord Deverell, either. That closed door was a powerful barrier to his staff.

Cass counted off another minute, each second tediously long, then blew out a breath and relaxed her posture.

"Crisis averted?" Northbrook murmured.

"Hardly," she replied in a low tone. "In fact, there are three crises. A damsel in distress is upstairs, a possibly injured sapskull is outside, and an intoxicated lord who may well be unconscious is in the study. Which would you like to address?"

"You do lead a most exciting life. Rather than account for my presence here, I'll go after your brother." For a tonnish heir, Northbrook was not short of understanding. *Injured sapskull,* he perceived at once, could only be Charles.

"Thank you." Cass bit her lip, looking at the study door. "I should stay here. But it'd seem wrong if I didn't see to her ladyship, wouldn't it?"

"Not at all. Let her lady's maid comfort her. We just heard other servants planning to return to bed; you ought to stay here in case the uproar was all a diversion."

"Caused by Charles? Nonsense. He's part of the investigation." Offering protection to the ladies of the household. Practicing dignified vigilance. Ha.

"The distraction could have been caused by her ladyship," Northbrook pointed out. "A lot of money is at stake in the tontine."

This tontine—what a dreadful affair it sounded. Northbrook had explained it to Cass and Charles when he'd hired them privately the previous week. Part an investment scheme, part a wager, it had been organized forty years before when ten younger sons of the aristocracy had each contributed an equal amount to a certain fund. The interest and principal were left to grow together over the years, untouched, as time reaped the lives of the contributors. When only one survivor of the investment group remained, he would receive the full amount of the fortune.

"A peculiar bet for friends to make," Cass had observed, "since it encourages them to pray for each other's demise."

"Who said they were friends?" Northbrook had replied. "And they arranged to stay in the tontine even if they inherited a title. So these men could also pray for the demise of an elder sibling or other relative in the line of succession."

Not much better.

The conversation had been held in a sky-bright drawing room in Ardmore House, the Duke of Ardmore's London residence. The space was as dainty and pale as a fancy pastry, yet a sense of dread had crept over Cass despite the sunlight and elegance. It was a feeling, honed by experience working alongside Charles for Bow Street, that something was not as it ought to be.

Charles didn't seem to feel the same, for he had asked, "What's the problem, then, after forty years?"

"The problem," Northbrook had replied, looking very tired and rather pale under his shock of black hair, "is that in the first thirty-nine years, only two men died. Their deaths were clearly natural. But in the last year alone, three more of the investors have passed away under mysterious circumstances. I would prefer my father not be next."

Death in men of about sixty years of age was nothing to be surprised about. But the supposedly accidental drowning, shooting, and poisoning his lordship described were, perhaps, out of the realm of both chance and coincidence.

"Would you really prefer his safety?" Cass had asked. "Surely you want to inherit your father's dukedom." No sense in avoiding relevant questions.

"What a horrible thing to say." Northbrook had studied her, then tipped his head. "Yet it's good that you said it. Someone's got to ask that sort of question. And the answer is no, I'm not keen to inherit just yet. Not if it means my father's life is cut short. He's an indifferent father and little better as a duke, but if he dies, he won't have the chance to correct any of that. And I dearly hope he will."

"Hope is nothing to live for," Charles pointed out.

"Fine. Then it's for my own sake. I'm ill-prepared for the responsibility just yet. May my father live to a great old age so I can squander a few more decades in debauchery and play."

Cass had looked at him cautiously. He was handsome, this bright-eyed, black-haired man, and dressed in the height of fashion. He looked much like every other good-looking and careless pink of the ton she'd ever seen. "I can't tell if you're joking."

"I'm always joking a little bit but serious underneath. Once you know that, you can see to my very soul and understand me utterly. It's a great curse."

He said this, of course, as if he were joking, but his blue eyes were deep and worried. She had smiled then, almost.

Yet Northbrook had hired the Bentons to watch not over his father, but Lord Deverell. She pointed this out delicately. After all, he needn't have hired Cass and Charles at all. Unless their hiring was an attempt to divert suspicion from him? Unless . . . unless . . .

Being an investigator was a devil of a job. It was so difficult to shut off the suspicions and questions.

In this case, Northbrook's answer was simple. "I will watch over my father as best I can," said the marquess. "Living in the same household, I'm well placed to do so. I ask you to watch over Deverell because he is my godfather. I have fond feelings for him and should not like harm to come to him."

That made sense. Cass could accept it. And for five pounds a week, she'd watch a chamber pot if she had to, and she'd stifle the question that kept coming to mind: Just how much did the heir truly want his father saved?

She had wondered that throughout the past week; she had also wondered whether the whole story of the tontine was a fabrication. Only when she overheard Lord Deverell discussing it did she relax—slightly—and trust Northbrook's word—cautiously.

But at this moment, with Charles outside and Lord Deverell silently sequestered, Northbrook wasn't being logical. As Cass pointed out to her blue-blooded employer, whispering in the return of nighttime quiet outside the study, "Lady Deverell wouldn't cause a distraction to allow her husband to be harmed. She will not benefit from the tontine if Lord Deverell is killed."

Northbrook was only deterred for a second. "Unless she's formed an alliance with some other interested party. We already know she is willing to form an, ahem, alliance with your brother."

Damn. He made a decent point. He even used the magic word *unless*. "You think like one of us," Cass granted.

"I will take the compliment with admirable grace."

She wasn't sure if it was a compliment at all, but she let

that pass. "I'll keep to my post. Thank you for seeing to my brother."

"Of course." When Northbrook stepped forward, the light about the study door traced the determined line of his jaw. He hesitated, looking down at Cass. One hand lifted, stroking Cass's cheek with a touch that was surprisingly tender. "Thank you for seeing to my godfather."

Her skin prickled; her lips parted—but before she could speak, he slipped back out the way he'd come.

And the interlude was over. The watch upon the study door resumed. Now, due to the fracas upstairs, there was every reason for Cass to be up and about. She could leave her hiding place in the shadows.

Her first step was locking the front door. Treacherous hands; they were still unsteady as they wrestled with the great key. At last, she clicked the lock into place. With fingertips that trembled, she touched the spot on her face that still tingled from Northbrook's touch.

The caress was odd, that was all. It was but another oddness in tonight's string of them. She and Northbrook worked well enough together when they had to, but they were certainly not friends. They shared no tender feelings, nothing more than a tie of business.

He'd seen to that the first time they met. It had been at the home of their mutual friends, Lady Isabel Jenks—noble by birth—and her husband, the former Bow Street Runner Callum Jenks. They'd been discussing some case, and Northbrook, who was there merely for pleasure and whose opinion had not been solicited, gave it all the same.

"She's so *plain*," he'd said of Cass.

And he so handsome. It had hurt to overhear that.

But he'd begged her pardon, and she'd set him straight about her capabilities, and he'd begged her pardon again. They'd worked together well enough since then.

She touched her cheek again, then shook off her wondering feeling. She'd a job to do, an earl to observe.

It really was not right that Lord Deverell remained completely silent, was it? If he had passed out from drink, he could die of it.

Cass was only feet away and ought to see to her supposed employer. Anyone would be upset by a footman toppling out a window; surely it wouldn't be unusual for a housemaid to speak to the master after the mistress had such a scare. She had the excuse of being new to the household, unfamiliar with his lordship's strict insistence on not being disturbed in the study.

She crept forward, ears drinking in the silence around her, then scratched at the study door. "My lord? It's Polly." Every housemaid here was called Polly. The Deverells found it easier that way to summon one when needed.

No answer to her greeting. She rested her hand on the door handle, easing the latch. "My lord?" she ventured, her voice a bit louder now.

No answer still. And shouldn't the study door have been locked?

Dread prickled between her shoulder blades. Again, something was not as it ought to be.

In one gesture, she flung the door wide and leaped into the room. Her hand slid into her pocket, finding the familiar butt of her pistol.

No answer. No response. No one here.

She looked around to be certain. There was the empty desk, the long velvet sofa with its back to her. The wall of shelved books and ledgers, everything in its place.

But heavy draperies stirred as if there were someone behind them. Seizing a penknife from a desk, she marched to the opposite wall and flung the curtains back.

No one. Nothing. The window was open to the summer

night, that was all. The curtains swayed from the breeze, not human touch.

Peering out, she looked for some sign of Charles. The lamps around Cavendish Square cast a glow bright enough for her to see that the earth outside this window was undisturbed. Much as she should have expected; Lady Deverell's chamber windows faced a different direction. Charles lay, if he still lay on the ground, around the corner and out of Cass's sight.

She left the window sash as it was. When she turned her back to it and again faced the room, she saw the earl.

On the long sofa, designed more for fashion than comfort, Lord Deverell snored. Between his outstretched legs, a stiletto pinned a folded note to the upholstery.

The blade had sliced his thigh, and blood soaked the once-beautiful velvet of the sofa. When Cass stepped closer, the air smelled heavy with the coppery scent of spilled blood, and with the brandy that had pickled the earl so thoroughly that he'd lost himself to sense.

Lord Northbrook had been right: Deverell was indeed in danger. Yet he was snoring right through the ebb of his own lifeblood.

How was Cass to keep a man from getting killed if he was determined to speed the process along?

Chapter Two

As a man of fashion, George used to stay up all night during the season as a matter of course, but he hadn't made a habit of it since his mother's brush with death the previous year. After spending a day and a night and a day with the physician, keeping the duchess alive despite her own best efforts to slip away on a wave of laudanum, George had been ready to fall into bed and sleep the sleep of the righteous.

His mother was in decent health now, though she remained in laudanum's thrall. And eventually, Lord Deverell would be all right, too—thanks, after another endless night, to Cassandra Benton.

He faced Miss Benton over tea in the Ardmore House drawing room in late morning. It was the same day Lady Deverell had screamed the house down, the same day that Charles Benton had tried to play romantic adventurer and fallen from a trellis—but it felt as if days had passed since the countess's cries had split the nighttime silence.

How Miss Benton had passed the hours after their parting, she had already told him: the wounded earl discovered, the physician summoned, the old earl's treatment. It seemed certain Lord Deverell would have bled to death in his stupor if no one had intervened. As it was, he would be all right.

"Or if he isn't, it'll be the brandy that kills him and not the knife wound," Miss Benton said crisply. She was as tired as he, surely, but her bright brown eyes showed no hint of fatigue and her black housemaid's gown was as tidy as her coppery hair. She was the most damnably capable person he'd ever met.

"Have some more tea," George replied. "I certainly will." It was overbrewed and bitter from sitting in the pot this past half hour, but he didn't mind that. It kept his brain alert. Sort of.

"I will, thanks. To your health." She clinked cups with him, then poured each of them another splash of tea. "I resigned my post as a housemaid before I left Deverell Place. Probably I ought to have mentioned that right away. You see, I lost my head when I called for the physician."

"Am I missing something? It rather sounds as if you did *not* lose your head."

"Yes, but a housemaid wouldn't have done what I did. She would have screamed and called for the housekeeper or butler. It was wrong of me to take charge of the situation." As she spoke, she crumbled a lump of sugar slowly into her cup with her fingertips.

"You don't sound the slightest bit sorry." George set down his teacup, giving up on the bracing power of the brewed leaf. "And Lord Deverell is no doubt grateful that you broke character."

"Eventually he might become so. For now, he's displeased that I entered the study while the door was closed." She raised her eyes to the ceiling. "It is his private domain, into which no servant is to intrude. If I hadn't resigned, he'd likely have given me the sack."

"Thus punishing a great favor that happened to accompany a small disobedience," George said. "If it helps, I realize how little sense that makes. But the question is, what shall we do next?"

She lifted her pale brows. "Am I to be involved still? I have other work to do, my lord. Charles's work."

That brother of hers. No one had come from within Deverell Place to check on him; Lady Deverell's screaming seemed to have killed the household's curiosity or humane feelings entirely. George had had the devil of a time getting Charles Benton home and hailing a surgeon to examine him. The false footman had broken one of the long bones in his right leg and wouldn't be up and about for some time.

But he was safe in his rented rooms off of Langley Street, a space that George gathered he shared with his sister. The rambling lodging house had seen better days and was far too close to Seven Dials for George's taste. It was well-kept, though, and despite being awakened in the dead of night, the landlady clucked over Charles like a mother hen.

Once he'd seen Charles settled, George had been sorely tempted to peek into Miss Benton's bedchamber. Manfully, he'd resisted the urge, but the rest of the rooms told a familiar enough story. Good pieces of furniture in the parlor and in Charles's chamber, but all long out of fashion and showing their wear. The Bentons had once had money; now they didn't.

The Godwins—the family name of the Duke of Ardmore—were much the same, thanks to the duke's fondness for gambling. But a duke could always get more credit, and thus he could live in a fashionable house in Cavendish Square and keep a houseful of servants and have a drawing room that looked like the inside of a cloud, if a cloud were also draped in silk and cluttered with elegant furniture and hung all over with those damned oil paintings the duke kept collecting.

George would prefer to have his own household. He had, once. But this arrangement was a compromise, and one that served him well enough. He had room enough in Ardmore House for his experiments, and he came and went as he pleased.

"I grant that your brother's indisposition will dump more responsibilities on your head," George said. "But I have paid for your time until the end of the week. And surely the events of last night—this morning . . . ?"

"I know the time period to which you refer," Miss Benton said drily.

"Yes, right. Well. When a man is stabbed in his own home, and a mysterious note left behind, surely that proves there's something suspicious about this tontine."

Miss Benton had extracted the note pinned by the stiletto that slashed Deverell's leg. It was written in block letters on fine-quality paper: FOUR LEFT. The suspected plot to eliminate members of the tontine was now made explicit.

At least, that was George's interpretation. According to Miss Benton, Deverell had dismissed its significance. He'd argued that it could mean he had four limbs left, or four remaining glasses of brandy in his favorite decanter, or—

"Four pints of blood left in your body," Miss Benton had suggested, but this was regarded as unhelpful by both Lord Deverell and the physician.

George was grateful that Miss Benton had accepted his

own theory. "I see dreadful things all the time," she said now. "Lord Deverell was not stabbed by a well-wisher, but by someone who longs for his end. Yet why would that person let members of the tontine know they are targeted?"

George had to think about that. "Suspicion. Fear. The onetime partners will all become ready to turn upon each other. Already my father has started carrying a pistol."

Miss Benton patted her reticule. "Wise man. I do the same. Yes, those are good reasons indeed. Though they will be wary, they will also all be suspicious and exhausted. And likely to shoot themselves accidentally upon seeing a mouse, thus saving the killer the trouble of going after each."

"You're not wrong." George sighed. "But I wish you were. There is no one so stubborn as noblemen of advancing years."

"You're not wrong either," she replied. "Deverell doesn't want to involve Bow Street. He wants to keep the whole matter private, from the stabbing to his wife's mysterious nighttime visitor."

"Which is why I need you to stay involved in this matter."

Miss Benton shook her head. "Although I failed to keep your godfather safe? I cannot shrug that off and keep my pay as if I've done excellent work."

"I don't blame you for what happened. Surely Lord Deverell doesn't blame you either. Nor do his wife or the physician."

"That doesn't matter to me so much as whether I blame myself. Someone got past my watch, and a man almost died. I'd best be back to Bow Street, where one sees one's foe coming."

She looked as if she were ready to rise—and on impulse, George held out a staying hand. It landed rather long of its mark. Where he intended only to gesture *wait, don't go,* he instead batted one of her knees.

It had the intended effect; she sank back into her seat. True, she also looked at him reproachfully, and she drew her knees in farther.

"Sorry about that," George excused. "I flail sometimes when I'm having a brilliant realization."

"And this was one of those moments?"

"Of course." He schooled his hands into calm, then organized his thoughts. "Here are the most important facts to me. First, you followed your instincts and checked on Lord Deverell's welfare. Second, you called for help at once and saved his life."

She looked as if she were about to speak, and he held up a hand again—less wildly this time. "Third, and most importantly to me, your failure bothers you. It bothers you that you didn't protect him completely, and it bothers you that someone hurt him. Those things bother me, too."

He watched her carefully as he concluded. "You care, Miss Benton, just as I do. Lord Deverell isn't merely a job to me. He's the man who gave me my first rattle as a baby and who taught me to shoot with a bow and arrow when I was far too young to be trusted with sharp objects."

"How old were you?" she asked. It was a stall, clearly. Her brows were drawn together and her head tilted, as though her thoughts were shifting to such a degree that they upset her balance.

"Too young. But I'm a wonderful shot now, so it was all worthwhile. Never mind that, though. Do you see what I mean, Miss Benton? I could hire another investigator, but I couldn't pay someone to care about Lord Deverell as I do. You care, and that makes you the right person to stay on this case."

In the ensuing silence, she took up another lump of sugar with the tongs, then held it up to the light coming through the tall east-facing windows. It sparkled like white sand; sunlight winked off the silver of the tongs. By contrast, Miss Benton was all sunrise colors of gold and copper and peach, with her black gown a sharp shadow. It would be a lovely image to view through his camera obscura, though if he ever fixed it upon paper, all the color would be lost.

But he was getting distracted, maybe staring a bit. When Miss Benton returned the sugar and tongs to the china bowl on the tea tray, the expensive *clink* of silver on Adams dishware snapped him from his reverie.

"Thank you," she said, her attention on the tea tray as if it had been the one speaking. "I had not thought how the matter might seem to you."

"Then you'll stay? Keep to the case?" He held his breath.

She lifted her eyes. "Yes. Through the end of the week at the very least, since you have paid already. Longer than that, if need be, and if you wish it."

"I wish it." He was blurting, he knew—but *God,* it was so good to know she believed him. He wouldn't have to sort out on his own how to protect his father and Lord Deverell and the other fools who'd formed the tontine so long before.

"One point that strikes me as strange," Miss Benton said slowly, "is that everyone in Deverell Place, from scullery maid to the earl himself, knows that Charles paid visits to Lady Deverell's bedchamber. But the earl is now choosing not to admit that."

"Quite natural, it seems to me," George replied. "He's preserving his own reputation. A man never wants to be known as a cuckold."

"True, though his lady seems determined he shall be." Miss Benton leaned forward, propping her elbows on her knees. "It was one scene of drama after another during the night, and it needn't have been. Her ladyship could have said she didn't know what had happened, she'd never seen the man before, he fell from the trellis before he ever reached her window. Instead, she tearfully told her husband that she and Charles had only exchanged kisses before he left."

"You doubt her tale?" Fair enough. George doubted it, too.

"My brother wouldn't climb a trellis only for kisses!" She rolled her eyes. "Well, he might. Charles does love a trellis."

"Never mind the trellis," George said. "Whoever left the note will soon know that Deverell survived, and that person will try again to kill him. You've got to get back into that household and keep watch again."

She slapped her hands on her knees, an unmistakable gesture of farewell. "If I must, but I can't stay any longer at the moment. I need to see how Charles fares, and then I'll go in to Bow Street and talk to the magistrate about covering his cases myself."

"Because you don't want to lose his salary?"

She stood, shaking out her skirts. "Obviously. It is what we live on. If I can do Charles's work while he's unable, the magistrate might not stop his pay."

That was a fair assumption, yet the necessity of it seemed unjust. "You work very hard, Miss Benton."

"And you don't work at all." She stood. "There, we've exchanged obvious observations."

He had to smile. Miss Benton had a beautiful speaking voice. Her accent was undistinguished, neither the swallowed consonants of the wealthy or the blurry vowels of London's working class. But the timbre, oh!—it vibrated through one like the playing of a glass harmonica. Swooping, vibrant, crystalline. She could have insulted him in every way, and he'd have leaned into the sound of her voice on the tips of his toes.

Thus it had gone the first time they'd formally met, too. It was at the Bedford Square house of his old friend, Lady Isabel Jenks—who had married a former Bow Street Runner, Callum Jenks, and assisted him in private investigations. Just recently, Lady Isabel had stepped back from active investigation due to her expectant state; still, one never found more interesting conversation than at the Jenkses' place.

On the occasion when George met Miss Benton, she was in deep conversation with Jenks about disguise. "The ton notices only the clothing of servants," she'd been saying. "If I'm placed among his staff, Wexley won't even realize we've met before."

Wexley. He'd thought the red-haired woman was familiar, and now he placed her. She'd helped rescue Lord Wexley, George's brother-in-law, from an attempted murder at a ball celebrating the man's betrothal to George's sister. It had been a year or more by now, hadn't it? Yet he knew Miss Benton's name, and her face wasn't the sort one forgot.

"Wexley would know her at once," George blurted to Jenks. "She's so plain."

This was, of course, the wrong thing to say. It wasn't even what he'd *meant* to say. Better for him to have called her plainspoken, or plain and straightforward in her manner. Plain of dress, plain of hairstyle; even those would have been marginally acceptable.

Yet what he'd meant was none of those at all. He'd

meant that Miss Benton was not a woman of fashion, so decidedly that she made fashion seem irrelevant. She was so capable that she made chivalry seem like self-indulgence and mannerly words a useless frippery.

Before he had the chance to bumble through any apology or explanation, the lady's head had whipped around. "Jenks," she said sweetly, fixing George with a narrow stare. "You might mention to the gentleman that the front of a lady's face has nothing to do with the brain behind it."

Jenks looked amused, damn the man. "Right. Lord Northbrook—"

"You might also mention," Miss Benton said, "that a woman's appearance has nothing to do with how good an investigator she is."

Jenks tried again. "I was about to—"

"*And,*" she added ruthlessly, "you could note that it is most rude to comment on the appearance of a lady when one's opinion has not been solicited."

Jenks gave up; he simply made a gesture from Miss Benton to George. "You heard the lady."

"Since I heard him, I'll warrant he heard me just as well," Miss Benton sauced back.

Isabel looked as if she wanted to laugh, but she schooled her features almost as soon as George turned suspicious eyes upon her. "Lord Northbrook," Isabel hastened to explain, "is a very old friend."

Miss Benton looked him over. "He doesn't look *that* old." She studied him for a moment, then snapped her fingers. "We've met before. You were at the ball celebrating the engagement of the Duke of Ardmore's daughter."

"I was indeed," George said. "You see, the Duke of Ardmore is my father, which makes his daughter my sister. So I was rather expected to be there."

"Well done, then," she replied, and turned away from him again to pick up the thread of her conversation with Jenks.

And there he was, standing like a ninny. He'd done wrong, and she'd put him in his place, and there was nothing for it but to grovel. "I beg your pardon, Miss Benton." He spoke up. "What I said was flippant and rude."

She did not face him again, but she went very still. The back of her neck looked vulnerable, a pale stripe between the collar of her dark gown and her fiery pinned-up hair. "It was honest" was all she said.

"No, it was flippant and rude," George repeated, trying to explain. "Those are the qualities I've cultivated. Not honesty. I assure you, honesty would get me nowhere in high society."

"Politeness would," Isabel pointed out with all the unhelpfulness of a lifelong friend.

"Men don't have to be polite," said George. "Especially not ducal heirs. But that doesn't mean they shouldn't be. And I should."

The stern posture had relaxed a bit; Miss Benton showed him her profile. "Yes. I agree. And if there's an apology in there—"

"Oh, there definitely is. I apologize for my flippant and rude words that were not at all honest."

"Then I accept it, with the understanding that if you ever insult my person or ignore my intelligence again, I will give you cause to regret it. *Physical* cause."

Strange how soothed he felt by her reply, coupled with a threat as it was. "You intrigue me. But not enough to want to discover what you mean."

With this, she granted him a smile. "Truth be told, Lord Northbrook, you're not the first to call me plain. I suppose I was piqued to have it be your first judgment of me, when surely the Jenkses have told you of my abilities."

"And those are the relevant qualities. Of course."

He hadn't forgotten it since—and not because of her threat. Because he'd been wrong, and she'd been gracious enough not to hold a grudge.

Since that inauspicious meeting, she had stayed with his godfather to make sure the man didn't bleed to death. She'd shared news with George by the stairs each night after toiling all day. She had agreed to continue working for him when she already had so many other jobs to do.

Yes, she was gracious indeed. And she worked damned hard, and he wanted her at his side. On his side.

She was pulling on her gloves now, her expression as distant as if she were already on the way to her next destination. The only reason George had a right to her time was because he'd paid for some of it.

But what to do for the remainder of the week? Would keeping a watch on Deverell be the most effective way to protect him, or would it be better to trace the old earl's attacker? What would be the best way to use Miss Benton's unique skills? Could he even *ask* her to keep watch, burdened as she was by the need to carry out her brother's work?

And then it came to George: the one thing that was more likely to yield answers than spying.

He sprang to his feet, cursing as he barked his shin against the tea table. "Miss Benton. I've an idea. For the rest of the week—or beyond, if need be."

She flexed her fingers in their gloves of tan kid. "You're not planning to ask me to be a housemaid again, are you?"

"No, no." He waved the possibility away. "You were a terrible housemaid anyway."

She laughed, a quick peal too soon cut off.

"We need to cast a wider net," George said. "Collect gossip. You need to be in the midst of the ton, not hanging about its fringes cleaning fireplaces and listening at doors when you can."

"Admirable summary of my time in the Deverell household," she granted. "You pay a good wage, and if it doesn't require me to clean out grates, so much the better. What do you have in mind?"

His idea was coming into focus, like lining up a camera obscura with just the right sort of light. "I want you to listen to gossip. Women talk about all sorts of things when men aren't around, surely, and such secrets might be relevant to this case. Someone saw something, or heard something, or knows something—"

"Yes, but what would you have me do? Parade through Almack's with an ear trumpet? You'd have to get me a voucher, and the proprietresses won't be eager to grant one to ordinary Miss Benton."

"So you'll have to be someone else. Someone fashionable and tonnish. Maybe even a bit fast, so you're always at the center of a swirl of gossip."

She looked much struck by the idea. "A noble by-blow would serve the purpose, maybe. Or shall I have made a scandalous marriage, which I must now escape?"

He grinned at her. "Perhaps both at once. How would you like to pose as my notorious cousin, arrived lately from the Continent?"

Chapter Three

"I don't like this plan, Cass," said Charles. "Not one bit."

Cass had expected her brother to say this; she'd predicted it word for word. She'd even echoed his posture, the crossed arms and stubborn chin, and mouthed it along with him.

Charles was never patient, and being unable to do what he wanted put him in a bad humor. His bedchamber bore every sign of a temper ready to snap, from the broken cake of soap atop his shaving stand to the discarded periodicals beside him on the bed. The room smelled of liniment; expensive, no doubt. The surgeon would have been expensive, too.

And now Charles couldn't work; he could only keep to bed and loudly dislike things.

He did not deserve sisterly compassion, and so Cass replied, "I don't like that you climbed the trellis at Deverell Place and fell off of it. And broke your leg. So, if you don't like Lord Northbrook's plan, we're even."

Stretched out on his bed atop the covers, Charles eyed his right leg—splinted and wrapped and propped on a bolster—with yet more dislike. "I didn't *fall*. The trellis broke. And I was collecting information."

Cass kicked the footboard of her brother's bed. "About Lady Deverell's breasts."

He almost smiled. "Secondary to my main purpose, I assure you."

She glared at him.

Now he did smile. Smirked, really, looking like a smug shark. A smug shark with coppery hair. "Fine, but my main purpose was no *less* important than Lady Deverell's breasts."

The devil of it was that he was perfectly sincere, and annoyingly able to pursue his own pleasures alongside an investigation. Charles's natural gifts with people were far greater than Cass's, and from him she had seen how to shape one's behavior to the situation. He was flirtatious with this person, stern with that one; dull-witted to bring out the superiority of an arrogant witness, then jovial with one who resented the law but wouldn't mind a friendly drink. The sluttish servant was a role, too—though one Charles played with particular relish, it being oriented to his own pleasures.

Just as Lord Northbrook behaved, telling Cass he cultivated rudeness and flippancy for his own enjoyment. Oh, these men.

"I don't have time for this," she muttered. "I have to get back to Ardmore House."

"Why do you have to stay there?" Charles was using his Grumpy Brother voice again.

She smoothed the bedcovers at his feet. "Because a bastard ducal cousin fleeing a marriage gone bad wouldn't stay in a hotel. And before you suggest I stay here at home—no. The Ardmore cousin would certainly *not* stay with a random Bow Street Runner who has a broken leg."

"I still don't like it." Charles's favorite weapon: persistence. It sometimes succeeded when far more dramatic weapons failed. Rather like erosion.

Cass was immune to erosion. She would not be eroded. "It's not as though I'm posing as Lord Northbrook's mistress," she reminded her brother. "I'm to be his fake cousin, and married to boot. I could have a nose like Napoleon and a chin like the Habsburgs for all it matters to his lordship."

She's so plain. Would she never forget those words? But they didn't matter. She'd be plain in silks and satins. Garbed in scandal, the most fashionable cloth of all.

When Charles still looked mulish at this reassurance, Cass realized, "That's not the problem, is it? What Lord Northbrook is planning? You don't fear for my virtue, such as it is. You thought I'd be here to take care of you." She sat at the foot of his bed with a thump that made him howl for his injured leg. "Do have the courtesy to look ashamed of yourself."

"How can I look ashamed when you're sitting on my broken leg? *You* should look ashamed."

"I never touched it. I only sat next to it. And you should know that I have to work, Charles. I can't play nursemaid to you."

He messed about with the stack of periodicals at his side, looking chastened. Almost.

"We were each of us getting five pounds a week from Northbrook for the Deverell House job," she reminded him. "What have you done with your first payment?"

Charles's brandy-brown gaze, so much like her own, slid away.

"Did the surgeon take it?" she pressed.

"No, Northbrook covered the fee. Said it was only right

since I'd broken my leg while working for him. An expense of the investigation."

"Thank the Lord for that." The Duke of Ardmore's financial troubles were legion, but his heir still commanded far greater resources than a pair of fallen gentlefolk who worked for Bow Street. "So, you still have your money?"

Charles picked up a periodical and began flipping through it.

"You'd be far more convincing if you weren't looking through an old issue of *La Belle Assemblée*." The magazines were clearly a gift from their landlady, Mrs. Jellicoe, who doted upon Charles and also collected fashion plates.

But Cass had suspected the answer to her question before she'd asked it—twice. Charles's money had gone for whatever caught his fancy: expensive handkerchiefs, flowers for a pretty lady who winked at him, drinks all around for the Bow Street Runners. Money slipped away from Charles as if it were meaningless. He had always spent like a wealthy person.

She stood again, rummaging through her reticule. "I've still got my fee for the first week, and you'll have to live on it somehow." She eyed Charles's trousers, slit up the right side to accommodate the bracing for his leg. "You'll be needing some new clothing once you're healed, for one thing."

He tossed aside the pictures of spring fashions from three years before. "If you give me your pay, what are you going to live on?"

"Good for you! You finally remembered to ask about my welfare." She pulled out coins by the fistful, raining shillings and pence into the basin upon the shaving stand. She studied the effect, then forced a final coin on end into the broken cake of shaving soap. "While I'm staying at Ardmore House, Lord Northbrook will cover my expenses. And he'll continue paying me at the same weekly rate."

His brow creased. "I still don't like it."

Slam. She slapped the cake of soap down so hard, the coin flipped out of it and went flying. "Don't you? Well, since you've done exactly what you *do* like for the past week"—*and for twenty-six years before that*—"then perhaps this will be good for you. It will expand your mental bounds."

Charles's mouth hung open.

It was so much like hers, his face; all angles and planes. They were the fair spit of each other, their grandmother had often observed, alike from their dark red hair to their strong jaws. With adulthood, Charles had stretched a few inches taller, but his face still mirrored her own. At his stunned expression, at the wounded look in his eyes, Cass felt as if she'd hurt her own self.

Crouching, she felt about on the floor for the fallen coin. When she laid hands on it, she stood again and dropped it into the basin with the other money. "I'll come check on you when I can."

Charles made a thunderous sort of grumble.

"Or"—Cass tried for levity—"I'll see if Janey can come peek in on you."

One of their favorite Bow Street informants, Janey Trewes was a sometime prostitute and frequent pick-pocket. She also sold clothes—sometimes right off her heavily swathed body—and was, overall, the most re-sourceful person Cass had ever known.

Charles groaned. "She'll have the five pounds off me in half a second."

Cass was quite sure he would yield the money, and hap-pily, should Janey slip a hand into his pocket. He had never admitted to tender feelings for her, but his face was an open book whenever the young cutpurse was near. "Then you'll have to ask her for tips on how to survive on one's own."

"Tips from Janey . . ." His cheeks were faintly flushed.

Cass rolled her eyes. "Behave yourself. Remember the old saying: 'Flirt when you have a broken right leg, be impotent forever.'"

"That's not a saying." Turning his head, he eyed her slantwise. "Is that really a saying?"

"It should be."

"Cass!" Leaning forward he tried to cuff her, then fell back against the pillows with a groan. "Where is your sisterly feeling?"

"It fell out the window at Deverell House," she said crisply. "But it had a rollicking good time first."

She left the room then. In her own tidy little bed-chamber, she packed a valise with her essential belongings. She hesitated over her favorite gown. Its deep green cotton print seemed so pretty hanging from a dress hook in this little room, but in the drawing room of Ardmore House, it would look cheap and plain.

Her clothing would never suit the role of a bastard ducal cousin. Perhaps she could say she'd disguised herself as a maid when she made her way to the bosom of her family.

She decided to take the gown, rolling and folding it with a care not even a lady's maid could have matched. She'd be entering a world of silks and satins and subterfuge, and the things Cass Benton liked were of no consequence to that world. But they were of consequence to her, and it would brace her immeasurably to know she had her favorite things around.

Which reminded her: there was one more item she wanted to bring along.

Returning to the small parlor that abutted both bedchambers, she picked up a miniature painting in a gold case. It lived on the mantel, almost the sole ornament to the plain little room.

Cass cradled the painting in her palm, looking at the familiar face done in pigments on ivory, then snapped shut the gold case that protected it. She peered into Charles's room. He was looking at *La Belle Assemblée* again, this time with real interest.

She cleared her throat to draw his notice from the magazine, then held up the gold case. "I'm taking Grandmama with me to Ardmore House."

Charles protested. "Why should you get to take her? She's my grandmother too, you know."

"I do know that. I just . . ." Cass hesitated. "I need something familiar with me."

The little painting, made when their grandmother was a gentleman's daughter hoping for a good society marriage, was all that remained of what had been a generous dowry. Two generations of marrying down had laid waste to the rest.

How the miniature and its case hadn't been sold for bills years ago, Cass didn't know—but she was grateful, and she would never allow it to be sold now. Grandmama was her namesake: a woman she'd never known young, but who had kept the strong-boned attractiveness and good humor so apparent in the miniature until the end of her life. Though she lost a husband and a daughter, though her son-in-law proved inconstant and undependable, she persisted. She provided.

In return, Cass had given her grandmother all her love

and admiration. When the elder Cassandra had died five years earlier, when Cass was twenty-one, she'd felt lost.

But if such loss was the price of love, it was well worth the cost.

So she copied her grandmother's example. She provided, finding a job for Charles and then doing most of the work herself. She would not be dimmed by grief, and she would not be caught with nothing. She might leave behind five pounds, but only because she was going to earn more.

And she would take Grandmama and her favorite gown with her.

"Very well, tuck Grandmama into your pocket," Charles said. "Then come sit and I'll tell you about our cases for Fox."

Cass plunked her valise onto her brother's bed and sank down next to it. "I didn't hit your broken leg. Don't yelp. All right, what have you got going with Bow Street? Something I don't know about?" Sometimes Charles went into court without her, though not often. Cass wasn't an official Runner due to her sex, but the magistrate was happy enough to have her work alongside Charles.

Charles turned the magazine around and showed a page to Cass. "Do you think Janey would look well in a bonnet like that?"

"Not if it was bought using the money I just left you. And Janey could steal a bonnet before you could buy her one."

"She should steal one for you. Your bonnets are always in a state."

"They're not in a *state*. They're just not as fashionable as the ones in *La Belle Assemblée*." She snatched the pages from her brother's hand. "Fox. Bow Street. Cases. What work do you need me to do?"

"Right." His brow creased, a rare troubled expression. "The new one you don't know about. It has to do with the Watch house by that lovely pie shop."

"The one on Hart Street?" She remembered everything that had to do with cases. Or pies. Both in their own way were a matter of survival.

Charles nodded. "I believe he's taking bribes."

She picked at a thread on the bedclothes. "You'd know."

"Unfair! Well, not unfair. But in this case, there's harm being done. Fox thinks girls from the country are offered honest jobs by the watchman, who then takes them to bawdy houses."

"Poor lambs," Cass said grimly. "So he's using their trust in him to betray them." No wonder Charles looked bothered. Even if they sometimes looked the other way or took the occasional bribe, Bow Street Runners held the public trust and safety as sacred.

"Yes, if Fox is right," Charles replied. "To know for certain, we've got to catch the watchman in the act of taking a bribe. I don't suppose you'd like to be a girl from the country in need of help?"

Cass snorted. "Hart Street. That's Felix's watch, isn't it? If he didn't recognize me right off as Miss Benton from Bow Street, it'd be a wonder. And playing one role at a time is enough."

When Charles looked as if he wanted to protest, she lifted a hand. "I'll come up with something. All right?"

The hard set of Charles's shoulders relaxed. As well they should. *I'll come up with something* was a magical phrase that shifted a burden from him to her.

"What else?" she asked.

Nothing else he described was so urgent. The usual round of pockets picked, heads coshed, watches stolen, drunkards bumbling about and breaking things. Simply being in court, ready to dart off as needed at a moment's notice, was an essential part of the job.

"I'm not sure how I can work in court and with Lord Northbrook at the same time," Cass mused.

"Have a twin. That was my strategy for getting twice the work done."

"Well planned. Very good," Cass said wryly. If he'd not had a twin, she wondered just how much he'd ever get done. Maybe without Cass to lean on, he'd have stood a little straighter.

Or maybe he'd have done nothing at all.

"I will try to keep up with these cases," Cass added.

This job for Northbrook was brief; Bow Street was their long-term support. She'd check in with their usual informants, maybe, and use some of her next week's wages from Northbrook to pay them for extra vigilance. Their friend Callum Jenks, a former Runner, had inherited a slew of underworld contacts along with the happy notoriety of closing the case of a theft of gold from the Royal Mint. These contacts were vouched for by Sir Frederic Chapple, a baronet deeply implicated in the theft of the gold sovereigns. Sir Frederic had eventually gone free, but even criminals had consciences.

Some of them. Sometimes.

"And what will you live on while you're shadowing the Watch and play-acting as a ducal cousin?" Charles jutted out his jaw. He was annoyed, perhaps, that she hadn't given him back the picture of the bonnet. "Not Northbrook's charity?"

"I'll be doing honest—well, sort of honest—work for him to earn a wage. That's not charity, and it's not improper."

"Unless he's like Felix, and he's leading you to his own dark ends."

"Even if that's so," she said, "what I do away from here is none of your affair."

Charles muttered something. Cass ignored this. She wouldn't mind seeing where Lord Northbrook would lead her, and how dark the ends might be.

Just for curiosity's sake.

She stood, then grabbed the handle of her valise. "I'll come check on you when I can," she said for a second time. "Mrs. Jellicoe will have meals sent up to you. Get well and don't jump out any windows."

"Ha." Charles was already reaching for the next periodical in his stack.

"And, Charles? Don't do anything I wouldn't."

"I definitely can't buy a new bonnet, then," he replied.

Brothers. "Cheer up. You can pretend to be a duke's by-blow instead," she said sweetly, then shut the door on his reply and made her way to Bow Street.

The Bow Street magistrate's court was as familiar to Cass as her own lodgings. It was an always-crowded room, smelling of sweat and cheap perfume and sometimes a meat pie or spilled ale if someone was eating while they waited. A few long wooden benches made neat rows, facing the railing dividing the public space from the officers' warren of desks and papers and shelves.

Front and center behind the railing, the magistrate's own bench took pride of place. From that seat and desk, Augustus Fox considered testimony and rendered verdicts. Long after regular hours ended, he'd been known to sift through evidence in his cramped private office. Portly and eagle-eyed, the magistrate was as fair as he was stern, and as much a fixture of the court as were the pillars that held up its roof.

Cass sidled through the ever-present crowd, ducking her head to avoid greetings and questions from Runners asking about Charles. To see one Benton twin without the other was, she knew, rare and strange. Too much about this past day had already been rare and strange.

The old leather valise bumped her thigh with every step, reminding her that she wouldn't be walking home again. Lord Northbrook had arranged to send one of the ducal carriages to Bow Street to retrieve Cass, and she had less than an hour before its arrival to arrange matters here.

She struggled past a drunken woman singing a song about Cupid, then a man who smelled of fish and who tried to embrace everyone who came near. At last, she burst through the crowd to the clear space before Fox's bench. He had just dismissed a case and was opening his mouth to call up the next.

"Mr. Fox!" she called, all but falling against the railing. "I need to speak with you."

He looked down at her with surprised blue eyes under heavy black brows. "On your own today? Where's that brother of yours? Here, come around, Miss Benton."

Another Runner opened the gate in the railing, and Cass slipped through to stand beside Fox. "Well?" said the magistrate. "What's on your mind?"

She drew a deep breath, braced by her employer's familiar scent of peppermint and pipe tobacco. "Charles was injured while on a private investigation."

"Injured?" The beetle brows rose.

"A broken leg. It happened last night."

"Ah." The brows slammed down. "I am sorry to hear it. He'll recover?" At Cass's nod, Fox added, "Do I want to ask for more details about the injury? Or the case?"

Cass shook her head. "Best not." It wouldn't do Charles credit, and they needed all the credit they could manage.

"Very well." Fox steepled his hands over his round belly, over which a plain black waistcoat stretched. "How long before your brother can resume work?"

"Six weeks." Her hand felt like a claw around the valise handle. "Maybe eight. But the surgeon said it would be at least six."

Fox stroked his chin, where grizzled bristles were beginning to poke through. "That's bad. He was to handle the Watch case."

"I'll cover his work," Cass blurted. "I can do it. I do have a private investigation to begin, so I won't be able to do a shift straight through. But I can cover his hours, if . . ." She swallowed. "If I keep doing Charles's work, can we collect his salary?"

Fox looked at her shrewdly. "How would that be different from usual?"

But he looked concerned too, his blue eyes kind. Cass and Charles had begun working for him five years before, as soon as they attained their majority at twenty-one, and he'd become the nearest thing to a father they'd ever known.

Still. Concerned though he might be, and not uncaring, Fox was an employer. And he needed work done, for the sake of the safety of London and its inhabitants.

"I don't know," he added. "It's not only the Watch case. We've got a terrible problem with pockets being picked at Drury Lane. We need someone there on site."

Everything was *we* with Fox; he had conscience enough for all his Runners and the whole city besides. This sense of obligation was hard on a man. In the five years Cass had known him, he seemed to have aged a decade—his hair graying and receding, his middle growing thick, the lines of worry slashing deeper around his mouth. But this same sense of responsibility for all that went on around him—for the safety of a city and its inhabitants—made

Cass willing to throw herself into a job that wasn't even her own.

That, and the salary. A person had to live on something.

"I'll see if I can get there during my work with Lord Northbrook," she offered. "The ton like their theater as much as the Runners do."

"Lord Northbrook," mused Fox. "The Duke of Ardmore's son? Do I want to ask for more details about your case?"

She could almost smile at the familiar question. "Best not," she said for the second time. "But I can manage it. The pickpocketing—I'll see it handled."

I'll come up with something, she had told Charles. Now she had told Fox the same. Future Cass had best be even more resourceful than Present Cass if she were to do all the work she'd promised.

The magistrate looked skeptical. "And the Watch case?"

"A watchcase?" piped up a familiar voice. "Need it fenced?"

Janey Trewes, pickpocket and informant and prostitute and clothing seller, stood before the bench. She was pulled in before the bench nearly every week for some trespass against the law, and each time she cheerfully paid fines and promised never to stray from the path of righteousness again. Fortunately, it was all a hum. If she stopped reporting on the seamy doings of Covent Garden and Seven Dials, the Runners would have a much more difficult time closing cases.

"It's not a case for a watch, Janey," Cass said. "You needn't . . . oh, never mind."

"Why are you here today, Janey?" Fox shuffled the papers before him. "Have you been picking pockets at the theater?"

He sounded weary; Cass couldn't fault him. Janey had

been hauled before the court innumerable times for that very offense. If she were to stop picking pockets at the theater, Drury Lane would become more secure than the Royal Mint.

"I was doing what I oughtn't've," Janey said with a shrug.

She was swathed heavily, as usual, a walking advertisement for the clothes in which she traded. Men's shirts over gowns over petticoats, belted with pinafores and tied at the neck with scarves. Her dark brown hair was sleeked back with a fillet of silk handkerchiefs knotted together. Cass would have bet the five pounds she no longer possessed that neither the handkerchiefs nor Janey's jangling string of gold and brass buttons had been acquired honestly.

"And you're sorry and won't do it again," Fox said, his hand already reaching for the gavel.

"Oh, sure." Janey grinned, showing crooked but white teeth. "Never."

And Fox's hand stopped. "Would you care to atone?"

"Care to what?"

"Atone. Make amends." Cass watched, mystified, as Fox struggled for another way of putting the matter. "Ah— would you like to make up for what you did wrong by doing something good?"

Janey thought about this. "Not really."

With a gimlet stare, Fox replied, "The correct answer is yes, if you want to avoid a fine."

"Yes, then. Unless it's somethin' I don't want to do. Then maybe I'll pay the fine and bing off."

Fox smiled. "It's nothing much. Check in on Charles Benton every other day, report to him on his cases, and report back to me. Especially the Watch case. Which is"— he shot a look of sympathy at Cass—"not the case of an actual watch."

Janey plucked at the end of her knotted silk hander-chiefs, her hands covered in fingerless gloves. "That's it?"

"That's it," Fox confirmed. "That's your atonement. His lodging is . . . what is the address?" Cass gave it to him, explaining Charles's injury to Janey, and the younger woman nodded her agreement.

"Aye, I'll do that. He never give me trouble when he'd got two good legs, and now he's got a broken one I c'n make sure he behaves." She narrowed her eyes. "For how long?"

"Why, until he's back on his feet," said Fox.

"And then I'll be—what was it? Atoned? And no fines?"

"No fines *this* time," Fox corrected.

"And you'll be as atoned as Charles ever is," Cass said. "Let me give you some papers to take to him, for I won't be able to visit him again today. Maybe not tomorrow either."

"Oh, aye?" Janey flashed that strangely charming grin again. "Got a ass-ig-nay-shun?" She pronounced each syllable carefully.

Cass had to laugh. "That word you know, but you swear you don't know 'atone.'"

"I know the words that matter to me. Girl like me, she hears about ass-ig-nay-shuns all the time."

"Yes, all right." Fox looked a little sheepish, as if he were already regretting his leniency. "Miss Benton, you'd best be off to one job or another. Janey, take whatever papers Miss Benton gives you, and hold them as fast as you would a brass button."

"Cor," she said, impressed. "Right, then."

As Cass bent over a desk and scribbled a few lines about Fox's arrangement with Janey, she heard the younger woman murmuring, "At. Tone. Mint. Atone. Munt. Attun.

Ment." Trying out the syllables, as if getting accustomed to the idea.

Cass folded the paper, then pushed through the gate and handed the note to Janey. "Thanks," she said. "Truly. Charles will be cheered up, seeing you."

"At. Own. Mint," Janey answered with a nod, taking the paper. "Every other day until he's on his feet agin."

She slipped through the crowd with the ease of a born thief. Cass took her own leave then, the cursed valise bumping her leg again with every step. She'd wait outside the courtroom for the ducal carriage, and . . . and soon she'd become someone else. She'd fool the ton. Collect their secrets. Save the Duke of Ardmore.

Keep Charles's job.

It wasn't that much to handle. Right? She'd come up with something.

She always did.

Chapter Four

"This is such a pretty house," said Miss Benton as George welcomed her into the entrance hall of Ardmore House.

At least, that's what George thought she said. Her lips shaped the words, but her voice was almost entirely drowned out by the barking of the Duke of Ardmore's dogs.

Everyone who lived here was accustomed to the dogs' snarls and growls. Though she'd called here before, Miss Benton was not. As their rumpus rang down the stairs, a wave of sound to which they treated the world almost every time someone arrived at the house, her brows drew together. "What a greeting," were the words shaped by her lips.

George leaned in closer, speaking into her ear. "You hear the dulcet tones of Gog and Magog. My father's dogs. They stay with him in his study and dislike everything."

"Rather like Charles," she replied. "Except for the bit about the study."

"Pardon me for a moment." George held up a finger, an I'll-be-right-back gesture, and darted up the stairs. On the first floor of the house, along with the music room and drawing room and a scattering of other chambers, was the duke's study.

If George wanted to see his father outside a gaming hell, this was the place to do so. Ardmore spent almost all his hours at home in here—when he wasn't dining, of course, or dressing for the day. The long hours were entirely unjustified by the slight amount of attention he paid his dukedom, though George supposed it still took time and effort to review a steward's letters and scrawl a reply, even of great brevity.

George poked his head into the duke's favorite room, and the cacophony made by the dogs increased. The two great hounds almost covered the floor of the study, a small chamber dominated by a desk, behind which the duke was sitting. Letters and invitations and bills littered the desk. Tradesmen, of course. Ardmore paid his gambling debts at once, which meant haberdashers and grocers had to wait ever longer.

Also dominant in the space was a large painting behind the desk. Until the previous year, the duke had long displayed a study by Botticelli. Three mostly naked women dancing by moonlight; George had liked the picture quite well. But Ardmore had traded it to the crime lord Angelus in payment for gambling debts. Only some of the duke's debts, unfortunately, and they'd since mounted again.

There was no shortage of paintings to take the place of the naked dancing women. Expensive oils in gilded frames hung thickly on every wall of Ardmore House. Art was the only thing the duke loved as much as a deck of cards.

Maybe this was why he'd now hung a painting that combined the two. A Dutch piece from the 1500s, it showed two men and a woman—all with distressed expressions—playing some sort of card game. George liked this one, too. The hats were excellent. The man on the left looked like he was wearing an artist's palette on his head, and the woman sported a bath sheet. The other man stared at them both with an expression of froglike dismay.

"Hullo, Froggy," George said to the painted man. "Eight of spades? You'll never win anything with that."

Ardmore's jaw clenched. This was his only reaction, ever, to George's greeting.

To be fair, George had in fact greeted a painted man several centuries his father's senior. He turned now to the duke. "Father. Our guest is here. Can't you calm the dogs?"

The duke eyed George balefully. He'd been skeptical of George's suspicions about the tontine from the start; the stabbing of Lord Deverell had convinced him only grudgingly that there might be something in the matter. But the installing of an investigator in his own household was, to quote, "foolishness. A lot of rough talk and dirty boots."

When George explained the investigator was, in fact, a young woman who spoke politely and wore clean boots, the duke had turned an interesting shade of red. Only assuring His Grace that the guest was a friend of Lady Isabel Jenks—which was almost the truth, since Miss Benton had once worked with Lady Isabel's husband, Callum—had returned the duke's complexion to its normal shade.

He looked a little ruddy again as George asked him to calm the dogs, both of whom were bristling at George as though they'd rather like to break the line of succession. "Sit," said the duke. Two great sets of haunches went down, though the barking and growling continued.

"That'll have to do," said the duke. "They'll quiet down soon enough."

Those damned dogs. George shut the study door, shaking his head to clear some of the racket out of it, then descended the stairs again. His father was right: the animals were beginning to quiet. By the time George reached the entrance hall again, he could almost ignore their snarls.

"Sorry about that," he said to Cass. "I thought we'd like to be able to use our ears. Hullo, someone's taken your valise."

"Yes, the butler greeted me. He said he'd have it brought to the green bedchamber. Then he said he'd bring tea to the drawing room, but I told him it was all right and I'd just wait for you here."

George had prepared the staff for the arrival of a "family visitor." Miss Benton had been retrieved from Bow Street in one of the duke's crested carriages, as George thought it best to begin making a show of her presence in the household.

Now that the dogs were reasonably quiet, he could try again to welcome her. "Come on up, then, to the drawing room. We'll sort out what to do next. Unless you want to rest first?"

"No need for that," she said. "I'm working for you. Let us begin."

As she spoke, she looked everywhere: up at the ceiling that soared above the entrance; down at the marble floor and the sculpted treads of the staircase. "I've never thought of Ardmore House as a place I might stay."

"And I didn't imagine I'd be living here at my advanced age, yet here we both are," George replied, ushering her up the stairs.

"How pretty," Miss Benton said again as they climbed past thickly clustered oil paintings framed in gilt, past polished wood and ornate plaster medallions traced in gold and heavy printed wall hangings. It was a compliment utterly simple, and sincere in its simplicity. She wasn't trying to impress; she was merely noticing.

As they settled in the airy drawing room, he found himself appreciating the prettiness of it—the overwrought, overdone, undeniable comfort of it—as he usually did not.

"Tea for you?" he asked when they had settled in a pair of striped-silk chairs before the fire. It was a warm day and the flames were low, but the scent of crackling wood was pleasant.

She waved off the offer of refreshment. "I'm all right. Let's sort out the details of my presence here. Who am I to be—did you decide? Your bastard cousin?"

"Half cousin. I plan to blame your get upon my grandfather, the previous duke."

A corner of her mouth lifted. "Dear me. The roots of this tale go back a long way."

"Everyone will believe it. The old duke had a weakness for women, just as my father does for cards and dice." He frowned, wishing for a teacup to occupy his hands. "I used to think it was funny."

"You need a shocking vice of your own. Then you would enjoy those of others more."

"I've been called lazy," he offered.

"Not exciting enough. No one is shocked by laziness in a ducal heir."

That stung a bit. "Perhaps I can begin smoking opium," he replied lightly, "but we'll wait on that until matters are more settled. I do apologize for delegitimizing you—is that a word?"

She was utterly unflappable. "You've made me a bastard. It's quite all right to say so frankly. I suppose my scandalous birth is so that I won't have appeared in society or Debrett's, and no one will know me."

"Exactly." She was admirably quick. "Where have you been living all these years, oh bastard cousin of mine?"

"I'd best be from the wilds of England—otherwise I shall have to know another language. I was raised in a village nobody in London has heard of."

"Very good, to say it with that sort of self-deprecating air. It shuts off questions."

She tapped the side of her nose, smiling. "I'm twenty-six. Does the mathematics work out for me to be your grandfather's daughter, or should I become a different age?"

"Yes, it's possible. The old roué was playing about with younger women until the day he died, when I was probably five or so." He counted on his fingers. "You'd have been two then; no need for an aging potion. The last of his by-blows, maybe? What an honor for you."

She lifted a ruddy brow. "Was it necessary for you to do arithmetic using your fingers?"

"I use my fingers for all sorts of things, Miss Benton. None of them are strictly necessary."

She didn't even blink. "An intriguing topic, but perhaps we'd better keep to the one at hand."

One of her hands slipped into her pocket. She had a watch in there, or something of that size. Through the gown fabric, he saw the outline of a little case as her fingers turned it.

She sat for a moment as if in thought, then withdrew her hand from her dress pocket. "You'd best call me Cass since we're to pose as family. And my false name had best be Cassandra too, or I'll always be forgetting to answer to it."

"Ah, Cassandra. The doomed prophetess."

"Not doomed. Cursed. No one believed her, though she was always right."

He granted this. His recall of Greek myth was imperfect

at best. "My Christian name is George," he said. "You are welcome to use it. It's everywhere and means nothing interesting. How do you like yours?"

"It's fine. I'm not always right, but people believe me."

"One generally is believed when one admits to human frailty," he replied. "Very well. You remain Cass. What is your last name for the time being?"

"Hmm. How about something intriguingly foreign? But similar to Benton, so I won't entirely forget to answer to that, too."

George cast about for names from the gothic novels he sometimes enjoyed. "Ben . . . Ber . . . Bah . . . hmm. Perhaps Benedetti?"

"Benedetti it shall be," she approved. "I was swept off my feet by a dashing Italian who proved cruel, and I have fled back to the bosom of my ancestral family."

"The very thing to explain your hurried arrival and lack of belongings."

"I am resourceful," she preened. "One has to be if one is to escape a cruel husband."

"Should we be expecting this dreadful individual to chase after you?"

"No, indeed." Her lips trembled, but her eyes were merry. "He lost all interest in me once he realized I had no fortune. He even paraded his mistresses before me."

"The blackguard." George stood, extending a hand to Cass. "You'll need a ring if you're married. Let me find something while you get settled into your bedchamber. The butler can show you to it, and you can share my mother's lady's maid. I'll begin introducing you now, Signora Benedetti."

"A 'missus' will do," she said as she rose. "I'm as English as you are, and there's no way to pretend otherwise."

She placed her hand in his. He remembered, fleetingly,

how he'd touched his tongue to her palm. What had he been thinking?

He hadn't been thinking; he'd simply done what he wished on the impulse of the moment. In this particular moment, another impulse led him to press her fingertips with his.

She pressed back. It was rather like a secret code, though he wasn't sure what it meant.

George rang for the butler and introduced the previously unnamed family guest as a connection of the late duke's, a Mrs. Benedetti. Bayliss was not without understanding of the previous duke's foibles. With a significant glance and a "Very good, my lord," he led Cass to the green bedchamber. It had belonged to George's sister before her marriage the previous year; all the more appropriate for a guest who was a relation.

Not that Cass really was. And with her wry, musical voice and bright mind, there was no danger George would forget that Cassandra Benton was unrelated to him by blood.

On the floor above the drawing room, George's parents had their suite of rooms. He knocked on the door to the duchess's chamber, not really expecting an answer. At this hour of the day, his mother was always in twilight: half-asleep, mostly unaware.

When he eased the door to Her Grace's chamber open, he saw that he was correct. The duchess lay in bed, though the curtains were open to daylight and she wore a morning gown. The room, like the rest of Ardmore House, was scrupulously clean, yet a dusty scent as of old dried flowers hung in the air.

"Mother," he said—again, not really expecting an answer—"I need to borrow a ring from you."

He'd have to get her lady's maid to unlock the jewelry box. George found Gatiss in the dressing room. She was a steady woman of late middle age who was mending a rent in the seam of one of the duchess's garments. In recent years, she'd rarely been asked for any errand related to jewelry; thus she arose eagerly, taking up the jewel case key and returning with it and George to the duchess's chamber.

"But Lily died," murmured Her Grace from across the room as her maid unlocked the jewel case. "Why do you need a ring if she died?"

George went very still. Gatiss, too, froze, her hand atop the jewel case. Of all the times for his mother to emerge from twilight into reality.

Yes, George had been betrothed once. And the lady had died. So George hadn't needed a ring for her, after all.

It was an old loss. By now it hurt only like the memory of a wound. The scar was tight where it had healed, sometimes tugging on the unhurt parts of him.

Slowly, George turned. Though she still reclined on the bed, his mother's eyes were open and clear. He had almost forgotten that their color was blue, like his own.

"Yes," he replied. "Lily died years ago. I don't need the ring for Lily."

Her hands moved vaguely, plucking at the heavy lace that adorned the neck of her gown. "Who are you going to wed, then? I have heard nothing of it."

"No one, Mother. It is for something that will help a family member." He toyed with sending Gatiss away and explaining the plan with Cass to the duchess, as he had to the grudging duke, but Her Grace was already closing her eyes again.

"Have the ring with the emerald." Her voice was quiet again, drifting away. "No one has worn it for years, yet it is very pretty."

There. He had his mother's blessing, though she knew not for what. He turned back to Gatiss.

"Open the case, please," he said. "Whatever this emerald ring is, I will have it." Some explanation was in order so he could control the story down in the servants' hall. He thought about what would cleave nearest the truth and also nearest the story the butler had already heard.

"A near relative of the old duke," he said delicately, "is staying with us for her protection from a cruel husband. She fled without her ring or most of her belongings, but I should like her respectable married status to be clear."

"Of course, my lord," said Gatiss, as if there was nothing strange about what George had said. He took the ring she indicated, slipped it in his pocket, then left the duchess's chamber and pounded upstairs to the remaining family rooms. Here he had his own bedchamber and the room for his experiments, and down the corridor was the green-papered room that would now belong to Cass.

She wasn't in there, nor was there any sign of her presence. The counterpane stretched white and pristine across the bed, and her belongings had already been stowed out of sight.

He looked about for her and located her in his second room, the one he had appropriated as a condition of moving back into the family home. It was the smallest of the bedchambers, dominated by a long, wide window that faced north and caught slanted sun at all hours. The window was framed by heavy draperies that could be drawn to block light when needed.

The space was furnished simply, with a chair before a long table holding his camerae obscurae. A set of narrow shelves ran the length and height of a full wall. On those shelves, he kept special papers, along with chemical concoctions in carefully labeled bottles of amber glass. The lamps that bookended the worktable were also shaded in amber glass. It was the sort least likely to be affected by sunlight or to interfere with a dark-roomed experiment.

Cass was lifting the lid of the larger camera obscura when George spoke. "Nosing around?"

She didn't start; she didn't even flinch. She only looked over her shoulder at him. "Did you expect anything less?"

"No. At least, I shouldn't have." He slouched against the door frame, bracing a shoulder against it. "You might as well have the run of the house while you're here, just as I do."

She closed the wooden lid gently, looking thoughtful. In the diffuse light from the window, she looked sharply cut: a straight nose, a graceful neck. Her shoulders were square in her simple gown, her golden red hair coolly lit like a crown.

"What does a marquess do with the run of the house?" she asked.

"The sort I am, not much," George said. "Northbrook is a courtesy title translating to 'Is the oldest or only son and will be a duke someday, but for now has nothing much to occupy him since his father is disinclined to share responsibility.'"

Her lips twitched. "Here I thought Northbrook meant the north side of a brook."

"It's a rough translation. But were you asking about me in general, or wondering about this room?"

"Both," she answered. "This room smells of oranges. Like you. I noticed it as I walked down the corridor."

He hadn't thought about his own scent in some time. A man usually didn't. "I sometimes work with chemicals that have an unpleasant scent. The orange oil covers it, and I got in the habit of having it added to my own soap lest I drag the results of an experiment about with me."

She trailed a fingertip over the nicked surface of the long table. "I wondered if perhaps you'd captured a schooner from the tropics."

"Sorry." He did his best to look contrite. "I could say I had if you'd be impressed."

She ignored this irrelevancy. "What do you use these wooden boxes for? You said you conduct experiments here. Will you tell me about them?"

The man had never been born who could resist a question such as that. George loped into the room to stand beside her, looking over the camerae obscurae. They must appear curious to her. One was a little peak-sided box of wood with a glass top hiding behind the wooden sides; the other was more than double the size of the smaller, about the length of a man's torso, and with a hinged lid. Each had a hole in one side, filled with a metal-mounted glass lens like a telescope's end.

"Each of these cunning boxes," he said, "is a camera obscura of a different sort. They are meant for making pictures. Or they would be if I were a better artist or scientist."

"Pictures—like the paintings that hang all over this house?"

"They can be." He plunged his hands into his pockets, considering how to explain. "Artists have been using them to help with paintings for centuries. I'm trying something quite different, though. I hope to hit upon a way to fix images from life using sunlight and chemicals."

Her eyes widened. "Images from life? You mean people as they really look, without the trouble of sitting for a portrait in paint?"

"That's the hope. I've had no luck yet, but there's got to be a way. I'll show you my work sometime, if you're really interested."

But his fumbling fingers had touched the gold circlet

in his pocket, and he remembered his earlier errand. "For now," he said, "I've a gift for you."

"No." She shook her head. "No gifts. Ours is only a tie of business."

She sounded so formal that he blinked. "Right. That's what I meant. This isn't a gift at all; it's part of a costume. A business costume."

He pulled the ring from his pocket, dropping to one knee on the acid-scarred carpet that covered polished floorboards. "Pretend I'm a dashing but cruel Italian, presenting you with this ring under false pretenses."

With a wondering expression, she took the ring from his palm. It gave him a queer feeling about his heart to watch her examine it, then slip it onto her fourth finger.

"Would I keep wearing your ring," she asked, "if you were cruel to me and I had fled from you?"

I would never be cruel to you. "Certainly you would." Grabbing the table edge for support, he stood and shook out his legs. The carpet did nothing to soften the floor. "Just look at it. It is a very pretty ring, and worth a great deal. You'd hardly leave it behind. Though if it matters, my mother's lady's maid knows I've got it from the jewelry box here. I told her you left your real ring behind with your other belongings, but I wanted you to appear respectable."

"And if the lady's maid knows it, the other servants soon will." She understood. "Very well. I do have a few more questions, though."

"Ask away. I am an open book inscribed with all the knowledge of the world."

"I am the luckiest of all women," she said drily. "First question: Why should anyone connected with the tontine care to know me? Second question: What shall I do for clothing if I go out in society?"

Clothing was a simpler matter to answer, so he took that question first. "Because you're meant to be a relative, my sister can kit you out. We'll have to tell her who you really are, as we told my father. Selina will be reasonable about the matter. She doesn't want our father killed any more than I do."

"All her tonnish friends will recognize her clothing, surely." Cass twisted the ring, a delicately worked gold band set with a single emerald. "Ah, well. I will embrace the secondhand clothing cheerfully. I'll be mad with gratitude that my cousin has loaned me her clothing, since everyone knows I own nothing to speak of. I fled with the clothes on my back and would be in nary a stitch without the kindness of family."

"Er—yes. You don't need to go on about your potential nudity to that degree, but that sounds fine. As for why anyone should care to know you, well . . ."

He fumbled for words. *Look at you,* was on the tip of his tongue. *Listen to you.*

He had paused too long, and she filled the silence herself. "Even as a duke's bastard, I'm plain and I've no fortune. And illegitimacy is nothing to boast about."

"But you have connections," he said, though this was not the right sort of reply. "And you are notorious—or you will be, if you can manage it."

"I will, and gladly."

They shared a smile. This was the first time George could remember that they were smiling for a united purpose, and not at cross-purposes or with one of them about to run off.

"Don't worry too much," he said. "My plans generally go as I expect they will."

"That is the sort of statement that makes people want to throw things at your head." She sighed. "Such schemes and secrets are much like a romantic novel. What comes next, George? You will give me lessons in how to behave in society, and I will fall wildly in love with you?"

Why wouldn't she stop touching the ring? It was most distracting. "I wouldn't argue with the second part," he said lightly, "but the first sounds like far too much work. And I'm sure you'd give me one of those withering glances if I even tried."

"Very true. Glad we're in agreement." She stepped back, turning toward the door. "And just so you know, falling in love with you sounds like too much work for me, so I likely won't bother with it."

George laughed.

As he'd predicted, she fired a withering glance over her shoulder. "I wish you wouldn't do that when I mean to puncture your pride. It entirely undoes my efforts."

He laughed again. "I can't do without my pride. It's my prize possession. Now, whenever you need me, I'll be in here or in my bedchamber next door to this one."

She lifted a hand, touching her cheek. "Next door? That's hardly any distance at all from my own room."

"It's as much distance as you want it to be," he said. "I vow that to you, as ours is a tie of business." He enjoyed the pink tint that overspread her cheeks, then added, "Now, what do you need to begin work?"

Chapter Five

The next morning, George hoped to see Cass at breakfast. But she'd arisen and eaten before he ventured downstairs, and his morning meal was its usual solitary affair.

Even so, the house felt different around him. Brighter, maybe, and richer and prettier. It was not due to the weather; his camerae obscurae had revealed nothing unusual about the amount of light spilling into his experiment room. No, it must be the brightness of having a plan.

The brightness faded as soon as he peered into his mother's room to bid her good morning. Even at full noon on the sunniest day of summer, the space surrounding the duchess was gray and dim—and today was an ordinary drizzly, foggy London morning. The scent of dried flowers was stronger today, along with the bitter scent of laudanum. Her Grace must have just taken a dose.

Gatiss, the lady's maid, bustled into the room. Her usual implacability bore cracks. "I'm afraid it's not a good day, Lord Northbrook. Her Grace doesn't care to dress or go downstairs today."

In the bed, the duchess slumbered silently, her cheeks

flushed from the influence of her favored drug. The only sign she was aware of the world around her was a puckered brow, a downward curve of the mouth.

Such was her reaction to a morning greeting from her son. George turned away. "There never seem to be good days anymore."

He'd been frightened when she'd taken too much laudanum the year before and almost died; frightened enough to stay up all day with her rather than falling into bed after a wasted night of . . . Lord, he'd no idea what he'd done.

She had lived. And he'd changed the way he lived, a little. He'd been getting pale and puffy and weary, living for nightfall and roistering. If his mother's example had taught him one thing, it was not to squander his health as she did.

He had never again managed to be frightened for her. Instead he was impatient, and guilty that he was impatient, and annoyed that he felt guilty.

"Isn't this Her Grace's day to receive callers?" he asked the lady's maid.

"It is, my lord." Disappointment etched lines about Gatiss's square features. "She's never missed her callers before."

Well. He couldn't make the duchess discard her laudanum bottle, just as he couldn't keep the duke away from cards. He was powerless in the face of their compulsions.

But no more of that now. Bright! Elegant! Plan! Cass! He tried to return his thoughts to the hopeful cast they'd worn before breakfast.

"I'll need your assistance later this morning, Gatiss. In a short while, my sister is going to bring over some gowns for our guest, Mrs. Benedetti." That would do; let the servants fill in any gaps in his explanation with their own gossip. "I am sure she will need the gowns fitted to her, and as quickly as you are able to accomplish it. Mrs. Benedetti and I will be going out tonight."

He and Cass had decided the previous day that they'd dive into society as soon as possible. He had selected an invitation almost at random from the ones always scattered over the occasional table in the foyer . . . the desk in his father's study . . . the foot of his mother's bed. This one was on heavy paper and beautifully engraved, which meant the hosts were trying to impress.

Which was just the sort of environment in which gossip flourished.

Gatiss looked pleased at the unexpected task. "I shall be ready, my lord." She hesitated, glanced at the duchess, then added, "It'll be nice to work with some pretty clothes. I'll be pleased to help the lady dress for the evening, too."

George thanked her and left the room, thundering down the stairs to the first floor of the house. Here were the drawing room—no Cass in there—and the music room— ditto—and his father's study.

George pushed the door open slowly so as not to rouse a flurry of barks and growls from the duke's dogs. Great hounds of bad temper and a particular dislike of George, they settled like bookends to the duke wherever he established himself.

But this morning they didn't bark, or snarl, or growl, though a whip-thin brown tail thumped the carpet. Mystified, George opened the study door all the way—and there was Cass, garbed in a pretty green gown and sitting on the floor with the two huge dogs around her like furry pillows.

"Good morning, Father," George replied to the duke's grunt of greeting, then looked down at the figure on the floor. "Hullo, Cass."

Either Gog or Magog—George could never tell which was which—picked up his heavy head and growled.

"Good morning." Rather than looking up at George, Cass took hold of the growling dog's scruff and looked him in the eye. "Calm," she said.

When the dog settled, its gaze dropping, she turned from him and petted the other dog as if he were the best-behaved creature in the world. "What a good boy for staying quiet."

"Surely," said George, "these are not the same terrifying watchdogs that no one but the great Duke of Ardmore has been able to tame."

The duke, his hair iron gray and eyes ice blue, grunted again.

"That must have been so annoying for you all," Cass said. "They started barking earlier when I stepped in to speak to His Grace, and I asked if I might try calming them."

George stepped farther into the room and crouched beside the non-growling dog, who looked at him with wariness—but kept its silence. "How do you know how to make them mind?"

Cass scratched behind the ears of the non-growling dog, causing its yellow-brown eyes to squeeze shut in delight. "If I didn't know how to handle an aggressive dog, I'd always have one at my heels as I walked about the city." She grinned, an expression of pure mischief. "Dogs are rather like the ton."

The duke grunted yet again. He could play a symphony with grunts, pitching them for every timbre and mood. George had sorted out their translation only imperfectly, but he rather thought this one meant, "How intriguing. Tell me more." Not that Cass would be able to interpret it.

"It falls to me," George said, "to ask how dogs are like people of the ton. Consider it done."

"They are social beasts," she explained. "They want

guiding, and if they get it, they'll fall right in line with the behavior one desires."

He opened his mouth—then shut it. "I would protest, but that is precisely the behavior we're hoping you'll elicit as Mrs. Benedetti."

"Damned nonsense," said the duke, shuffling papers. "I was never in any danger before. No need for all these elaborate schemes."

George looked at Cass. She lifted her hands, declaiming responsibility, as the non-growling dog whuffed a protest at the pause in the ear-scratching. "I have tried to persuade him to the contrary."

"You persuaded me in the end," the duke said.

George craned his neck to examine the features of the duke. "How did she do that?" he asked, as wary as the dogs. Because Ardmore never smiled, yet his steely eyes held a touch of humor now.

"She said if I went along with the plan, I never had to get you a gift again. Not for your birthday, not your wedding, nothing."

"Oh." George sank to the floor, stretching out his legs along the carpet. The dog that had growled slunk over and put its head in his lap. Idly, he petted the canine head, thinking over the consequences of *no gifts*. Everyone liked getting gifts. "What about Christmas?"

"Nothing," Ardmore and Cass chorused.

He cast about for another occasion. "Midsummer Day? Or what about Easter?"

"*No,*" came the chorus again.

"That seems hard on me, Father, considering this plan is for your benefit."

The duke grunted again. This one was percussive and meant "Shut it."

George did not shut it.

"I moved into this house four years ago at your request," he reminded his father. "To help you keep watch on my mother, because you were worried about her health. Now I'm worried about you and I've moved someone in to keep watch on you."

The duke glared.

"You're welcome!" George said heartily. The formerly growling dog that was now not growling picked up its head and looked at him with disappointment, then collapsed to the floor again for more petting.

The duke grunted, but just quietly enough that they could ignore him.

So George did. He turned his attention to Cass. "What are you doing here? The dogs are keeping watch now."

"I know. I wanted to meet them after they gave me such a loud greeting yesterday." She smiled. Her red hair was a braided coronet that made her eyes as warm and bright as amber.

Steady, George. "You're joking," he said. "No one wants to meet these dogs."

"Indeed I did. I introduced myself by looking them in the eye, then holding them by the scruff. To a dog, it's like a bow or handshake. See? It's just here." She laid a hand on the neck-adjacent region of the better-behaved dog.

"I know what a scruff is," George lied, trying to sort out where it would be on the dog draped beside him.

"You must take hold quite calmly," Cass added, "as if you're entitled to your position. That is what convinces them you are."

"You were right. It really is the same at many parties I've attended. Less neck-grabbing, of course, but the confidence and pretense . . . yes."

"I told you it was a good analogy. When Gog growled at you, I gave him the cut direct. Just as one would to someone who got drunk at a party or cheated at cards. That sort of behavior won't do."

So Gog was the one toad-eating him now, jealous of the ear scratches Magog was enjoying. "How do you know which one's Gog? I can never tell them apart." They were equally unpleasant to his eye.

"He's a little bigger. And look, his paws are quite black, and Magog has one that's a light brown. Gog thought he was in charge, but he must learn that he's not."

"I am," said Ardmore.

"Of course, Your Grace," said Cass in a tone that did not indicate agreement.

The duke met her eyes. She met his right back and smiled. George had the feeling that given another moment, she'd bounce up from her seat on the floor and take his father by the scruff of the neck.

George would dearly love to see that, but it would not contribute to his father's peace and safety. He rose to his feet, then extended a hand to Cass. "Let's leave the duke to his work. It's nearly time for you to get fitted for your evening as Mrs. Benedetti."

This was only an excuse to remove her from the tenuous good cheer of the dogs and the decidedly absent cheer of the duke. But as they stepped into the corridor and made their way to the stairs, George heard the front door of the house open and his sister's voice float up from the entrance hall.

"I decided not to bring my cat this time," she reassured the butler. "Ardmore's dogs are intolerably rude to poor Titan. She stays at home with Lord Wexley."

Amazingly, the dogs held their peace at the sound of this arrival.

George motioned for Cass to follow him, and they descended the stairs to greet Selina. George's only sibling, Selina had always been cheerfully delighted with her place in life. She had wed the previous year at the age of twenty-one, and the young Lady Wexley was now yet more delighted with her husband and household. She had pounced upon the scheme to introduce Cass into society and had brought over—George peered through the open front door with dismay—far more gowns than one person should be expected to own.

Cass looked a little glassy-eyed as footmen carried in the drapes and swags of fabric. Selina directed them up to the drawing room as having the best light.

"It's all just fabric," she excused with a little shrug. "Wexley plays with grain futures or some such thing. How can he begrudge me my own fun with clothing?"

"Admirable husband," George agreed. "A very wise man."

"Mrs. Benedetti," Selina added with a wink, "I wanted to have you come to my household, because I was sure one of the footmen was stealing the spoons. But then I caught Titan at it, so all was well. Yet now I get to have you around anyway, just as I wished."

Cass blinked. George rather enjoyed seeing her so discombobulated, since he'd never witnessed anything shake her calm before. "Why . . . would you want that?" she managed.

Selina leaned in close—mindful of the servants brushing by with yet more clothing, George was glad to see. He leaned in too, listening. "You helped to save my husband's life," murmured Selina simply. "Last year, from that mad girl. You're a good person to know."

Cass seemed not to know what to say to this.

"I agree," said George, enjoying his own part in flustering Miss Benton.

When at last Selina's carriage had disgorged its final gown and trunk full of unmentionables, everyone went upstairs to the drawing room. As the largest chamber, it would do for a makeshift modiste's shop, especially since the duchess did not intend to receive callers today.

Unnoticed by George, Selina's lady's maid had also swooped into the household, and she was now draping gowns over every item of furniture in the room.

Selina stood at the center of it all, tapping her chin. "You're a bit taller than I—and more slender, you lucky thing. But never mind that. One can do wonders with ribbon and pins, at least if one is my lady's maid. Cobbett, do what you can with this blue. She will be a dream in it."

"Gatiss will help, too," George said. "I arranged it with her."

Selina rounded on him. "Good. Fetch her, then leave us. This is women's work."

George allowed himself to be shoved to the doorway, glancing back at Cass all the while. At the sight of silks and satins draped all around, she'd lost the easy confidence she'd had with the dogs. A pretty blush had pinkened her cheeks.

As George prepared to shut the door behind him, his sister caught his hand. Her nails bit into the skin as she drew him up short. "I never thought you'd go in for a scheme like this."

Selina looked pleased, but he was puzzled. "Like what?"

"Like, you put a ring on someone's finger and spend a lot of time with her."

Oh. So she'd noticed the emerald ring Cass wore. "Part of the costume," he said. "Part of the plan. To help Father. That's all."

Selina arched a brow, dark as George's own, and fixed him with a stare. It was a pity icy blue eyes ran in the family; they were so disconcerting.

"Besides, you shouldn't be shocked by the trappings of the plan." He shook free of her feminine talons. "I'm not afraid of rings. Or women. I was engaged once."

"I know." Selina looked thoughtful. "But that was ages ago. Ever since then, it's as if you've freed yourself of all the scheming parents wanting to marry off their dears. Including *our* parents. You are the envy of all tonnish bachelors."

"Hardly a point for comparison," he replied. "Ca— Mrs. Benedetti is nothing like Lily. And I'm nothing like the George I was then."

Though the truth was, he wasn't sure of that, because he hardly remembered the George and Lily from eight or nine years before. They'd both been young and free of care and certain that they would always be both. Never would they have worried about their fathers being attacked, or the existence of a wagered fortune that depended on the deaths of men they'd known their whole lives.

"I'll summon Gatiss for you now," he said, and was grateful to let the door shut behind him this time.

After hours of being fitted and poked and pinned into gowns that weren't her own and that she could never have afforded, Cass felt well and truly like a duke's bastard.

She was used to gowns that fastened up the front and stays she could lace up herself. Now, from the skin out, she was dependent on servants to dress her in every stitch she wore. She wasn't sure if she liked that—but oh, she liked this blue silk gown. It was bright and dark at once, the shade of those expensive blue paints that long-ago artists used on the Virgin's veil. Short sleeves puffed elegantly at her shoulders; a slim band marked the high waist. And then it was just a clean fall of blue silk, more and more of it, until the hem, which was embroidered lavishly in all the shades of fire.

It made Cass feel like dancing, kicking up her heels and watching the little flame colors flash and wink in candlelight. But she didn't know how to dance, and she wasn't sure if these long white gloves were meant to be above her elbow or bunching below, and the slippers on her feet felt flimsy and frail compared to the practical boots she usually wore. Her hair was twisted in complicated curls, and the duchess's maid, Gatiss, had cooed with delight as she poked a few amber silk roses into the twists.

So, yes. A duke's bastard: between worlds and dressed above her station.

She found George in his second bedchamber, the experiment room with all the shelves and those wooden boxes he'd called camerae obscurae. The heavy drapes were open, and rosy sunset light spilled into the now-dim room. A metallic smell drifted through the air.

"Greetings," she said. "I've been as experimented on as any of your papers."

When he turned to look at her, she caught her breath.

Not that George in evening dress was so different from George in day clothing. He always wore a well-tailored coat and one of those fashionably high starched cravats.

But George in evening clothing, with a small glass bottle of chemicals in his hands and a preoccupied expression on his face and a red sun falling low behind him, was a sight for which she was entirely unprepared. It was a peek at the man beneath the coat and cravat. Trying things, wondering about things, not caring about the hour.

God, it was an attractive sight. Especially when she noticed his hands in work gloves that were all marked and spattered with mysterious chemicals.

He blinked, seeming to take a moment to realize where and when he was, then smiled a greeting. "Are you worried about this evening?"

She stroked the line of the gown, waist to hip. "No one in such beautiful silks could be worried. If I dressed like this all the time, I would be a pillar of unshakable calm."

Capping the bottle, he returned it to its place on one of the long shelves. The metallic smell lessened at once. "You have money saved, don't you? You could buy such gowns for yourself."

"No, I couldn't. No matter how much I earn or save. I've been frugal for too long to spend money on anything I don't have to have." Thus the inexpensive bonnets about which Charles twitted her.

And no, she didn't have money saved. Savings were for those in the middle of society: the newly wealthy, the tradesmen and merchants who'd made good. People in Cass's way of life couldn't afford to save, and those in the top-lofty ton didn't bother.

George nudged aside one of the lamps on the large table, then pushed it back to its original place. "What about Charles? Would you spend money on him?"

"I do, all the time. On things he needs and on the inconsequentialities he wants. But those cost far less than a silk gown."

Sunset painted his face with a faint blush. "What about me?"

"What about you? Would I buy you something pretty, do you mean? A beautiful silk?" She laughed.

But he looked oddly serious. "Would you use your money, or what resources you have, to help me? If I weren't paying you a wage to do so?"

The question surprised her, but the answer was easy. "Why, of course I would."

"You answer so quickly. Just like that, you say that you would. For anyone." He turned away to fuss with the lid of the larger camera obscura. "It is a compliment to the goodness of your heart."

"You're acting strange, and what you said doesn't sound like a compliment at all. But it *is* a compliment to you." Now she was the one blushing, and she hoped the dim bleed of warm light would cover it. "Because no, I wouldn't say that to anyone. But yes, you I can answer. Just like that."

"You are generous."

This time it *did* sound like a compliment. Cass didn't think she was, really, but she liked the sound of it and didn't want to protest.

When he dropped the lid of the camera obscura and faced her again, he looked different. Always handsome, now he was incandescent. A beautiful thing such as she craved and could never have for herself, no matter what she saved or how long she waited.

Somehow they'd got far away from the simple greeting, and the purpose of the evening. Or *she* had. She wished her gown had a pocket so she could have brought along the miniature of Grandmama. A reminder of her real self—the self that never wore silks and didn't associate with the likes of a duke's heir—would have been welcome just now.

Cass cleared her throat. "Let's go over the plan."

He frowned, all languid Lord Northbrook again in a moment. "Must we? I trust you to handle this. I'm paying you to handle this."

She folded her arms. "Don't be lazy."

"No, anything but that." He rested his weight on the edge of the long worktable. "All right, fine. One last review."

On his fingers, he ticked off the now-familiar names of the survivors of the tontine. Besides Ardmore and Deverell, there were Braithwaite. Gerry. Cavender. She was to listen for those names, to speak to the men themselves if they were present tonight. The question foremost must always be: Who will be targeted next?

"My father won't be in attendance. He's much likelier to be found in one of Angelus's gambling hells," George said wryly. "And Deverell won't be at the ball either. His wife has put it about that he's taking a rest cure, which everyone knows means he is going to drink in a different part of England. He'll be back in London soon enough, probably sooner than he ought."

Deverell was such a strange case. "You mentioned once that he was your godfather," Cass said, "so I presume you've known him some time. Has he always drunk so much?"

"Not that I recall. Though men hardly behave in front of children the same way they do in private."

"It might have grown upon him over the years." Cass sighed. "Like so many vices."

"Again, you make me feel positively ashamed that I lack a defining flaw."

She eyed him closely. "I did call you lazy just now. And you once called yourself lazy, too."

"True." He tugged off the much-used work gloves and

laid them on the table. "It lacks the elegance, shall I say, of gambling or drinking or toying with women's hearts."

"I am not interested in elegance," she said. "I'm interested in solving a case. Once we find the pattern behind the deaths of the men in the tontine, we'll know who's next. And maybe we'll even know why."

George pushed himself upright and drew a pair of evening gloves from his coat pocket. "Let us go, then. We'll be unfashionably early, but we care nothing for elegance."

Just like that, they were an instant away from leaving the house. Together. But not together, really; not ever.

Cass hesitated. "Could I . . . what about a kiss for luck?"

Stupid request. Irresistible, though.

When George stared at her, she explained, "It seemed the sort of thing your Benedetti cousin might say."

"Well. For the sake of getting into the role, then." In a second, he had dropped his evening gloves on the floor, crossed the room, and taken her face in his hands.

As she caught her breath, he lowered his head and pressed his lips to hers.

It was a sweet brush, a slow savor of mouth upon mouth. She shut her eyes and tried to think of nothing else in the world; to sink into the sensation and wrap herself in its boldness.

It was not so easy to turn off her thoughts.

What did she hope would happen? Would the world shift? Would he drop to one knee again and offer her a ring under his own name? Would his heart pass into her keeping? Would hers become his?

No, this was too much to hope for. After all, it was just a kiss. A nice one, as George smelled pleasantly of laundry soap and that faint scent of oranges, and his lips were firm and his fingertips gentle. But if the kiss had been nicer still, surely she'd have thought of none of these things and would simply have surrendered to it.

She couldn't afford to surrender.

She was desperate to surrender.

He pulled back, and her eyes opened. He was blinking as if dazed. "I needed that. I hadn't realized how much."

Cass realized. "*You* are the one who is worried."

"Not *worried*," he contradicted. "Merely . . . apprehensive."

"Yet you were asking about my own fears." It was rather sweet. She picked up his dropped gloves and pressed them into his hand.

He looked at them as if he didn't quite know what they were. "Ah, well. You're the one with a part to play. All I've got to do is be myself."

Silly of him to say such a thing. He didn't realize that it was far easier to be someone else.

Chapter Six

Most Runners worked alone, but Cass never had. She hadn't been alone since the first moment of being knit into existence.

This was why, surely, she was glad for George's company as she entered the sprawling London mansion of Lord and Lady Harrough. There was no denying the comfort of having one's hand in the arm of a confederate—or compatriot, or co-conspirator—as one began one's first evening in the skeptical embrace of the ton.

True, she'd been at tonnish events before, but only on the fringes to work as a Runner. She had never attended a ball as a guest.

Over the next several minutes, the *nevers* piled up.

Never before tonight had she descended from a private carriage and handed her wraps to a servant. Never had she been greeted by a hostess, a smile of welcome bestowed upon her. Never had a flute of champagne been pressed into her hand, to fizz floral and sweet on her tongue as a duke's heir introduced her about, again and again, while chandeliers burned bright overhead and perfume and laughter floated in the air.

Never had she worn such silk, or all but demanded a kiss of a man far above her touch.

She should never have touched him, yet she wasn't sorry.

A sign she was exploring the bounds of her assumed identity? Good for her; what a talented investigator she was.

To orient her to the space, George made a circuit of the ballroom with her. The room had been no more than half full when they'd arrived, but more and more people drifted in by the minute. Already there was too much noise to hear guests announced, and the violins were no more than a distant squeak unless one walked right by the musicians.

As they strolled the perimeter of the room, her gloved hand resting properly on his arm, George described the people they passed. This lady was a good friend to his sister, Selina; that one was always eager to gossip but was never included in it. The gentleman to their left liked to pretend to stumble against women and so grope them; the one to their right would try to slip the emerald ring from her finger if she danced with him. And look! Lady Deverell was here, which must mean his lordship was recovering well—or drinking so steadily, he didn't notice her absence.

Cass listened to his cheerful monologue with about seventy percent of her attention. The remainder ought to have been devoted to observing and filing away facts in her memory, but in truth, she was *experiencing*. Her fingers in a glove of buttery kid, resting on George's corded forearm. The candles overhead; the scents and sounds of the sweeping room.

Experiencing was not the same thing as *observing*—yet she couldn't make herself stop. There was so much wealth here, and so much company and so much champagne, and none of it for any particular reason. It was just the way these people lived. Merely an evening's entertainment, a way to pass the time.

Good Lord. How strange, and how lovely, and how troubling.

It was all right for her to be rapt, she decided, in her guise as a country girl dragged from her homeland, then returned to it in marital disgrace. Certainly Lady Harrough had been gratified by Cass's greeting, which had probably been both wide-eyed and gape-mouthed.

Lord and Lady Harrough possessed a title of recent vintage, George had told her, which mattered very much to the sort of people who cared about titles. They had piles of money, too, and one of the largest homes in London— but the wealth came from shipping or mining or some other thing that also mattered, and not in a good way. Likely one's family was supposed to have been given a treasure by William the Conqueror. It all seemed very silly, but the unwarranted sense of inferiority meant that their hosts were eager to please and eager to form connections. Which meant good food and much gossip.

Cass snagged another flute of champagne, admiring the wink of her gold and emerald ring on the white surface of her glove. It was all a bit dizzying. This would have to be the last champagne she'd allow herself this evening.

George leaned in to speak by her ear. "Got your courage up?"

She drained the flute, enjoying the pop of bubbles on her tongue, then set the empty glass on the tray of a passing servant. "Yes. Ready to work. Whom would you like me to meet first?"

"Braithwaite," George decided. "Christian name Lionel, and he's affable enough that he might invite you to use it. One of the surviving members of the tontine."

"Along with your father, Deverell, Gerry, and Cavender."

"Very good," George replied. "Braithwaite was the younger son of the late Earl of Allenby—remember, all ten of the members were younger sons when they formed the tontine. His elder brother inherited the title right enough and has had a fine big family."

Cass understood. "So Braithwaite is well out of the line of succession. He'll have spent his life confined to a younger son's allowance."

"Such a man could have been tempted to hurry fate and gain a fortune of his own."

"Possible. Or he might simply be a doting uncle." Cass lifted her chin. "Lead on, and I'll see if I can spot which sort he is."

Their quarry was speaking to a friend, but George interrupted Braithwaite's conversation with all the confidence of a man whom others were inevitably pleased to see. The older man greeted him politely, and Cass sized him up as they completed the introductions.

Lionel Braithwaite was a handsome fellow of about sixty, with deeply tanned skin, curling gray hair, and the sort of strong features that aged well. Though his clothes were of excellent quality, they were several seasons out of date—Cass could thank her landlady's fashion periodicals for this knowledge—and were beginning to show wear.

"Mrs. Benedetti is"—George paused significantly—"a near relative of the late duke, my grandfather."

This code was instantly understood to mean *illegitimate daughter*. Braithwaite regarded Cass with interest. "I am honored to meet the lady."

"The honor is mine," Cass said. "Which is the first scrap I've managed to clutch about myself since returning to England."

It seemed the sort of thing a grateful, harried, unconventional duke's bastard might say.

Braithwaite's mouth curled with humor. Even better, the muscles of George's forearm went all rigid beneath Cass's fingertips.

"What interesting relations you possess, Lord Northbrook," said the older man.

Interesting was not a compliment, but it didn't have to be. *Interesting* meant *arousing interest,* and that was the whole purpose of Cass's presence.

"You have no idea," replied George. "I'm not certain I do either."

"Nor do I," Cass said. "But I am clutched to the welcoming bosom of my family and am eager to find out."

She could almost *feel* George rolling his eyes. This was fun.

"I wonder, Mrs. Benedetti," said Braithwaite, "if you would favor me with a dance?"

Cass's smile froze. *Dancing.* How had she not considered the possibility of dancing? She could move her feet to the tune of a fiddle in a pub, but to dance in a ballroom? Those twining, intricate steps that took months to learn with the help of professional dancing masters?

"I should be delighted," she replied.

This polite sentence had always struck her as funny, as if its second half were missing. *I should be delighted, but I am not.* In this case, it was perfectly true.

"The next one, Braithwaite." George spoke up. "As the lady has promised the first dance to me."

The older man bowed his assent, and Cass drew away after George, who was already pulling her in the direction of the musicians.

"Why did you say we are going to dance?" she hissed. "I can't dance. I don't know how."

He held up a staying finger, then spoke a few words to one of the violinists. When he returned to Cass, he took hold of her hands and tugged her into some sort of elegant contortion.

"You can manage this next one. It'll be a waltz. I'll push you about the floor and twirl you, and you can put your hands all over me and look delighted."

Other couples were beginning to drift up to the musicians, and the center of the ballroom cleared. "Then what?" Cass was beginning to feel alarmed. "Will all the dances be waltzes?"

"They won't, no. But given your fictional background, it's reasonable that you wouldn't have learned to dance. There's no harm in saying so." He placed one of her hands on his shoulder. "Or if you like, we can pretend that you twisted your ankle so you can sit out."

"The Bentons and their leg injuries," she grumbled. "All right."

"You can blame it on me," he said generously. "I'll tread on your foot and mess up your graceful fairylike flit across the floor."

How could one not laugh at that? "It's arranged, then," she agreed. "And maybe for the best. If Braithwaite will honor the poor weak-ankled signora with his company, I can talk to him instead of dancing."

"Thus prying far more information from him than you could if you were tramping through a country dance, exchanging half a sentence at a time," George said. "I told you my plans were always good."

Fortunately for George, there was no time for Cass to reply before the violinist's bow touched string—and with a tremulous sweep, the musicians dipped into the stutter-step of a waltz.

George released Cass's hand at his shoulder, then touched her waist. Their other hands remained clasped.

"One, two three," he murmured, pushing lightly with the hand that cradled her midsection.

Cass gripped his shoulder and stumbled back—or she would have if he hadn't held her steady. Her smooth-soled slippers instead slid backward on the glossy floor as George stepped forward.

"Excellent!" He beamed at her, his blue eyes crinkling at the corners. "You're dancing. Here, let's try a twirl."

"No! Let's not—oh." Before her protest was spoken, the spin was completed. Then there was another shove backward, another little spin. She bit her lip. "I'm going to step on your feet."

"Do your worst." He pulled her closer, humming a little. "I won't even feel the stomp of your fragile little shoes."

She wanted to make a clever reply, but nothing sprang to her lips. She was *experiencing* again, from head to toe. His hand was on her waist, and she held the hard line of his shoulder, and they were part of a twirling crowd of elegant Londoners, and just for now, she was not herself. She was a duke's bastard, dancing.

Cass was jostled and grabbed every day in Bow Street. She'd had lovers' hands on her bare skin. Was it the silk gown, then, that made her so aware of the light touch of George's hand at her waist? The unfamiliar stays, lifting her breasts and rubbing at their sensitive tips?

The knowledge, maybe, that everything from her gown to her name was borrowed and could not last?

"I know you're here to work," he said, "but I hope you'll enjoy yourself all the same."

"Um." She slid back, then fell against him when he twirled her in a new direction. Her mouth went dry.

"I've been to dozens of balls like this, maybe hundreds, since my Oxford days," he continued blithely, seeming oblivious to the upheaval within her. "They're all pleasant enough if you get good things to eat, though I always get pinched by some old dowager who remembers my undignified days in leading strings."

Talk. She needed to remember how to talk. "Do you dance with them?"

"Those pinchy-fingered dowagers? Oh, sometimes. They're terrible dancers but delightful to talk to. Then there are the shy wallflowers, who are just the reverse."

Slip. Slide. Turn. "I'm not sure which sort I am."

"Delightful to talk to," he replied promptly. "You must be; our plan depends on it. Plus my sister, Selina, will be talking about you all evening. Telling everyone how charming you are."

Lady Wexley—no, she'd said to call her Selina, hadn't she?—had promised to gleefully and in greatest confidence spread the news of the family's unfortunate and slightly scandalous guest. The secrecy of this information would, of course, ensure its immediate and wide distribution throughout the guests in attendance.

"Am I charming?" Cass turned over the word, liking it. "I've never had such a compliment before."

"It's not that much of a compliment, I have to admit. 'Charming' means acceptable to know. 'Pretty' means tolerable looking. 'Accomplished' means literate."

"You didn't have to tell me all that," she said. "You could have let me enjoy the nice words." So it was not a compliment, but a polite obligation. Just like the hand at her waist, and the one that clasped her fingers so lightly.

Thus she asked, "What does 'plain' mean?"

George's fingers tightened at her waist. "It means you're never going to let me forget anything, are you?"

She tipped her head, pleased with this reply. "You weren't going to forget. Were you?"

"No. No, I wouldn't forget anything I said to you. Worse luck."

She relented. "You don't have to remember. I'll remember what people say to me. For the case." She twirled, though unfortunately at the wrong time. "Sorry. Another time, you ought to come to the Boar's Head and we'll dance a hornpipe together."

"You'd regret inviting me at once. I'd embarrass you in front of your friends."

"Turnabout is fair play." She followed his lead, getting the timing of the next spin right. It put her head in a whirl. "Before we leave the floor, point out Gerry and Cavender to me, if they are here. I shall work my investigative magic upon them."

It was closer to dawn than midnight when they returned to Ardmore House. George parted with Cass when they reached the third story. She went, he assumed, to her bedchamber, while he went to his experiment room.

Lighting one of the amber-shaded lamps to dispel the darkness, he peered at the paper he'd set into place before leaving for the Harroughs' ball. He had painted a heavy sheet of paper with a solution of silver salts, then laid it upon the glass top of the smaller camera obscura. The camera's cunning method of reflection would shine an image up onto the paper, he thought, and—perhaps—imprint upon it. He had placed the camera before the window, so it looked out upon the facing buildings of Cavendish Square, and left it to stew in the diffuse evening light.

By the ruddy glow of the lamp, he spotted no results. Everything was a uniform pale shade, the paper still damp. He would leave it longer, though daylight would quickly darken the entire sheet if it rested on the glass. Inside the camera obscura with the paper, then, and a wooden board atop the glass to block it. The only light would enter through the lens. It would be a small amount, a little image if it worked. But it just might. By evening, he would know if this trial had succeeded.

Carrying the lamp to the doorway to light his steps, he tugged at his cravat and was already dreaming of bed.

Then a whisper split the nighttime silence. "George."

A female whisper.

"Cass?" He held up the lamp. "Cass? Are you all right?"

A pause. "I . . . need your help." Her bedchamber door was open partway; her form made a shadow around which candlelight spilled.

In an instant, he'd doused the lamp, returned it to its place on the worktable, and stepped back into the dark corridor. Cass was no longer in the doorway, so he tapped at the door before pushing it open further.

"Yes, come in, come in," she replied. He entered the room.

"Close the door," Cass said. She sounded impatient.

She *looked* impatient. Impatience was in every line of her body, from her half-unpinned hair to her bare toes peeking beneath the hem of her gown. Impatience was scattered about the lamplit room: slippers on the floor, gloves bunched and draped on the vanity, stockings tossed over the top of a dressing screen.

At the sight of her discarded clothing, *impatience* was not the sentiment that settled upon George. He forgot that he had been tired or that his cravat was scratchy about his neck. He could think only that a woman was shedding her clothing in his presence, and then it was difficult to think of anything at all.

George was casting about for something to say besides

what have I done to deserve this—good or ill—when Cass spoke again. Impatiently, of course. "I can't get this gown off."

He shut his eyes. He must pretend not to notice the erotic clutter of castoff garments. "Thank you for the information. Let me summon Gatiss for you, shall I?"

"No!" She sounded shocked. "I'm not going to wake a servant at three o'clock in the morning just to undress me as if I were a baby!"

Undressing. Lord. This conversation was not going to veer back in a safe direction, was it? Yet it must continue. George required his eyes to open. "Assisting women with garments is the purpose of her position as lady's maid. She expects to be woken when she's needed."

"She might expect it, but . . . I don't want to do that." Cass bit her lip. "It doesn't feel right. I'm used to doing for myself, and this is the first time I haven't been able to. But that's not Gatiss's fault."

"It is," George said. "Because she helped dress you in whatever contraptions you now can't undo."

"They're not contraptions. They're just clothes. But they fasten up the back, and I can't reach. Can't you help me?" She turned, presenting him with her back. "It'll take three minutes. There's no reason to wake up Gatiss for something you could do in three minutes."

George sighed. "I might be your fake cousin and your real investigative partner, but I am also a man. You're asking me to undo your clothing. I might get ideas." *I'm already getting ideas.*

Beautiful ideas in which he continued removing his cravat and progressing to his bedchamber. But in this version of the fantasy, a redheaded temptress accompanied him, and she undid his buttons just as he unfastened hers, and they fell onto the sheets and . . .

A hand touched his. "George. It's just me." Earnest brown eyes met his. "I'll ring for Gatiss if you really don't want to help, but . . . it's just me."

Oh, he was willing to help, all right. That was the problem.

He wouldn't let on. He mustn't. "Right. Sorry. Can't think what came over me. Do forgive my maidenly bashfulness and turn about."

He knew who she was. He didn't need reminding of that. She wasn't Mrs. Benedetti; she was Miss Benton, and it was all a role, and he had a job to do just as she did. And right now, that job was undoing the damned buttons. It was irrelevant that they were the buttons on Cass's gown, and that they would open the bodice of her dress. It did not matter in the slightest that she smelled of sweet flowers and her tumbling-down hair shone like copper and bronze.

He undid the damned buttons, gritting his teeth against everything else in the world. There was a short march of them, covered in the same blue silk as the gown. They seemed to grow tinier and more sleek with each movement of his fingers, slipping away like minnows.

She was saying something now. It was words and sentences, but he could hardly take in what she was saying. For he'd finally undone the buttons; the fabric parted; and there was her shift, nearly transparent, and the top of her corset. They had been hidden beneath the rich silk; they hid still her skin, and he wanted only to undo more and more until every layer between them was stripped away.

"What do you think?" she asked.

He found it difficult to swallow and shape a reply to what she'd asked him. Whatever it had been.

"George?" she pressed.

"I shall become capable of listening in a moment." He turned his mind to chemical solutions. Acids and salts. Unsuccessful experiments. "There. All right. Speak freely."

"I was saying"—her voice was tinged, again, with impatience—"that I thought the evening was a great success. Your idea of the wrenched ankle was a good one. Braithwaite was only too happy not to dance."

"Most gentlemen are." Did he have to unlace or unbutton anything else? Surely he'd done penance enough for whatever sins he had committed today.

Or perhaps not, as he was continuing to commit the sin of lust. He really couldn't help it. *Acids salts unsuccessful experiments think think think.*

Cass was oblivious. "He was only too happy to talk about Gerry too, since the man wasn't there. Braithwaite said Gerry's gout is worsening, so it's hard for him to get about. And Cavender told me—"

"I can't do this," George blurted. "Your gown is falling off and—Look, just ring for Gatiss. Or anyone. The cook or the scullery maid. The stableboy if you must."

She turned her head to the side, regarding him aslant. "Why, Lord Northbrook. You can't be thinking I have designs on you. Me, with an illustrious man such as you?"

The amusement in her voice did nothing to dampen his growing arousal, though he tried to respond as lightly as she. "If you did, you'd be at least the tenth woman this week. I haven't kept count higher than that."

She reached a hand up to her shoulder. Feeling about for his fingers? No, she was only tugging at the edge of the now-unbuttoned bodice. From the front, she likely looked almost dressed. She could have no idea of the view with which she now presented him.

"The curse of the titled heir." She sounded sympathetic. "It must be dreadfully dull being harassed with female attentions all the time. I'm sorry."

"Do you mean that?"

"Of course I do. But don't worry." She turned about, removing that enticing view from his eyes, and patted his cheek. "You're quite safe with me. Why, you're far too young for me. You can be no more than thirty years old."

"Twenty-nine," he grumbled. "I am your senior by what, three years?"

"You might think so. But twenty-six in female years is at least double your own age, and if you add twin years on top of that . . . gracious. I've lived a lifetime already, and I've no interest in breaking you to saddle."

His brows lifted. They were not the only part of his person that did so.

So he motioned for her to turn around again. In for a penny, in for a pound. As her partially unfastened clothing presented itself again, he said, "What if I've been well-trained already? Put through my paces by the best?"

Why was he saying these things? He shouldn't be, just as his fingertips shouldn't linger over the lacing at the back of her corset. Teasing it wider and wider open, when it was already quite wide enough for her to slip it free.

He was hard and growing harder by the second.

"Who has trained you? Merry widows and expensive whores?" She used the same tone of courteous interest with which she'd earlier collected information about the members of the tontine.

"The former; not the latter. I don't pay for sex."

"Certainly not; I should have guessed. You are far too

attractive. Women swoon at the sight of you. They trip and fall into your arms, and sometimes onto your—"

"Don't finish that sentence."

She shrugged. The movement of her shoulders caused the blue silk to slip down farther. "Very well. I'm glad you're not a virgin. No one thinks about sex more than virgins. This way, we'll be able to think more about the case."

His fingers fumbled the corset laces. "I take it you're not a virgin either."

"What would be the point of that? There's no value to virginity if one's not going to be sold off in a good marriage. And even if one is, once the ceremony's done, it can't be undone. Even if the bride's been plucked. And the groom *always* has been."

"Who have you . . . been with?" He dropped his hands from her clothing, clenching his fingers tight. "Sorry. None of my affair."

She felt the edge of the gown and corset again, then thanked him as if he'd handed her a cup of tea. Taking up a dressing gown, she and her unfastened clothes disappeared behind the privacy screen.

"It's none of your affair, true," came her voice. "But I don't mind telling you. They were men of the moment, and they served their purpose."

This was intriguing. "What purpose?"

The blue gown was flung over the top of the screen. He almost groaned. "One was for pleasure," Cass said, "because I liked the look of him. One was for protection, to get away from a threat. And one was for comfort, because I didn't want to be alone."

She said this so matter-of-factly, as if there was nothing shameful in being lonely, or in doing anything—even taking another person into her body—to seize upon companionship.

George had become trapped, perhaps, by the mindset of the beau monde. The fashionable folk of London could admit a need for a new hat, or for a pair of fine grays, or a trustworthy servant. Never could one admit a need for something real, though, that could not be bought. Something like companionship. Safety. Purpose.

The pleasure of encountering a like-minded soul.

Of the two of them, he was the noble, yet he'd never taken a lover for any reason so noble as those.

"So. What were we talking about?" Cass asked. "Oh, yes—the tontine. What I learned at the ball."

And as if she hadn't just told him too much and not enough at all about her sexual past, she launched into a description of the conversations she'd taken part in and overheard. Garments came and went from the top of the dressing screen as she spoke, so that George was as transfixed by these as by her recall of the evening.

"Might I emerge in a dressing gown?" she said during a pause. "Or will you be scandalized again?"

"Don't let that stop you," George said.

He cast about for somewhere to sit. Before the vanity table was a fragile little affair of cushion and wicker-work; he ignored that in favor of a more solid-looking armchair beside the fireplace. Across the room from the vanity table and the dressing screen. A safe distance, or as safe as one could get while remaining in the same room with a woman flinging her clothes everywhere.

Cass emerged from behind the screen, wrapped from collarbone to ankle in a tawny silk that made her look like a flame. She seated herself at the inadequate chair before the vanity and began pulling the remaining hairpins from her locks.

"Lady Deverell was there tonight, too," she noted. "Which you noticed, since you danced with her twice."

"Hunting for information," George said lightly. "As you were."

"That's what Charles said about his relationship with Lady Deverell. Of course, he hunted for information inside her gown."

George eyed Cass pointedly, meeting her gaze in the vanity mirror.

"You were not looking for information inside my gown just now," she sniffed. "My gown was incidental to the conversation."

"Yes, I remember that from a few moments ago when we were discussing our romantic histories."

"I don't recall using the word *romance*." Hairpins pattered through her fingertips to the surface of the table. "But let us move along. Cavender, I noticed, was dressed more fashionably than most men there. More fobs, a higher cravat, a narrower waist to his coat."

George stretched out his legs. "He looked like an old man playacting as a young one. It was strange. I don't remember him aping modern fashion so slavishly in the past."

"But his wife died some years ago, did she not? Perhaps he's looking to wed again, and the clothing is his courtship plumage." She rubbed her fingers over the heavy silk knot that closed her dressing gown. "It was all cheap and showy, though. Almost like a theatrical costume. It looked all right across a ballroom, but up close, the fobs were base metal and the man's coat was shiny. Not wool, but some other cloth."

"So he wants to look richer than he is? That's hardly damning. Most people want that."

"True. I'm not sure if it means anything." Cass took up a brush, then began to draw it through the long length of her unpinned hair. "Lionel Braithwaite was a little shabby, the reverse of our theatrical Mr. Cavender. He was dressed in clothing of good quality, but it was old. The rare man who lives within his means, perhaps? He was charming, too. A delightful conversationalist."

"That's not relevant," said George.

"It is. If people enjoy talking, they often tell me things. But in this instance, he didn't say anything of note. He was cheerful and didn't seem at all worried about a threat. Which was, itself, of note."

George's cravat was beginning to feel scratchy again. He picked at the elaborate knot that fastened it. "How is not saying anything important something important to notice?"

Cass set the silver-backed brush down with a heavy *click,* then divided her hair into three sections. "Braithwaite's calm means that the threatening note and the earl's stabbing are not publicly known. Which means the remaining men in the tontine don't know they're a target."

"That seems a great deal to gather from a normal conversation. But it makes sense."

"Of course it makes sense," she said. "People follow patterns. If Braithwaite acted unworried, most likely he is unworried. Which tells us that our shadowy attacker is holding back, for now. But we don't know why, and therefore we don't know for how long."

They both fell silent. He was transfixed by the rapid movement of her fingers, plaiting her hair into a long rope of copper. When she bound the end, she turned on the seat, facing George from across the room.

"I think," she said, "we ought to involve Angelus in this

investigation. Your friend Lady Isabel has met him. Your father knows him as well."

George recoiled at the name of the lord of London's underworld. Few had met Angelus, but everyone knew his name, and almost everyone in the beau monde had borrowed from his bottomless purse at some point. "Why on *earth* would we want to involve a man from whom my father is attempting to extricate himself financially?"

"Because Angelus knows so many people's financial problems. He might have an inkling who would be most likely to need the tontine's saved-up funds now, after nearly forty years of peaceful waiting."

George had to grant this. "I can consult with my father tomorrow. We'll find the time for this."

Cass looked amused. "Find the time? What do you do with your days, that you must go seeking for a free moment?"

Why was his cravat so *tight?* "A fair question, if an impolite one. I do whatever I want to. I've a title and no responsibilities."

It wouldn't always be that way. Overseeing a dukedom was an all-consuming role involving Parliament, rents, tenants, staff, estates, agriculture, livestock, and investments.

That is, it *could* be. The Duke of Ardmore didn't sit in the House of Lords. He hired stewards—good and competent men, as far as George knew—to run his estates as best they could. And all the while he gambled, debts mounting, living high and indulging his sickness at the faro-table.

Ardmore did whatever he wanted to, and he wasn't much of an example to follow.

"I do whatever I *choose* to," George corrected.

It was not much different from his previous statement, but it seemed better. More active, less dissipated. More controlled, less indulgent.

Cass didn't look impressed. "And what is that? Tonight, for example. This moment. What are you choosing to do?"

She sounded skeptical, but this he disregarded. An opportunity presented itself, and if there was one thing the son of the Duke of Ardmore understood, it was how and when to take a chance.

"Whatever you wish," he told her. This was more accurate, because if he'd done what he wanted, his fingertips would be rolling her nipples to tight peaks at this very moment.

If she wished that, he'd do it in a moment. The heavy silk of the robe draped over her breasts like a stroking hand.

His words were spoken lightly, but she seemed to weigh them as if they were a proclamation.

"Thank you," she said. "That is a comforting offer."

This, he hadn't expected. "Is it? I confess, I didn't know what feeling my statement might inspire."

"Oh, it is. I'm not often told things can be as I wish. Remember that I have shared my life with Charles since before birth."

Ah. Should he say he was sorry for that? Grateful to be able to offer something different? It sounded nice, having a brother and never being lonely—yet he knew this was not the impression she'd intended to give.

He had waited too long to speak, for she replied now. "May I take you up another time on that offer of doing whatever I wish? Right now I wish to sleep, and there's no way you can help me with that."

He ceased tugging at his cravat. "I could. I could read a very boring book to you."

"No need for that. Thank you." She smiled; it was sweet, and a little sad. "We'd both best be left alone with our thoughts now."

That was the last thing he wanted, especially now that

his thoughts were sure to be about her. Her bodice unlaced, her hair down, and—most seductive of all—her knowing eyes upon his.

"Good night, then," he said. "Let it be as you wish."

Her smile was everything he himself could have wished for.

Chapter Seven

"This is a call among friends, not purely a case," said Lady Isabel Jenks to Cass. "Of course we wanted to welcome you and Lord Northbrook to our home."

Leaning closer to Cass's ear, George murmured, "And this way it's more unofficial than if we met at their offices, and we don't have to follow the law strictly."

Cass laughed. But Callum Jenks, her old friend, had the ears of a bat and had overheard George, for he said, "We always follow the law."

"If it's best," Lady Isabel said cheerfully, dark eyes dancing.

"Which it is," Jenks said in his gruff way.

Not even romance, riches, and relocation—more of those troublesome R words—had smoothed his blunt edges. Cass was glad of it. Over the years, she and Charles had visited Jenks many times in the rented lodgings he'd used to inhabit. Much like the Bentons' own rooms, they were a relic of better days, inexpensive and clinging to respectability only due to the tireless efforts of a determined landlady.

But the previous year, Jenks had become tonnish. After he'd saved Lady Selina's then-betrothed from an attack,

London's elite had realized his connection with the glamorous and violent Royal Rewards case. The theft of a fortune in gold sovereigns from the Royal Mint had fascinated all England, and Jenks had been one of the Bow Street Runners who'd located much of the stolen gold.

Now Jenks was married to a marquess's daughter, a pretty woman with dark hair and eyes and a sphinxlike face that lit with kindness every time she smiled. When Jenks left Bow Street to establish his own consulting practice with Lady Isabel, the beau monde had flocked to present him with cases.

For a grocer's son, it was all rather strange and—Cass suspected—sometimes exasperating. There was no denying the financial rewards of becoming fashionable, though. Jenks had exchanged his rented rooms for the couple's tidy gray-brick house in Bedford Square fronted by a green space with well-grown trees. It had full servants' quarters and both a drawing room and a morning room; luxury indeed.

Though it was early afternoon, the latter space was where Lady Isabel and Jenks had settled their callers. In the past week, Cass had entered more fine homes than she had in the year before, but this was her favorite of them all. The morning room was a neat, sunny space papered in a pleasant yellow print, furnished with new but comfortable pieces and smelling of sweet pastries from the trays of dainties set before the callers.

Cass had declined to take any of these. Her stomach was unsettled, either from the late night of polite revelry or the recollection that George had seen her in her dressing gown and knew how many lovers she'd had.

Not that he, cheerful and heedless as always, seemed affected by either of these facts.

"Good sunlight, even at this hour," George observed as he joined Cass on a settee covered in ivory silk as soft as a dove's breast. "This is east-facing, yes? Maybe the north-facing windows of my experiment room aren't ideal. With more intense sunlight . . ." He trailed off, looking all about with interest.

Had she really asked him to unfasten her gown the night before? It seemed so far away, the silks and buttons and talk of sex. All so innocent on the surface, not a single touch of bare skin to skin; all fraught longing below.

This was better. Daytime was better, and being in the company of others, and digging into the seamier side of George's suspicions about the tontine. No more balls and champagne for a while; if Cass wasn't careful, she'd get her head turned not only by his lordship but by the role of Mrs. Benedetti.

"Mr. Gabriel has arrived," announced the butler, a thin gray man named Selby.

"Show him in, of course," said Lady Isabel, just as George said, "Who is Mr. Gabriel?"

"An affectation," said a voice from the doorway. "You will forgive it, I hope, understanding my desire for privacy to be equal to your own."

And the final member of their gathering stepped into the morning room.

Over her years with Bow Street, Cass had met criminals both petty and powerful, but to her knowledge, she'd never encountered Angelus in person. He proved to be a hale man of about fifty years, with silver-shot black hair worn dramatically to his shoulders. He was dressed all in black save for white linens, the silver embroidery on his waistcoat, and the heavy silver head of his ebony cane.

She recognized him at once.

"I've seen you," she blurted as the older man seated

himself. "Recently. With Lord Deverell. You called upon him one night and discussed the tontine with him."

At her side, George tensed. "You *know* him?" he whispered. "Angelus?"

"Felicitations, Miss Benton, on recognizing me." The king of London's underworld accepted a steaming cup of black tea from Lady Isabel. "I should chastise you for spying and for listening at doors, but it is your job, isn't it?"

So he knew her name. "It is my job, yes. And I suspect if you minded, you'd have let me know long before this moment."

He eyed Cass over the rim of his teacup. She tried to keep very still as she took his measure in return, like a rabbit hiding in plain sight from a predator. In Angelus's eyes, there was something of the panther. Hooded, observant, ready to pounce. One should be very careful around such a man, who could destroy with a figurative swipe of his paw: a mere sentence, an order, a rumor. All more damaging than a physical blow.

Yet his voice was pleasant, and as carefully schooled as Cass's own when he replied, "I have been managing the funds of this bedamned tontine for years. Lord Deverell wanted a loan from me based upon his contribution. Wanted out of the tontine entirely, rather, but without having to go to the trouble of dying."

Lady Isabel handed him a plate piled with almond biscuits. "Your favorites, I think? And one can't blame a man for not wanting to die to collect money."

"One can't," agreed Angelus, "but I didn't turn over a share of the money to him either. It would be unfair to the other investors."

"I suppose all the survivors see the tontine as an investment," replied Lady Isabel.

As the others also took up sweets and teacups, George

shook his head. "An investment they're entitled to claim in full? All five of them? They cannot think so."

Angelus selected a biscuit from his plate. "It would not be the first time a bunch of blue-blooded, middle-aged Englishmen thought themselves entitled to something that oughtn't to be theirs. As much of the world can attest."

After launching this cannon-shot, he then turned to Lady Isabel to congratulate her and Jenks on the forthcoming arrival of their child.

"How did you know? We've hardly told anyone." Lady Isabel's hand fluttered to her midsection. "There are months to go, yet."

"I have ways of listening at doors, too." Was that a wink? Did he *wink* at Cass?

"That's just disturbing," said George.

"I never claimed it wasn't," said Angelus, crunching through an almond biscuit. "Though in this matter, it was simple to determine. One had only to note that you no longer accept cases that take you afield. And far from looking ill, you appear healthy and blooming."

"She changed her pattern," Cass realized. "And you knew what it meant."

"I always know," replied the older man. "It's more disturbing that way."

All right, Cass was beginning to like Angelus. She suspected that when the panther pounced, it would not be on her, or anyone present in this room.

"Congratulations and disturbances aside," said Jenks, "my wife asked you here at the request of her friend." He nodded toward George. "Lord Northbrook suspects foul play related to the tontine formed by his father and nine other men some forty years ago."

Still eating biscuits and drinking tea, Angelus listened to George's theory about the recent mysterious deaths, the unsuccessful attack on Lord Deverell, and Cass's involvement in the investigation under an assumed name.

"You ask good questions," concluded Angelus when the tale was complete. "For one hundred thousand pounds, many men would not ask questions at all. They'd seek their own solutions, maybe with one of those knives that almost did for Deverell."

George blanched. "One hundred thou—no, surely not. The tontine is worth one *hundred thousand pounds?*"

The older man shrugged his black-clad shoulders. "I've managed the investments well. And they've had decades to grow. The last survivor will be a rich man."

Such a fortune was so immense, Cass couldn't even speak the amount. "They're already rich men, though," she said. "Or so they seem. We wondered if you knew anything to the contrary about any of them."

"I have a list of the ten investors." George took a folded paper from his coat pocket and handed it over.

Angelus unfolded it and scanned the handwritten lines. "Henry Rose, deceased. Ellis Murchison, deceased. Thomas Whiting, shot. Gregory Knotwirth, drowned. Francis Lightfoot, poisoned." He took up a final almond biscuit, pointing it at George. "Bad odds, being in this group. Half of them dead before they reached their dotage."

"A tontine is no health tonic," George said grimly.

Nodding his agreement, Angelus set aside his plate and cup. "Two of them don't have a cause of death listed. Henry Rose? I don't know the name."

"He died of consumption perhaps thirty-five years ago," George replied. "Ellis Murchison is the other man who died young, ten years or so after Rose. Some sort of liver disease. He turned all yellow, my father said."

"And then no deaths for nearly twenty-five years," said Cass. "No suspicious accidents or sudden illnesses."

"Right," said George. "I believe something changed recently in the circumstances of one of the survivors. Something in the past year or two that meant he couldn't wait for time and chance to bring him a fortune."

Angelus drew a fingertip down the list, name by name. "If so, the news has not come to my ears, nor the borrower to my door. Only Lord Deverell has tried to get money of me, yet he was almost a victim. Were any of these deaths investigated through Bow Street as suspicious?"

"No," said Cass. "None of them."

"Are you certain?" George twisted on the seat, regarding her more closely. "Don't you want to look at records, or—"

"She's sure," interrupted Jenks. "She remembers Bow Street cases like you remember what you wore to parties."

George twisted back, now looking at Jenks. "Is that meant to be an insult?"

Jenks eyed him mildly. "Why? Is it insulting?"

Cass stifled a smile.

Angelus, ignoring this conversational diversion, pulled a bit of pencil from a pocket and began marking on the list. "Knotwirth vanished last year, didn't he? There was betting about it at White's, whether he'd turn up safely or be found dead. More than one gentleman needed my assistance"—a loan, Cass guessed he meant—"in covering a debt of honor."

She hoped he charged a towering rate of interest to those who wagered on a man's safety.

"It seems cold, in hindsight," George said, as if he could read Cass's thoughts. "But Knotwirth was known to vanish, sometimes for days on end. He was a scatterbrained sort, and his fondness for eating opium didn't help."

"He drowned, you say." Angelus was still making notes on the list.

"Accidentally," said George. "Or so one guesses. It took ages for his body to turn up."

Lady Isabel was managing the bleak subject with complete composure. "How could one be sure the body was Knotwirth's, then? Surely the condition was not good."

"The teeth," said her husband. "He'd several of gold."

"And they weren't stolen by mudlarks?" she asked.

"They were. The jaw was missing just the teeth that had been gold in life."

Lady Isabel's brows knit. "It's not much to go on."

"It's as much evidence as there ever is," said Cass. "Unless the unknown person happened to be carrying a card case that didn't degrade and wasn't stolen, and his clothing still had its labels. But as that never happens, at least coroners can tell a bit about the height and even the age of a person."

"True enough, and they had to conclude it was Knotwirth," George said. "We'd all been looking for him."

"Had you?" Angelus asked, sounding as if he thought the opposite were more likely true.

"Well, his wife had," George admitted. "No one else thought it was a particular surprise when he vanished. As I said, he was an opium eater."

Angelus looked back at the list. "And the man who was shot? This wasn't at first regarded as a suspicious death either. Was he a duelist or a terrible hunter?"

"Thomas Whiting," George said. "A terrible hunter. He went out alone and was found all sprayed with shot. His gun had misfired, or something of that sort." Now *he* sounded as if he thought the opposite were more likely true.

"What about the man who was poisoned?" asked Lady Isabel.

"Lightfoot." George sounded grim. "He was morose over the death of his only son from consumption. Calling

Lightfoot's own passing an accident was a kindness to the family, to allow him a churchyard burial."

"So he ended himself." Angelus scribbled another note.

"Maybe," George granted.

Talk, talk, talk, and no further clues were surfacing. Cass gritted her teeth; they were solving nothing. "There's no pattern here. If there were, Lord Deverell would have drunk himself to death, and your father would be bashed on the head by a falling painting."

"Or choked by a deck of cards," Angelus suggested.

George made an unspeakable noise.

"What I mean," Cass explained, "is that the earlier deaths made sense with the men as they were known in life. The attack on Lord Deverell draws attention to itself. There's no way it could pass for a natural death, even should it succeed. And who will suspicion inevitably turn to?"

"The other members of the tontine," said Jenks.

Isabel laid a hand on his, an unconscious gesture of intimacy. "Is it possible," said her ladyship, "that someone would want to kill Lord Deverell and avert suspicion by blaming the tontine? Who would gain by his death other than the remaining survivors?"

"This is a grim conversation," said George.

Cass rubbed at her temples. When was the last time she'd slept as long as she wished? "It is, but there are to be more just like it. There will have to be if we're to sort this out."

For a moment, George's fingers touched hers—then they were gone. "I can find out the terms of Lord Deverell's will, if that will help. At a guess, his wife and the daughters of his second marriage would benefit from his death. But that's not to say they'd be well off."

"Had he no children of his first marriage?" Angelus was looking at George as if he already knew the answer.

"One daughter," George said calmly. "Lily. She is no longer living."

Lily. Cass had heard that name before, from Selina. Hmm.

Lady Isabel nibbled at some confection of cake and glaze, her expression thoughtful. "It cannot be right to look for his attacker within his household. Why should his wife and daughters wish for his death? Lord Deverell is a gentle-natured man, and Lady Deverell does as she pleases."

So it had seemed to Cass, too. Yet even as a terrible maid and superior spy, she hadn't pierced the secrets of Deverell Place in a week—for if she had, surely his lordship would never have been in danger. "Without living in a household for some time, one can never know what goes on within it," she said to her hostess.

As a guest under the Ardmore roof, Cass had quickly seen that not even the privileged and titled were spared from ordinary human heartaches. The duchess was ill, the duke was lonely, the dogs were afraid, the servants were weary of it all.

And George? She couldn't capture him in a single adjective. There wasn't a word for what she thought of him—at least not one that remained the same for any significant length of time.

All this she knew about the people of Ardmore House, but she didn't know *why,* and *why* mattered in a case far more than *what.* And George was part of this case, as much as Lord Deverell and a stiletto and a note that said FOUR LEFT. George was the one who had seen the case for what it was.

Angelus folded the list and slipped it back into his pocket, along with the pencil. "The ton is more bloodthirsty than I ever knew as a youth. Fancy betting on one's survival at the expense of others."

To Cass's eye, George appeared tired for the first time

today. "I wish the tontine had never been formed. Have you any insight into the most likely culprit behind these attacks—if attacks they even were?"

The lord of the criminal underworld looked at George with pity. "In my experience, people are neither as complicated nor as clever as they wish to believe they are. Which of the survivors gambles and is constantly short of money?"

Lady Isabel bit her lip. Jenks locked eyes with Cass for a moment, then squeezed his wife's hand.

At Cass's side, George's shoulders sank. "You mean my father."

Slowly, Angelus nodded. "The Duke of Ardmore always needs money, and last year he lied to me about the painting he owed me. Why should we believe he would not go to the necessary lengths to secure himself a fortune?"

"He's my father," said George. "I can't believe—no."

Cass wasn't sure whether she should reach out to him or not. "Because you think he's not capable of hurting people?" she nudged.

To her surprise, George hesitated before answering. "It's not that. More that he's not capable of planning to such a degree. He looks only to the next game, and maybe to the one after that. He's got a gambler's heart, such as it is. Risk and games are his lifeblood. He might gamble for other shares in the tontine; he wouldn't kill for them."

From the thoughtful expression on Angelus's face, he—like Cass—was far more convinced by this analysis of the duke's flaws than he would have been by an insistence on the duke's good character. "Even so," said the older man. "Someone is reckless, and you believe that same someone is willing to kill. You do not know who. It's wise to have Miss Benton staying with you."

George tried for a smile. "For my father's protection. Yes, I told him this."

"And for your own," Angelus replied. "Spying and listening at doors has never been more important, Lord Northbrook. Lives may depend upon it."

"If the members of the tontine are targeted, then I'm not in danger," George said.

Cass shook her head. "If someone is targeting the tontine, and they know you're investigating, and they're desperate, you could be in grave danger."

"You can't do better than having Cass look after you," Jenks said. "No one will suspect it."

Cass laughed. "Because I am such a delicate female, looking after a large strong man?"

George looked pleased. Jenks looked stern, but that was how he looked ninety-eight percent of the time.

Lady Isabel looked amused. "I think my husband meant the compliment to your acting skill rather than to Lord Northbrook's heft. But of course he is a big strong man, too, and cannot speak about emotions."

Jenks regarded his wife. "I'm having another emotion right now. Can you guess it?"

"Not in front of friends, darling."

Angelus struck his cane against the carpeted floor. "Flirt later. Plan now. What will you do next?" His black brows raised, he regarded each of the others in turn.

Now George looked blank. Isabel looked troubled. And Jenks, of course, looked stern.

Cass sighed; only one answer came to mind. "We do just what we've been doing for the past week. We gossip."

Thus charged anew, Cass spied and listened, gleaning knowledge wherever she could. The next week flew by in a whirl of calls and teas and dinners, with a new gown—thanks to Selina—on each occasion.

She owed her embrace by society to Selina too, who seemed to enjoy the secondhand adventure and introduced Cass to all her acquaintances. Elegant old Lady Teasdale, with sharp eyes and a dry sense of humor; young Mrs. Gadolin, whose deep pockets were matched only by her frank eagerness to be thought tonnish. Lady Helena Selwyn, a brittle woman of careful dress and manner who turned every conversation to the accomplishments of her young sons. Any number of pleasant, wealthy young women on the verge of marriage, or just married.

Cass had been charged with placing herself at the center of gossip, and surely she had reached it. The women of the beau monde seemed to talk of nothing except what other people were doing, or what they *might* be doing, and with whom.

There was far more talking than there was doing, with the result that every action was picked over and dissected until all the life was gone from it.

It was strange to Cass, but she rather liked it. For the first time, she was experiencing leisure, and the novel realization that she had resources enough to solve a case—given time and clues, too.

Besides the proper sorts of calls and teas, Cass tossed in a more scandalous outing every day or two. George was a great help with this, reminding her that she ought not to rap at the door of White's and ask for him; nor should she be seen smoking a cheroot in public, whether it made her cough or not—and it did. She also trespassed against the *oughts* of society in smaller ways, by carrying her own bandbox and hopping herself down from a carriage. Only some of these mistakes were intentional.

The women of the ton seemed to welcome Cass for her

novelty, and since she'd nothing else to recommend herself, she traded upon it with little subtlety. The familiar five names of the tontine survivors—Deverell, Ardmore, Gerry, Cavender, Braithwaite—she dropped into conversation and listened for echoes of gossip, but they simply sank without ripples of information. For her own amusement, then, Cass mentioned George to see what tittle-tattle surrounded the ducal heir.

Nothing shocking, alas. Much giggling from the unwed maidens; much exasperation from Selina. "Better than most young men," sniffed Lady Teasdale. Lady Isabel looked at Cass with a curiosity that made her regret mentioning his name.

Damn. The noblewoman had taken on her husband Jenks's noticing ways.

But it wasn't all leisure, Cass's time in society. She wasn't always in society, for one thing. Cass stopped in at Bow Street whenever she could. If anyone were following the eccentric Ardmore cousin around London, they would indeed wonder about that lady's fascination with the magistrate's court.

There was little progress on the cases left before Charles. The Watch thought to be entrapping young women had done nothing wrong—at least when anyone was watching.

"Janey is doing as much of that as she can," Fox told Cass during one of her visits to the courtroom. A social call, it almost felt like, in her grand clothing and with a ducal carriage waiting outside.

Cass opened her mouth to protest Janey's involvement, but before a syllable left her lips, Fox held up a hand. "I know. You said you'd see to it. But really, Miss Benton . . . how? When you're not even here?"

She fumbled for words, but there were none to be found. Informants were not puppets, to be yanked on and made to do one's bidding. A Runner's success depended on relationships with people like Janey, and those had to be built from trust and cultivated over time.

Fox was right. With Charles injured, Cass had to be here to do the work. And right now she simply couldn't.

She retreated from that thought, skittering away like a startled crab. "What about the pockets being picked at Drury Lane?"

"They're still being picked. When are you going there under your exotic new identity?" Fox's tone was not unkind, but it held reproach. Cass felt all the shame that she'd once felt when her grandmother looked at her with disappointed eyes.

Overall, the passage of the week gave her a feeling of not being in the right place, not doing enough. Her work in Bow Street was being neglected or covered by someone else—and how was Charles to keep his job if a Benton didn't do the work?

At least Charles had been forced to restrain his spendthrift ways while confined largely to bed. With the start of a new week, George paid Cass another five pounds, and this time it stayed in her own pocket.

She felt guilty about taking the payment. Keeping it for herself. Not using it at once, not *needing* it at once.

And maybe not even deserving it. After all, no one else from the tontine had been attacked. The Duke of Ardmore was beginning to grumble—well, was grumbling more loudly—about the plan. About being watched, or having to be careful. About it not being so serious; after all, Lord Deverell's wound had healed enough for him to return to society, and if one didn't look for a limp, one would never know it was there.

Did she need to be here anymore, in Ardmore House?

If she didn't, would she admit it to herself—much less to George?

Oh, she was in danger, but not the sort for which an investigator was used to watching out. No, she was in danger of believing in it all: the role, the fantasy, the notoriety.

One had to believe it to be convincing in a role, but every investigator could tell tales of a role that had sunk in too deeply. The false dockworker who couldn't shake the rough language when he went home. The sometime pawnbroker who saw worthless trinkets posing as items of value everywhere. The pretend pimp or madam who couldn't help but wonder how many men one passed on the street each day had given coin for sex, had treated a prostitute roughly or given her a disease.

Comparatively, this was a lovely role, but it would be all the more difficult to shed because of that. Someday soon she'd change sleek silks for stiff cotton; a bath brought by a servant for a cold morning wash in a basin.

She ought to guard against the inevitable end, but if she carried it always at the forefront of her mind, she wouldn't be who she needed to be for George.

Not for George. For the role. The job. The case.

Yet the two were tied together, and she was entwined with all.

The most difficult part came each night, when she told George what she'd learned, and then they looked at each other as if that couldn't be everything. There must be something more to come. The silence was tight, a tension that filled her from belly to breast, until every night she almost burst out with a "stay with me"—but instead he said good night, and she said it back as if there was nothing else on her mind, and she turned the key in the lock more to keep herself in than to keep anyone out.

If she really were a duke's bastard, she would take him to bed. Wouldn't she? Surely she would. Everyone thought she was the sort of woman who would do such a thing, and they were living in the same house, and they were both unencumbered, and . . .

It wouldn't be the first time Cass had taken a man to bed on a case. But it was the first time she'd thought about it so much without leaping in to get a result. More and more, she wished they were together by choice, not because he'd hired her. She wished there were no case at all—though if there never had been, she'd never have come to know him.

Maybe that would have been for the best.

She wanted to take him to bed because she liked him. His words, his laughter, his curiosity. The gentle way he treated her and the burning way he looked at her. She liked it all.

But liking something, wanting something, had never been reason enough for Cassandra Benton to pursue it. She knew too well: it would be difficult enough to leave this case with her head turned by luxury. If she surrendered her body to George, her heart would follow, and she would never recover from the impoverishment.

Chapter Eight

Any time George needed a respite from his thoughts, he came to the walled yard behind Ardmore House. Here he had once hung a block of wood and painted target circles upon it for a bit of archery. He could fire a few arrows to one side of the yard, away from the bustle of servants going to and from the small garden, the shed with tools, the washtub and boiler, the cook's small flock of chickens.

Here he was solitary, but not alone. On this particular morning, barely past dawn, he couldn't be alone. His thoughts were too persistent. Intrusive, really. Obstinate. Unexpected.

Much like Cassandra Benton.

Since that night of the Harroughs' ball, he'd never been able to forget the sight of her bared skin and scattered clothing. She wasn't only Miss Benton anymore, or resourceful Cass. She was a woman, lovely in her trust of him. He held it gingerly as he would a glass ball, unwilling to let it go, unwilling to do anything that might harm it.

Caught by it.

He took up bow and arrow. Nocked the arrow, tightened

his fingers around the string. Held the tension, tested it, let the arrow fly.

Shh-whup. His ears caught the whisk of the arrow through space, the *thump* of its metal tip into the wood target.

It was a short distance to shoot; hitting the target was as easy and unsatisfying as cracking a rotten nut. But it kept his arms in good trim. And that was more important day after day: his grip on the glass ball had become ever more determined—and ever more slippery.

The more he thought about it—Cass—trust—those discarded stockings . . . the more difficult it was to remember that she was here because of a case. A genuine need; a true danger.

Peck. Scratch. Peck peck peck.

Little taps and scratches on George's boots drew his notice downward. A feathery back, a dainty head with a leathery comb. *Peck peck peck.*

The cook's precious chickens. Let out of their coop each dawn, they pecked at George's boots with mild interest.

"There aren't any insects on my boots," George informed the chickens. "Or seeds or whatever it is you love."

The chickens ignored this sage insight and continued abusing his boots.

George scowled. He attempted to ignore the attack on his footwear, aiming and letting another arrow fly. *Shh-whup.*

Ting!

Uh. Hmm. That one had bounced off the stone wall, rather far above the target. It lay on the ground now like a reproach.

"Stop pecking," he told the chickens. "You messed up my aim. You'll be put into a soup if you keep that up."

Again, the chickens ignored him. They did, however, lose interest in the boots when those items proved not to be edible, and they swaggered away to peck and scratch outside the kitchen door.

Now George *did* feel alone. There were too many questions on his mind, and he wanted to forget them. He wanted them, really, not to exist at all.

But they did, and no number of arrows or chickens would undo that.

Was he right about the case? Wasn't he? He'd doubt everything if it hadn't been for that note left beside his wounded godfather. FOUR LEFT. But there were five survivors left still, and when would the person who'd left the note—attacker or assassin or trickster—do something more?

Why was he trying to protect his father, who clearly disbelieved in the danger?

Why was he living here still, when both of his parents needed help and neither would take it?

And why should anyone trust in his judgment, when he'd never done anything more significant than waste paper and chemicals on failed experiments? His recent experiment with the camera obscura had imprinted vague lines on treated paper, an image of Cavendish Square if one squinted and prayed. But after a few minutes in daylight, it had darkened and faded into nothing. As apt a symbol as any: everything he tried led eventually to nothing.

He asked too many questions now, and thought too much about the answers. The influence of one Cassandra Benton.

Narrowing his eyes, he fired another arrow. *Shh-whup. Thump.*

This one hit the target.

A breeze ruffled his hair. This passed for fresh air in London in summer: damp gusts with the promise of rain, then a heavy whiff of acrid coal. This passed for leisure:

arrows fired at a bit of wood amidst every pedestrian and unpretty item necessary to run the household. He wasn't solving anything this way.

All right, then. Why shoot? Because arms in good trim were worth having. Because the sound of the arrow twanging on the bow string was pleasant. Because a marquess bred and raised to a title from birth couldn't give rein to temper and annoyance, but he could fire an arrow into a block of wood and yank it out again.

So he did. He retrieved the arrow from the ground, then yanked out each of the arrows he'd fired into the target. He touched his fingertip to the wounds left in the block of wood. Eventually it would be shot so full of holes that it wouldn't hold an arrow anymore, and he'd have to replace it.

When he turned in the direction of the house, hand bristling with arrows, Cass was standing at his heels.

His shoulders jerked. "Ah—good morning. Didn't hear you approach."

"Of course you didn't. I have the velvet tread of a panther."

George raised an eyebrow. "Velvet tread? Have you been into my gothic novels?"

"Maybe. It's also possible you were distracted playing Robin Hood." Her mouth was a tight line, pulled not by humor but something more prosaic. Distraction? Preoccupation? "I have to leave for a while. I just wanted to tell you because we had planned to go to Gunter's today."

He squinted at the colorful sunrise sky. "Surely not before six o'clock in the morning."

"No, but I don't know when I'll be back. I received a note last night from Bow Street. There's a case I need to work on."

You're supposed to be working on my case, he thought, but he refrained from pointing this out. She'd never hidden her need to continue her brother's work during his recovery. At the moment, dressed as she was in a plain dark gown that Selina's modiste would never have touched, she was clearly not Mrs. Benedetti. She was Miss Benton, the Bow Street Runner.

"Has something happened?" he asked, curious.

"Something is always happening, and I need to find out what it is. I'm meeting an informant in Billingsgate. And after that?" Her shrug was elegantly noncommittal. "I'll do whatever needs to be done."

"Billingsgate? Where people sell all the fish? It must be . . . how far?" As George tucked away the arrows again, he tried to calculate the distance in his mind, then gave up. "Well, it's some miles from here. Would you like use of the carriage?"

"Oh, no." Now Cass did smile. "I can't go to Billingsgate in a crested carriage; what a spectacle I'd make. I'll walk a few streets to get away from the nobs, then hire a hackney."

The nobs. He snorted. He liked getting away from the nobs sometimes himself. "Would you like company?"

"I can go on my own."

"I never doubted it. You're the investigator, and you don't need my presence. But I'm very handsome and you might like having me around to look at."

A chicken scratching nearby paused, regarded George with a beady eye, then stalked away.

Cass appeared no less skeptical. "You say the most sensible things, then the strangest things."

"Part of my appeal," George said. "But my question

was sincere, and no more nor less than what I meant. I know you don't need company, but would you like it?"

"Would I like it?" She sounded bewildered by the question.

"Yes. Company. Would you? I ask because I know you are used to working with your brother as a partner. Of course you would not request my presence because you want to gaze upon my masculine beauty. At least, not *only* because of that."

"You praise yourself more than you do any lady," she said, but she was smiling again. Which was, of course, why he'd made such foolish jokes.

"Come along if you like, then," she agreed.

Which was also why he'd made such foolish jokes. On that, at least, his mind was clear and he'd no questions.

Stowing his bow and arrows in the cluttered shed, he noticed a slouchy gardener's hat. He clapped it onto his bare head, then joined Cass in slipping through the back gate and into the mews. From there, they made their way around to Cavendish Square. It was all but empty at this hour, its green expanse and walking paths peaceful and silent under the rosy-pale sky. Behind the quiet facades of each grand home, George knew servants were already bustling about, their work never done. Sleep and peace were privileges for the few.

But look at the sky one missed if one slept the day away; look at the company one missed. At George's side, Cass strode quick and determined. Her marvelous hair was covered by a simple hat of cloth and straw. The shoulders he'd seen bare were garbed in a sensible spencer that buttoned under her breasts and did little to make him stop thinking of them.

His mind was a bordello around Cass Benton; it had

been ever since the Night of the Stockings. The Night of
the Torturous Undressing. It deserved capital letters in
his memory.

Not that Cass needed to know that.

"Do let me know when we've gone far enough from
the nobs," George said lightly, "so that we might hail a
hackney."

They'd reached a street corner already awake and busy.
Cass looked up and down the street, then nodded. "This
will do." With her blessing, George hailed the first vehicle
he spotted, then directed the driver to Billingsgate.

"You can pay him as well," Cass said once they'd settled onto the worn, greasy squabs. "Since you've a mind
to be so involved in this case."

"I was trying to be polite and helpful," George
pointed out.

"Paying the driver would be both."

With this, he could not argue. Fortunately he always
carried a notecase in his coat. It was almost the end of the
quarter and his purse was thin, but he'd money enough for
traveling around London.

He looked about him with interest. Grimy windows,
through which the streets outside appeared a hazy dream.
Stubs of candle within smoky lamps, unlit now. Seats on
which innumerable other arses had planted themselves.

When had he last taken a hackney? His Oxford days,
maybe. Ripping around the streets half-drunk and laughing with friends. Pursuing pleasures instead of his studies.

A private carriage was another luxury he hadn't thought
about much. Like sleeping when one wanted to, working
when one wished. He really did get his own way a lot of
the time.

"So what is this case?" George broke the silence. "Do

you think it has to do with the tontine, your meeting with the fishmonger informant?"

Cass was clearly deep in thought, her mind already at her destination. "She isn't a fishmonger," was all she said.

"She? How intriguing. I thought you were one of a kind. That is—you *are* one of a kind, but I thought you were the only—"

"It's all right. You needn't talk yourself into a fit. I know what you mean."

This was all she said, though, so he tried again. "Is this rather dangerous?"

She blinked. "Buying fish? Not really."

George folded his arms. "Buying fish? So we're cooks' assistants now? I mean meeting an informant, of course."

Her hand strayed to her gown pocket. "Sometimes. But you needn't worry; I'll protect you. I've a pistol, and I'm good with my fists."

"Oh, I remember." He rubbed his midsection, recalling how she'd turned on him in the surprised dark of Deverell Place. Less than a fortnight ago, yet long enough for the memories to become essential to him. "Is it strange that such talk is attractive to me?"

She rolled her eyes, but did not look displeased. "No. It's not strange to want someone else to manage trouble for you."

But that wasn't what he'd meant. He'd meant the attractive bit. Cass was splendid, with her pockets and her weapons and her matter-of-fact ways.

Before he could say some of this, or maybe even all of this, the hackney jolted to a stop. Cass craned her neck to look out the window, then nodded. "We're here. Hop down, my lord—you're about to become a Runner."

* * *

Cass hadn't meant that literally, that George would become a Runner. Or a runner, without the capital *r*. Almost the moment they descended from the hackney, though, a boy brushed against Cass's side.

She knew the move well: a pickpocket's bread and butter. She slapped a hand to the pocket of her gown. Empty! Her pistol was gone. And worse, her miniature of Grandmama. She'd been foolish to bring it, but she was in the habit of having it with her.

She'd been careless.

Lunging, she snatched for the boy's collar, but he was quick as mercury and slipped from her grasp. The crowds about the wharf were thick. She couldn't lose him. Shouldering her way after him, she cried, "Catch him! He stole—"

Before she spoke another word, George was off in pursuit. With his broad shoulders, he made a path through the crowd; his gloved hands reached, his legs scissored in long strides. Cass gathered up her skirts above her ankles and pelted after him.

It was like running through a tunnel, crowded and odorous. The wharf squatted on a hairpin bend in the Thames, hemmed in by huge buildings of brick and stone, then open to the water. Porters carted fish around; fishmongers laid it out on tables and booths beneath low wooden sheds over which they watched with gimlet eyes. And people crossed and laced and ducked and wove, and somewhere in the crowd was Grandmama's picture. George was pulling ahead, and Cass's skirts were tangling about her ankles, and the cobbles were slippery under her feet. She lost sight of them both in the crowd for a moment.

Blindly, she shoved, not minding the famously coarse language of the fishwives. Where had that boy got to?

Where was George? If only she'd been quicker, she could have prevented—

And then she slipped past a ruddy-faced woman, hands on hips and squalling, and it was as if she'd walked into a different part of London. The crowd had backed up, making a perfect open circle, and at its center stood George. And the struggling boy. And, surprisingly—or maybe not?—Janey Trewes, swaddled and swathed as always, whom Cass had arranged to meet here, and who had a gift for being exactly where she was needed.

Cass shoved past the muttering onlookers to join the little group at the center of the circle. Somewhere George had lost his odd hat, and his gloves were dirty. They were clenched on the boy who'd picked Cass's pocket: one on the boy's shoulder, and one about his wrist.

"Smart," Cass said, nodding toward the double grasp. "In case he slips out of his jacket and tries to run for it."

"Lemme go!" yowled the boy. "I didn't do nufink!"

He was small and thin and grimy from soot and mud. Likely not an errand boy fetching fish for a household, but an opportunist. A thief, come where the crowds were.

"Check 'is pockets," Janey said. "If he's innocent, off he goes."

Cass crouched before the struggling boy. "I'm going to check your pockets. And if you have my things, I'm taking them back." His glare was pure hatred.

His jacket, threadbare and too short at the arms, yielded a wealth of goods. Cass's pistol, yes; Grandmama, in her gold case. There was a spill of coins, too; Cass looked at them dubiously in her hands.

"Those is mine," said the boy. "Can't prove they isn't."

"True." She stood, slipping her possessions back into her pocket—then, thinking better of it before onlookers, held fast to them. "What's your name?"

He said a word that would have made a fishwife gasp.

Janey laughed. George murmured, "Odd choice on your parents' part."

Around them, the crowd began to break up. If the running lady had got her items back and was asking the boy's name, there was probably not going to be a fight or a killing, or even a knocked-over booth of fish. How dull.

Pasting on her sternest expression, Cass replied, "I'm not calling you that. You deserve better. And a word of advice: you're good, but not good enough. I felt the dip as soon as you made it. Either get better before you start stealing again, or go to Ardmore House in Cavendish Square and ask for a job."

Now George laughed. "My father would love that."

"I could teach 'im," Janey said thoughtfully. "How to pick a pocket, like, so's no one 'ud notice."

"That is not why we arranged to meet this morning," Cass reminded the younger woman. "You already have apprentices enough to fill half of London."

"Could always use another," Janey said cheerfully. "Hold now"—she referred to the boy by the filthy word—"I might have a jacket as'll fit you better." She began unwinding a rolled garment from around her head, where it had perched like a turban over a white maid's cap. It proved to be a series of child's jackets, knotted at the sleeves. She wrestled one free and held it out to the boy.

George released him. His eyes, pale and mistrustful, darted from George to Janey to Cass to Cass's handful of items, then back again.

"Jemmy," he said sullenly.

"Is that your real name, or are you under the impression that's how you say 'thank you' to the lady?" George asked.

"A lady!" Janey sounded delighted. "Go on, then."

Jemmy scuffed his bare foot on the cobbles. "Thank

you," he mumbled, then snatched the jacket from Janey's hands. He dragged it on over his old one, then folded his arms tightly. "Can't take it back now."

"Of course not," Cass said. He really was so thin, so dirty; he must be cold. Likely hungry, too. In a moment, she decided. "Here. These are your coins." One by one, she dropped them back into his eager hands, keeping a wary grip on her own pistol and miniature. "Mind you don't take anyone else's, now."

"I won't!" This was almost certainly a lie, of course. He took a step to flee; Janey caught his shoulder, bent to whisper something in his ear, then nodded and set him free. He hared off, lost in an instant among the ceaseless movement of people.

Cass looked doubtfully at Grandmama. Her pistol. How to keep them safe?

Shrugging, she slipped the miniature into her bodice, where her spencer and stays would hold it tight. The cold metal went instantly warm against her skin. She hesitated over the pistol, not liking the idea of stuffing it into her garments.

"Do you want me to carry that for you?" George asked. "I could put it in the pocket inside my coat, where a pickpocket couldn't get it."

"Then we couldn't reach it easily." Cass tapped it against her palm, then handed it over. "But it's not loaded at the moment, so I suppose it won't be much help anyway. Thank you."

He tucked away the little gun. "I told you I'd protect you, didn't I? Yes, I'm pretty certain that's how our conversation went."

When he winked at her, she smiled. "That's not how I recall it, but it's what you did. At least—you protected my belongings, and that means a great deal to me."

"I should love to see what you keep in that little gold case." Holding her gaze, his blue eyes were warm. Did he mean the gold case protecting the miniature? Did he mean he'd like to undo her bodice, where she'd stowed the precious item?

Or was she being wishful, thinking he might be looking upon her with desire? Especially when all around them was tumult, and the odor of fish so strong it almost covered the stench of the river.

"I . . ." She fumbled for something to say that would not sound ridiculous.

George rescued her. "But never mind that now. Will you introduce me to your friend, if she will allow it?"

Naturally, Janey allowed it. The pretty young woman was all impish flirtation as she made the acquaintance of George, Lord Northbrook, who used *far* better manners with her than he had *ever* displayed with Cass.

"I need to speak with Janey for a bit," Cass then said to George. "Bow Street business."

"Right. I'll make myself scarce, shall I? I'll just . . ." He looked around. "Buy some fish? Yes. I'll buy some fish."

Off he went, and Cass eyed Janey curiously. "Did you tell that boy where he could find you?"

Janey shrugged. "No harm in that, was there? I'll teach 'im to be good."

"What sort of good? A good boy or a good pickpocket?"

"Why not both?"

Cass had to allow this. Janey was indeed a good woman and the finest pickpocket in London. So she asked, "Why did you want to meet at Billingsgate?"

"Got to meet somewhere." She twisted the knotted row of jackets back into a coil, then wrapped it around her head like a turban. "And I wanted to be gettin' a fish for me dinner. Charles would have it as a treat, and Missus Jellicoe said as she'd cook it for us."

So her brother was Charles now. It was only fair, as they'd always called Janey by her first name—but again, Cass had the feeling of events passing her by. Charles was making connections without her, and those would make her old life new and unfamiliar when she returned to it. "Where is Charles getting the money for fresh fish?"

"Coins all over his washstand," Janey said, as if this were perfectly normal. "Keeps one in a broken cake of soap, too."

"He keeps a coin in his soap? Still?" How well did Cass remember jamming it in there on end, a fruitless gesture of annoyance. But it had fallen to the floor, and she'd replaced it on his washstand.

"He *is* washing," Janey said. "See him every other day, I do, and the soap is smaller ev'ry time. Must be as he puts the coin in again each day."

"*Charles,*" Cass muttered. Using her wages to buy fresh fish. Keeping a coin in a cake of soap. What was he about?

She had to grant that fish was not an extravagant purchase, though it was an unusual one for her brother. And if he drove the coin into the soap, just as Cass once had, then maybe he had taken her words to heart. Maybe he was trying to be a bit wiser with money, or more careful about work.

Or maybe he thought it looked smart. One never knew with Charles.

Cass shook this off and returned to the subject of work. "You're helping with the Watch case? Is that what you speak to Charles about?"

"Whatever's needed. But mostly that, aye." Janey nodded, looking grave. "Some toff was asking about a girl who disappeared. Lord Randolph, 'is name was. She was some servant that had run off to London, and *he* said he wanted her back because he was worried for her, and me friend Mary Simpkins said as she'd heard he was cruel to young women, so the lass probably ran away—lass, that means girl, that's just how Mary talks."

"I know the word," Cass said drily. "And I know Lord Randolph's reputation." It had been soured around the time of the famous theft from the Royal Mint. Lord Randolph had lost himself a mistress and, in retaliation, set up a bawdy art exhibition in the wilds of Derbyshire. He didn't move often in society, but when he did, he was a discomfiting sort. "So Mary thinks Lord Randolph is responsible for the girl's disappearance?"

"No, no. Mary thinks the Watch is being more careful, now, because there's a toff nosing into the matter. So there hasn't been any more girls gone as we know of."

"That's . . . good? Yes, that's good," Cass said. Better for London's young women to be safe, even if the case stayed open longer. Just as it was better for George's father and his old compatriots to remain safe, even as the tontine case ground to a halt.

And Cass seemed never in the right place to help with either. Not even able to hold on to her own belongings.

But able to count on George to retrieve them, on Janey to follow the case. This was a strange sensation, not only to lay one's trust upon another person but to have it repaid.

"Thank you," Cass said for the second time in a short while. "You're a great help to Bow Street, and I've no doubt to my brother."

Janey made an unintelligible sound like *faughhhhh*. "It's my attun-mint. You know that."

"The reason doesn't matter. It's a great help." She asked Janey about the other cases before Bow Street, those

Charles had been working as well as those that had come up since both Bentons had absented themselves from the courtroom. Janey's memory for names and faces was good, though she'd yet to master the legal jargon of the courtroom and stumbled over many of the words.

With a pang of envy, Cass said, "By the time Charles is well, you'll have made yourself indispensable to Fox." It was such a good feeling to be needed.

Janey flashed her charming grin. "And haven't I been indis—like you said—all along? Best informant that Mr. Fox has, he says."

"Then it's true. Fox never exaggerates or lies."

Janey looked doubtful at this description of such a paragon of honesty; then her grin returned. "Ah, that lord of yours is back! And what a big fish as he's sportin'."

"Uh," Cass replied, now rosy herself. She wheeled in the direction of Janey's gaze to see that yes, George was making his way back to them, and he was carrying a large flopping fish—thank the Lord, not in his arms, but in a straw basket he must have bought off one of the fishwives.

When he reached the two women, he thrust the basket at them. "Here. I bought a fish, just as I said I would. Its eye is staring at me and I don't like it. Which of you wants to take responsibility for it?"

Cass tucked her arms behind her back. "Not I. You could give it to your cook."

"Or you could give it to me," said Janey hopefully. "I was goin' to buy one, but now I won't have to."

"The lady wins." George surrendered the basket to Janey, a look of relief on his face. "Happy birthday, for whenever your birthday is, and don't say Lord Northbrook neglected that occasion."

"It's next week!" Janey beamed at him. "Thanks to ye, and I'll be off."

As quickly and subtly as the boy Jemmy had slipped away, Janey and the basket and the fish were gone.

"She's going to give that fish to Charles," Cass pointed out. "Basically, you bought my brother a fish."

George lifted his brows. "That sounds like a euphemism, but I cannot imagine for what."

Cass chuckled. "Don't ask questions you don't want to know the answer to." She dusted her hands against each other, not that this did her soiled gloves much good. "Well, what now? I should have kept a few of Jemmy's coins to hire us a hackney back to Cavendish Square."

"Not yet." George looked down at her, bareheaded and rumpled, with a mischievous twinkle in his light eyes. "We look disreputable—at least I do—and I'm not ready to stop enjoying it. If you'll permit me to ask a question that I *do* want the answer to, might I take you to breakfast? I know the perfect place."

Chapter Nine

"Pie," Cass said in the decided tone George was becoming very fond of. "I love pie. That's what I want for breakfast."

"An easy wish to fulfill. Will you have the meat sort, or the sort with fruit in it?"

"All sorts," Cass said promptly. "Any sort. Put something in a crust and bake it, and I will eat it."

"You make the matter simple," George decided. "We'll have an all-pie breakfast, if my friend is willing."

He'd brought her to Antony's, a restaurant slipped among the many inns and hotels and public houses of Piccadilly. The hackney that had brought them here from Billingsgate had been scarcely faster than a walk through London's thickening traffic, but it was still not even nine o'clock in the morning. The tonnish wouldn't be awake for hours, and the *chef d'oeuvre* at Antony's would not offer a formal service until noon.

But George knew he'd be here with his assistants, preparing meats and vegetables for the luncheon dishes they'd serve.

A knock at the back door brought a grumpy-looking

Frenchman to answer it—one whose expression changed from impatience to delight when he saw who stood there.

"Lord Northbrook, *et sans chapeau!* You have had an adventure this morning?"

"Only a small one," George replied. "But I did lose my, er, *chapeau*. To be fair, it was all the lady's fault." With this, he introduced Cass to Antoine.

"Antoine Fournier." The *chef d'oeuvre* bowed low over Cass's hand. "Enchanted to make your knowledge."

"Don't listen to that jumbled talk of his," George told Cass. "He only does it to be charming. Really, he speaks English better than either of us."

With a sniff, Antoine straightened. "Certainly better than you." He was about George's age, with dark hair and mobile brows and the slight thickness about the middle that came from living amongst the glorious foods of his own creation. As he had every time George had seen him at the restaurant, he wore an impeccable white garment that was not quite a shirt and not quite a jacket, and around his waist was a broad apron of the sort butchers wore.

Around him, from within the kitchen, divine smells issued forth. George inhaled deeply, forgetting the stinks of the Thames and none-too-fresh fish and dubious hackneys. "Look here, I freely admit I'm an uneducated clod compared to you, and not nearly so charming."

"He is being modest," Antoine said to Cass. "This means he wants something."

She grinned. "Of course he does. But I think it's what I want, also. You see, he thought you might give us breakfast. Pies, especially."

"Is that all? *Bien sûr,* come in! Have *le petit déjeuner!* I will make you the best pies you have ever experienced." He opened the kitchen door more widely, ushering them through.

As George followed Cass, Antoine held him back, the teasing manner now sincere. "You are always welcome here. You know that. Whatever you want—no pay."

A brisk nod from each: the masculine equivalent of words of friendship and gratitude. To speak the words themselves would have been intolerably sentimental.

Antoine directed them through the kitchen; George had a brief impression of giant stockpots bubbling, a large table on which several assistants were chopping vegetables and rolling out dough and performing other food-related tasks. His feet rang on the flagged floor; above him hung gleaming pots and pans and aromatic bunches of herbs.

And then they were through into the main dining space, currently empty save for themselves.

The ceiling was a light gray-blue, like the color of the London sky when sun won out over fog. The walls were paneled and plastered in the most fashionable of colors, with still-life paintings of succulent fruits adorning them. The white cloths covering the tables were crisp, complemented by shining flatware and glass drinking vessels. The space fairly invited diners: *come in and sit—we have a space all ready for you.*

Yet the diners did not come, at least not in the numbers needed for the restaurant to remain solvent. It was a mystery to George.

George scrutinized Cass's features as she took her seat in one of the chairs at Antony's. Did she like the place?

"This is nothing like the Boar's Head," observed Cass.

"Is that your favorite restaurant?" He sat across from her.

"Too grand a word for it. It's a public house near the Bow Street court. I can't tell you how many times Charles and I took a quick meal there." Cass settled her skirts around her on the chair. "If his name is Antoine, why is the restaurant called Antony's?"

"Because every Frenchman who starts a restaurant seems to be named Antoine and call it Antoine's. I encouraged him to think of something a little more English."

"And he listened to you?"

"He ought to have. I gave him the money to start the restaurant."

George hadn't meant to admit this. As he'd feared, Cass now looked about with growing curiosity. "So this is really *your* restaurant."

"No, no. I don't do anything here." He waved his hand. "Someone else cooks, someone else waits, someone else—"

"Arranged it all? Gave the capital to start it up?" She arched a brow.

"Shhh, you will shame me. And it wasn't that much, really. It wasn't even half of my quarterly allowance." Though it remained an expense, quarter after quarter, as George made up the difference between Antoine's costs and income. "Besides, isn't it worth it to taste such foods? Oh—you haven't tasted them yet. Well, once you get your pie breakfast, you'll agree that it was money well spent."

"How did you come to invest in a restaurant?"

He racked his brain to remember. "I think . . . it was because of the food at a ball a season or two ago. Two seasons now, it must have been. It was of such surpassing excellence that I found the cook and told him he had a marvelous gift. I forced him to become my friend and filled his head with all sorts of grandiose schemes for starting a restaurant. So you see, I had to pay for it after all that."

"You didn't. You could have eaten and enjoyed the food and left it at that." She bit her lip, looking around the room. "You certainly spend your money differently from your father."

George tugged off his gloves and tucked them away. "He's the one who inspired me to do this, by counter-example. If a bit of money could make a difference, shouldn't I use it well instead of throwing it away? I mean, I already have enough cravats. At least until next season."

Cass eyed his cravat, which was surely a sartorial disaster after the morning's exertions. "Wisely said."

"I do keep a hand in the place, a little," George admitted. "I wanted a place where the tonnish could dine without having to deal with a crushing ball or worry about meeting one's mistress."

Cass looked interested. "Do you have a mistress?"

"Certainly not! They are far too expensive. And so is backing a restaurant, which I didn't realize when I began. I must get some more fashionable people into the habit of dining here, so that other fashionable people will come to look at them."

Men and women of the beau monde were so often separated. Yet they needed each other, in the most basic sense, for survival. Why act as if they were two separate sorts of creatures who could not be trusted together—like lions and lambs?

Which was the lion and which the lamb, men and women would never agree. But they would also never tire of talking of it.

"I do have one idea for decreasing this restaurant's expenses." Cass poked at the white cloth over the table. "These cloths. They look lovely, but ask your friend if he'd prefer not to be put to the expense of laundering them all the time."

"How much could that possibly cost?" George scoffed.

When Cass muttered something that sounded like *no sense with money at all*, he had to defend himself. "Even a common chop house has white linens on the table."

"So don't be common. Don't let this place look like a chop house. Make it lovelier."

He shook his head. "What's lovelier than a white cloth on the table?"

"I pity every woman you've ever courted." She sighed. "How about something completely different? Top the tables with glass mosaics or punched-tin sheets. Something to make it look like its own sort of place, so people can't judge it against the other places they know."

"The power of uniqueness," he mused. "It's worked well for my friend Lady Isabel. She married a Bow Street Runner and dresses in all sorts of odd things, and no one knows what to make of that, so they assume it's all right."

"She has money, so it *is* all right. And if this place turns a profit, it'll be all right, too." Cass paused.

"What's got your tongue? Another suggestion?"

"No, an observation. I only noticed that the power of uniqueness has worked for you, too. You live within your income and make experiments with a camera obscura and dance every dance at a ball instead of acting too bored for words. And somehow people like you."

This touched him, so of course he had to hide it. "There's no 'somehow' about it," he said. "I'm a very likable fellow. People cannot resist me."

"And the tender moment passes into oblivion." Cass began to tug at the fingers of her gloves.

"It need not." George held out a hand. "Allow me, my lady, to help you with your gloves."

She smiled, extending her hand, and he pulled at the forefinger of her glove. Just a little tug, a little pull at the rough leather, and it came loose and slipped from the shape of her finger. It drew at the rest of the glove, a gliding over skin that left it only half on and her wrist bare.

She sucked in her breath, and he felt it in the pit of his stomach.

"All right?" When she hesitated, he added, "I will respect your wishes. If you pull away, I won't pursue."

She slid her hand closer, dun-colored kid on the pristine tablecloth. "Then how can I ever bear to pull away?"

This woman. His lips curved. "If you don't want to, I'm not going to try to convince you otherwise. I've told you from the beginning, I'll keep the distance you want me to."

"And how much distance do you want to keep?"

He rubbed a hand over his eyes. "Not enough, God help me."

"You act as if you're courting me." She sounded mystified.

His hand dropped to the table with a thump. "Certainly not. If I were, you'd be under far more illusions about me and you'd be much more impressed."

"Then I like this better." Within the half-off glove, her fingers played.

He tugged it off the rest of the way, then handed it to her and made quick work of its mate. "Besides," George careened on, "I've undressed much more of you than this."

"You have." Cass looked at him curiously. "I can't tell what you're thinking about that."

I'm thinking that I've not undressed enough of you. Not enough, God help me.

It wasn't just about wanting to take her clothes off and enjoy the pleasures of the flesh with her—though there was certainly plenty of that, and he'd been a fool to think he could strip off so much as a glove without wishing for more.

No, it was that he wanted her close. Choosing him, belonging with him. He wasn't a fellow who had done much with his life, but with her, he thought about what was possible.

And if that didn't sound like a man in trouble, then he ought to hire another investigator to examine his head.

"I'm thinking . . ." he began, casting about for something neutral to say. A movement of the kitchen door saved him. "That the first pies are here. Ah! Thank you, Antoine."

What the Frenchman set before each of them was no pie George recognized. It looked like a tiny tart, its edges crimped and golden brown and ready to crumble. Within was not the usual custard or fruit, but some mixture of bubbled, browned cheese and egg from which bits of crisp pork and onion peeked.

"What do you call this, Antoine? I've never seen such a pie. Er—it *is* a pie, isn't it? The lady rejects all food but pies."

"I do not!" Cass replied. "And this smells like heaven. And it has a crust, so it must be a pie."

"Scabs have a crust," George said. "Would you consider them pies?"

"That is disgusting. Of course not. You're desperate to make me forget that we were talking about something serious before, and it's working. I can hardly hear my own voice over the sound of my growling stomach."

Antoine looked pleased. "This is called a quiche. New in France, and very good idea. Make a tart shell, put in any food with egg, and bake it."

George poked it with a fork. "Will I turn into a Frenchman if I eat it?"

"*Vous n'êtes pas si chanceux.*" With a sniff, Antoine turned toward the kitchen. "Eat. I complete one more pie."

"I speak French, you know," George called after him. "I understood that."

Antoine made a particularly Gallic and rude gesture before passing through the door.

George snorted. "He said I wasn't lucky enough to be French. Can you believe it?"

Cass did not appear to be listening. She was already forking up bits of the pie that did not look like a pie, making little happy-mouth moans that made George want to bang his head against the wall. "Don't make sounds like that," he said. "Or I shall forget what I said about not pursuing."

"I'm just eating pie," she said. "And I don't recall drawing back."

"Um," responded George. The look in her eye was pure mischief—then her eyes closed as she took a bite, and the expression on her face was pure pleasure.

He couldn't recall when he'd last had any sort of pure feeling.

So he took her example, applied himself to the strange little tart, and found it very pleasant. There was much to like about salty eggs and cheese, crispy pork, browned and savory onions in a crust.

Cass finished first, her expression doleful as she regarded a plate that held only crumbs. And then she looked around the space again, her brows knit. "You've not had diners enough come? With food like that?"

George brandished his fork. "See? It doesn't make sense, does it?"

"Well . . ." She cleared her throat, a little smile tugging at her lips. "Might I make another suggestion." It was not posed as a question.

"Please. Yes. I can't promise that I'll take them, or that Antoine will, but if you can't make suggestions, you'll puff up with unspoken words and won't fit in the chair anymore."

She eyed him. Then she reached out her fork, took the last bit of quiche from his plate, and popped it in her mouth.

Once she'd swallowed the bite over his protest, she said, "That was my tithe. And here's my first thought: don't try to make Antony's a place for the ton. Let it be for the merchants and their wives. Cits and whatever else you like to call them."

An interesting notion. "People with money, you mean, but without blue blood."

"Right. This is a business, so you need people with money to come here. Not only that, you need the sort of person who pays his shot."

"Ah. Yes. The nobility are usually terrible at that."

"And," she added, "there are far more merchants dining out in London than there are dukes or that sort of person."

"Because dukes keep their own French cooks?"

She looked at him with patient tolerance. "Because most people aren't dukes. One-quarter of your immediate family is made up of dukes, and another quarter is a duchess, but that's not the case for most people."

"Your arithmetic is unassailable. Very well, I see. More customers equals a happy restaurant. Ah! Our next pie? Thank you, Antoine."

The plates the chef laid before them this time were much more familiar: a semicircle of thick pastry with sweet, fragrant juices bubbling from the slits in the crust.

"A pasty?" Cass asked. "What sort of fruit is inside it?"

"It is not a pasty, but a pie for the hand." Antoine ticked on his fingers. "*Elles contiennent les pommes, les baies sucrées, les—*"

George rolled his eyes. "Oh, stop. You're impressing the lady with all that French, and she's meant to be *my* breakfast companion."

He poked at the pie, then hissed as it burned his fingertips. "This isn't baked. You'd never have had the time. How ever did you cook it?"

Antoine beamed. "It is fried! Melted lard, thin dough, fruit stewed in sugar." He kissed his fingertips. "All in a few minutes, you have a breakfast pastry."

"You are a great talent," Cass said. "I am very impressed. You don't even have to speak French."

George must have looked rather stormy at this comment, for Antoine winked at Cass and said, "For the sake of my hide, I return to my kitchen. You come back when you wish, yes, Miss Benton *si charmant?* Any day. You knock at my kitchen door."

The Frenchman withdrew with a waggle of fingers that made George want to slam that kitchen door and bolt it. Ungracious since he was dining on the man's generosity, but there it was.

"Don't look like such a thundercloud," said Cass. "I can be impressed with his skill without wanting to . . . to pretend to be his cousin and stay in his house and take on his case."

George lifted his brows. "Your completely fictional scenario intrigues me. Are you saying you're impressed with me?"

"I'm saying the world cannot handle two of you, Lord Northbrook." She poked at her pie. "Still too hot."

"I don't think that's what you were thinking about me. Not really. But if you're too bashful, I will let it slide for the moment." He relented. "You made it look easy at Billingsgate. Knowing what to do and whom to talk to."

Such confidence she had. Not the puffed-up confidence of lordlings at White's, who had been convinced that their maleness and money would see them through any situation. Cassandra Benton's confidence came from experience and common sense. From having faced situations those lords would never dream of, and having made her way through by wits and will. She always knew what to do, and George could think of nothing more beautiful than such a knowledge.

She waved off the compliment. "You do the same in a ballroom. And I wouldn't have done much of anything if you hadn't collared that boy who picked my pocket. Really, it's all practice and effort. That's what completes cases. Every case needs to be completed and set aside, because there will always be another."

"What if you can't complete a case?"

She looked troubled. "Then I can't set it aside."

As their pies cooled from broiling to warm, she told him about the cases she was pursuing. Charles's cases, Charles's work. She'd made it her own, taking it upon her heart. The country girls taken to brothels by the Watch; the pockets picked and throats cut and wives sold. Never had George imagined London was such a dangerous place, and he said so.

"We didn't see that London today. This was only a bit of adventure for you." She shook her head. "There are parts of this city where people would kill for a fish, or a loaf of bread."

"Do you go to those places often?" He tensed, awaiting her reply.

"Rarely. Only when I must. I hate going to those streets, because nothing I do there makes a difference. A penny given to a child to buy a bun? It'll be stolen by someone bigger. Helping Charles arrest a man who drinks too much and breaks shop windows with his fists? He might use those same fists on his wife and children, but at least he offers them safety from others."

She picked up the hand-pie before her, looking at its shape as if it were unfamiliar. "When people are desperate to survive and half-starved, they don't care about Bow Street. Who cares for the law if it stands between an empty belly and the first meal in a day?"

"They have nothing to lose," George realized aloud.

"Nothing," she agreed. "And there's always a child being hit, or a girl from the country taken to a brothel, or a dishonest member of the Watch."

"But to help even one of them—that's not nothing. To help one person, even once." He regarded her, silent and still, and said quietly, "It's not nothing, Cass. In fact, I think it's everything."

She looked up at him then, and a flicker of sunlight caught the irises of her eyes. They were warm and wide and, he thought, hopeful.

She had that strong chin, that sharp cleft. Her skin was lightly freckled with gold. He was accustomed to thinking of her as all angles and points. Not in an unattractive way; it was merely that she gave the impression of being utterly shielded. But sometimes, when he looked at her unawares and she didn't catch him at it, her straight brows with the soft downward curve at the ends gave her a worried look, and he would have given anything he possessed to know what was on her mind, and what it would take to slip behind that shield of hers.

Finally, she was setting it down, and what was behind it was so unguarded that he felt her vulnerability, again, as that precious glass ball entrusted to his keeping.

"I'm a good investigator," she said at last. "But I do the work to help Charles pay the bills, not because I love it. I don't love it. Every time I can't close a case, it's like a bruise on my heart."

"Because you care about them all. Just as you cared about Lord Deverell." He had to ask. "If you don't like investigating, why do you choose that way of helping Charles?"

"It matters to him. And that means *I* matter. And you can't imagine how few ways there are for a woman to matter in London in this Year of our Lord 1819."

She said this so frankly that he had to think it over for a minute. "I can imagine," he finally said. "Or try to. I often feel powerless myself."

"You?" she scoffed. "A courtesy marquess and an heir since birth?" She finally took a bite of the pie, and he lost her for a few moments to gustatory bliss. This rather spoiled the effect of his reply, not that that stopped him from making it.

"Cass, none of that means a tick if I can't help the people I care about. I cannot convince my father to stop laying waste to Ardmore's future, and I cannot draw my mother out of the laudanum bottle." He sighed. "I would dearly love sometimes, Cass, to matter."

"Those are their cages, not yours." But the proud lines of her face softened. "You care, too. Any heart can be bruised, can it not? You've had fewer choices than I realized."

Her kind words were too much. He backed into flippancy. "Ah, well. It's a great big cage, and well furnished. I shouldn't wish for escape. There's no denying it's an easy life, even if it's none of my making."

They ate for a few minutes, and it was a simple pleasure. A genuine one, to eat good food from clean dishes in fine company. The pie's filling was hot, but not too much so, and sweet and tart and flavorful, and it was no act to become enraptured by pastry for a few gluttonous moments.

And then a thread of memory snagged on his consciousness, making him set down his food and pose a question. "Are you willing to leave London for the case? There is a chance we could make a vacation of it to Chichester."

"A vacation?" Her eyebrows were all skepticism. "Surely you misspoke. I am on a case for you."

"Yes, yes, of course I misspoke. I mean to call it a

business journey, during which we would work very hard and you would not enjoy yourself at all."

"You mean the opposite, and now I don't know what to say."

"Let me say it for you a different way: several members of the tontine are planning to go to Chichester in three days' time. I've been invited as well, and I hadn't decided whether to accept, but perhaps I ought. There will be a match race at Goodwood, and a house party at the Duke of Richmond's estate, and—you're looking a little green."

"Too much pie," Cass gasped. "Or too many dukes. I'm fine. I just—Isn't there something I could watch for in Covent Garden?"

"I'm certain there is. But not related to the tontine." He paused for maximum effect, then said casually, "It's your duty, and you'll make a difference, and you've been paid to solve that case. But if you want to stay and do Charles's work, I understand."

Unconcerned, he picked up his pie and took a large bite. When he set the last crust down again, she was watching him with narrowed eyes. "You're baiting me."

"Of course I am," he said cheerfully. "Is it working?"

"You really think I would make a difference? Going to Chichester?"

"I would consider it a great personal favor. You are my bodyguard, remember. Angelus and Callum Jenks both said you ought to keep me safe."

She laughed. "You don't need me for that."

"I might not. But are you willing to take the chance?"

Half-consumed, her pie was dripping syrupy purple juice onto its plate. Cass poked a fingertip into it. "I'd love to see more of England than London," she said slowly. "I never have. But how can I do what I wish when I resent Charles every time he does the same?"

"If you won't, you won't," George said. "But *I* can do what you wish."

"I said *can't,* not *won't.*"

"And I said that I can. And if you'll allow it, I will. No need for guilt or resentment. Cass, this is part of the case, and you ought to come. If it helps, I could order you to come or threaten you with the sack."

She looked mulish.

He *felt* mulish. "Honestly, Cass. It sounds as if the moment you start wanting something, you shy from it. Because wanting something breeds resentment."

"It does," she agreed. "Because there is too much wanting and never enough of anything else."

Ah, well. He knew that feeling, too. Though he'd every privilege, he had no one to smile at him in the morning.

Cass was adding, "You're a persuasive fellow. I think I shall have to visit Charles again before I agree, though. Perhaps tomorrow or the day after."

"Whenever you like," he replied. "You're only poking your finger into that syrup now. Have you finished eating?"

"No!" She picked up the half-eaten pie in one hand, heedless of the sticky syrup. "It's a sin to leave pie unfinished—or it should be. I'm bringing it with me."

He had to smile. "Let's go, then, pie and all." He stood, took out Cass's pistol from his pocket, and handed it back to her—to the hand not currently holding a pie, that was. Then he removed his notecase and selected a banknote.

"Antoine said not to pay," Cass reminded him as she too stood.

"He says that because he's gracious, and I pay because I'm gracious. Also, he worked and provided us a meal."

She waved her hands at him, pistol and pie, then pulled a face. "Don't. Don't pay. Just thank him."

Bewildered, George wondered, "Why is that better?"

"He made this meal as a gift to us. Because he's not only your business partner, he's your friend."

"He is my friend," George repeated. "Yes. But I don't want to take advantage of his skill."

"Which means you never would." She looked from one of her hands to the other. Pistol to pie. Work to leisure. "Just as you said to me. You ask and you offer, but you do not pursue."

"Yes, well, I don't want to take advantage of you either—and I mean that in a way entirely different."

"You couldn't." She smiled. "I wouldn't let you."

"Do you know, I believe you. And I'll abide by that, just as I said."

But what would happen, he wondered, when the case was done? Would she set him aside, grateful for one fewer unsolved burden?

And wouldn't that be for the best?

Chapter Ten

In the end, Cass decided to accompany George to Chichester even before she visited Charles again. Simply wanting to do something was, after all, no reason to go darting in the other direction.

Well, it *could* be. But in this instance, the trip was part of the tontine case—or so George had said, and she very nearly believed him.

And it *was* true that Angelus and Jenks had both told her to watch over his safety. Really, then, she was just being responsible. Even if George had first posed the journey as a—dare she think it?—pleasure trip.

So it was that she called upon her own lodging, feeling very much like a visitor while dressed in Selina's borrowed finery. The main room held an air of neglect; her own bedchamber seemed a cubby belonging to someone else entirely.

When she poked her head into Charles's room, odors of liniment and perspiration struck her. He was prone on the bed, from which he greeted her, "I'm bored."

She sat on the end of the bed in a rustle of silk, taking

care to avoid jostling his injured leg. "I believe it. But what do you intend for me to do? Play cards with you?"

"I'd thought you might, rather." So hopeful, he looked. And so rough. Under his eyes were shadows, and his chin bore several days' stubble.

"You've not been taking care of yourself," she pointed out. "You know what you need? A mother."

Charles grabbed a bolster and stuffed it behind his back. "Spare me your lectures. Either entertain me or leave."

"You are spoiled and crochety. I thought seeing Janey every other day would keep you in a fair mood. Where is she, by the bye? Has she visited today?"

"She'll be here tomorrow." His fingers worried the coverlet, even as his expression remained sullen.

"Is she good company?" Cass pressed.

"Very." Faint color stained his cheeks. "Not in any improper way. She's just . . . sunny."

"Don't take that for granted, Charles. Especially in gray old London, sunniness is hard-won."

"I know. She's quite a help, actually. Keeping an eye on that fellow in the Watch house."

That stung, though Cass had known from Janey's own lips that she was assisting Charles. "I said I would think of a way to handle that."

He shrugged, tugging loose a knitted thread. "I thought of one instead."

"You mean Janey thought of one." Yet Cass wasn't sorry Charles had pursued answers a different way—especially since she herself had thought of nothing. "Are you paying her?"

"I am," he said. "She's working for me. She's still not caught Felix leading a girl off to a bawdy house, though, so there's nothing clinging to him but suspicion."

"Hmm. So, no results."

"None. I'm worried," he admitted. "Fox might not hold my post."

"Of course he will," Cass said. "You're the best investigator he has now that Jenks has left Bow Street."

The lie tripped easily off her tongue, and usually Charles played right along. Not today. "You are, Cass. Not me." A ghost of a smile. "I might have been good enough value when he could get both our work for my salary, but I won't be if you don't return soon."

Just so, he heaped the responsibility for his recovery onto her shoulders. And wasn't she already trying to do more than one person was capable of?

She had made the decisions of an adult since childhood, and Charles had made none at all. As Grandmama took care of them both, Charles was ready enough to accept favors and coddling. "Women are better at that," he excused himself, not allowing their efforts to be any credit to themselves at all.

It wasn't just that Charles was spoiled. They had spoiled him, because he was male and it seemed right to them all.

And now he sounded lost, her big, tall, heedless, careless brother. For a moment, her heart squeezed. There had never been anyone closer to her than Charles from the first moment of her existence.

But he was a grown man who had caused his own problems, and she couldn't help him solve them. Not this time. Not today.

"I have to go," she said. "I only stopped in to tell you that I'm traveling to Chichester tomorrow, or near enough, for some sort of match race on the Goodwood course. All the men in the tontine will be there."

"That tontine case," he grumbled. "I wish I could be of some use. But every time I go downstairs on these crutches, it takes half an hour. It's not even worth the bother."

"You'd better have Mrs. Jellicoe hire you as a housemaid, if you don't intend to be leaving our rooms," she said tartly. "The main room is dusty enough. You could do something about that."

He gaped. "Cass! I'm injured."

Really, it was a wonder she had never broken Charles's leg herself.

"Dusting is not so bad," she pointed out. "I've done the job myself when we were stationed at Deverell House, if you'll recall. You don't get much sleep as a housemaid, but then, you weren't sleeping much at Deverell House anyway."

It would have been a good parting line, but he looked so befuddled. She'd always saved the sharp side of her tongue for others before. For people who attacked the unit of Cass and Charles.

Leaving Charles behind for the tontine case was like shedding a weight. One that was part of her, keeping her grounded; one she'd been born with and never known life without.

She was light and free. She was incomplete.

What a surprise that the first person who understood was a marquess who seemed to carry every privilege about himself. She ought to have known from Bow Street that one could never judge from appearances—yet it saved so much time and trouble. She was counting on just that when she posed as Mrs. Benedetti, the notorious cousin hungry for gossip.

She stood to leave, but first planted a smacking kiss on Charles's head. "Bleah. You need a good bath, no matter how long it takes you to arrange it."

"And then what?"

"That's up to you."

He turned his head toward the wall. "I'll sort it out later. I've already done enough for today."

Whatever you wish, George had said to her once, and it was intoxicating. She ought to *say* whatever she wished.

So she did. "You always say that. Later; you'll do something later. Well, there's no later. We live now, and how you spend today is how you're spending a piece of your life you'll never get back."

Charles snapped upright, roaring. "I've a broken leg!"

"You do, yes. And you still have your brain. You and Janey could work together as a team, a real one. You've both got one foot on the right side of the law and one foot wrong. We always made more from the bribes you took than from the Bow Street salary."

Ugh, she was doing it again—making suggestions, solving his problems. Yet at the look of hope that returned to his features, she couldn't be entirely sorry.

"All right," he said. "I'll see."

"After you bathe."

"After I bathe." He swung his feet to the side, wincing as the stiff brace on the broken leg tapped the wall. "Go on then, I can right myself. It'll just take time and some contortions I'd rather not have anyone witness."

She laughed. So easily, her mood aligned with his. Maybe this was part of why she tried to lift him up. "All right. I'll visit you again when I return from Chichester."

"One piece of advice. Do you remember what you told me before you went to stay with Northbrook?"

"I told you a lot of things. I'm delighted that you not only listened but remembered some."

"Don't do anything I wouldn't do." Charles looked pleased with himself.

"I'm not planning to," she said breezily.

Since that removed no possibilities whatsoever.

* * *

The match race, Cass understood from George, was to take place at Chichester because London was growing so hot. Londoners were eager to escape town but not miss any of the season, so the *haut ton* dragged the season to the coast.

She accepted his explanation, just as she accepted the presence of his large camera obscura in the carriage with them, along with other paraphernalia to do with his experiments. If she'd had a pastime she enjoyed as much as he liked mixing up chemicals and slathering them on paper, she'd have brought that along, too.

"I shall try a new combination of silver salts," he was saying, still talking nineteen to the dozen after hours in the carriage. "And maybe the sea air will turn them more slowly."

Yes, she felt keenly the lack of a purpose of her own. This was her purpose, this helping, but it didn't feel the same as a concrete goal. Totting up numbers and making them end in the positive. Mixing chemicals and fixing an image to a sheet of paper forever. Establishing a restaurant and giving it the funding it needed. So few of the problems she helped solve were ever concluded so tidily as George's were, or could be.

But at last they arrived, and then there was much to occupy her thoughts. They passed first by Goodwood House, the seat of the Duke of Richmond. Though humbly named, it seemed as large as any of the monarchy's palaces. It was of clean stone, not a bit smudged by coal smoke, and flanked with copper-domed turrets that gave the grand structure a rounded, welcoming feeling.

Cass and George would not be staying here. As a supposed ducal bastard, Cass was not a worthy houseguest, and for politeness' sake, George had suggested he and his father remain with her. "For safety's sake, too," he had said.

Instead they would be staying in a coaching inn, also on the duke's property. Ardmore was vocal in his displeasure: all the best card games would take place at Goodwood House.

"Go back and forth," George had said unsympathetically. "Though if you want quantity of wagering, not merely high stakes, the racecourse is where you ought to be." Goodwood Racecourse, too, was on the Duke of Richmond's land, which set Cass to wondering how much of England was parceled out for its few dukes.

Though the match race would not take place until the next day, Richmond had been entertaining guests for the better part of a week, and Ardmore was eager to hare off to the main house for the whirl of gaiety and betting.

"Go on, then," George told him as they descended from the carriage. "I'll see us established at the inn."

When Ardmore had departed, all but running in the direction of the main house, George turned back to Cass. His expression was a little of everything that began with A. Amusement, annoyance, anxiety . . . and she had thought R words were troublesome. "I'll send the carriage for him later," he said. "We'll have our things brought in first."

"I'll help carry in the bags," she suggested.

"Mrs. Benedetti," he said with a faint smile, "you forget your place. Look, there are already flocks of servants coming to take everything and stow it away."

"Then what am I to do?" She looked around her, wondering. The sun here was bright and the sky pale and clear, and the air had a lightness that made her feel as if she had to cough. Where was the smoke and grit? The yellow fog, and the stink of the Thames? Why was it so *quiet?*

It wasn't unpleasant. It was just . . . strange. And her belongings, which didn't really belong to her at all, had been spirited off to a room in what all these dukes regarded as lowly lodging, but was likely finer than any place she'd stayed before taking George's tontine case.

She separated from George once inside the building. He went off to see to the disposition of his camera obscura, and she allowed herself a few minutes to explore. Who else was staying here rather than at the main house—a guest but not quite a guest?

She became distracted poking into the different common rooms, finding all appointed beautifully in creamy wooden panels and cloth wall hangings. This was no ordinary coaching inn; there was no touch of the public house to it. No taproom with dark ceilings and spilled ale. No sullen servants with indifferently clean clothes.

Instead, the building was set within a glorious sweep of gardens, abloom with flowers and flanked by tidy rows of vegetables. Outside every window was something pretty to look at, and within every room was quiet and peace.

This was true luxury: not a presence, but a lack. A lack of fog, of mess, of the presence of servants. A lack of the noise of the streets.

It must take an enormous amount of effort to maintain this sense of calm and peace. But when one was a duke, one could have things as one liked.

In a small sitting room, she came upon some of her fellow guests. Whether George had arranged matters thus or whether it was by chance, they made a little party of the tontine survivors.

Cavender was there, looking as cheaply fashionable as ever. On a stage, he would have made a marvelous impression. Gerry was a quiet man who seemed to walk only with great pain. He had gout and used a cane and traveled with his own physician. This was not sufficient reason to remove him from suspicion, but Cass mentally shuffled him farther back in her file of likely suspects. An ailment could be feigned, but if so, he'd been feigning this one for years on end.

Braithwaite was not to be present in Chichester, and she found she missed his friendly face. Which, she had to remind herself, might be the face of a murderer.

And Lady Deverell was there, rattling on and consuming cakes, both at a tremendous rate. "There is to be a velocipede race and an archery competition tomorrow, too," she said to Gerry, who appeared as little interested as a man might be who would take part in neither. "My husband is at The House"—these words were clearly spoken with capital letters—"to arrange all sorts of wagers, and I shall join him for dinner."

"Is everything to be wagered upon?" Cass ventured from her seat beside Cavender.

"Of course!" he said in a bluff tone. "Otherwise how would anyone know whether they were winning? And then how'd you know if you were enjoying yourself?"

"Always such a japester," Gerry said in a little dried-up voice, his hands holding fast to the head of his cane.

Lady Deverell looked sharply at Cass. The countess's face, as Charles had noted, was pretty as ever at age forty, with wide blue eyes. She also had a quantity of soft brown hair and an even larger quantity of bosom.

"You are familiar to me," said that lady. "Forgive my abominable memory. Have we met?"

Her smile was friendly, but her eyes were shrewd, and Cass's breath caught in her chest. *Yes, I was your housemaid for a brief while, and now I'm investigating whether one of these two gentlemen with us is a possible murderer.*

"I daresay I've been in caricatures," she managed to toss out carelessly. "This hair of mine is rather a spectacle."

"It's your behavior that is the spectacle, rather, if you end up in a caricature," said her ladyship. "But it is not for me to judge, but to enjoy."

And that lady, who had once had no qualms about kicking over an ash pail and telling Cass to do her work better the next time, offered her tea. And Cass, who mistrusted the shrewd eyes but whose tongue was tied, accepted a cup.

"I know where you've seen her!" Cavender leaned forward, all helpfulness. "She met me at that ball at the Harroughs', and you were there, too. Must've clapped eyes on her then."

"That must be it." Lady Deverell smiled prettily. "I regret that I did not make your acquaintance then, Mrs. Benedetti, but here we are now. A friend of Northbrook's, you know, must be a friend of mine. We must have a comfortable coze and not let all these men distract us with their wagering."

My brother has seen you bare and screaming for help, Cass thought unkindly. And then, justifying the unkindness: *and you left him on the ground, injured, for someone else to take away.*

But all she said was, "Of course, my lady." With Gerry and Cavender there, she could say little else.

Cases were solved when one recognized a pattern and anticipated what would come next. And Cass recognized the pattern of the ton as a whole. There was surface gilt, the trappings that spun like Catherine wheels to draw one's attention to their brightness. Beneath that, everything was the same: worry. The women who ran society were worried. They had money and leisure but nothing to do of significance, and they were one party, one plan, away from facing their own lovely inconsequence.

She recognized it, because she felt it herself. That growing sense of dread, the feeling that something was not right.

The worry that nothing she did mattered, or even *could* matter, just as if she were a real lady of the ton.

By the time Cass extricated herself from Lady Deverell—that lady leaving only to return to the main house and dress for dinner—she was completely done in. How could so much gossip contain so little helpful information? Though with those men there, who *would not leave,* Cass couldn't mention the tontine, or ask for information about them. All she could do was inquire after Lord Deverell, and that nobleman seemed hardly to interest his wife.

Cass shook her head, hoping to clear it. Then, catching a liveried servant at random, she asked for directions to her bedchamber and requested a supper on a tray.

Once she had eaten, she cleaned her teeth and washed her hands and face and felt like a human again. She knocked at the door to the room beside hers, hoping the servant had been correct and that George's room was between hers and Ardmore's.

Indeed, it was George who answered the door; a George with coat off and shirtsleeves rolled up and cravat undone. "Oh, hullo," he said carelessly. "Want to see what I've set up in here? I've been very clever."

Cass entered a room that must have looked much like her own before a marquess with a fondness for chemical experiments got to it. Where Cass had a small bureau, a writing desk, and a washstand, George had pushed all of these together and somehow got a plank of wood to lie atop them.

"See?" He gestured. "A space to work."

The larger of his two cameras reposed on the make-shift table. Around it were different sorts of paper in dark sleeves, plus the familiar noxious compounds in amber bottles. "My father asked if I wanted to dine at the great house," George said, "but I had a tray brought up. If we're to be here all weekend, we're going to work. Just as I promised you."

He grinned at Cass, and it was impossible not to grin back. "You did promise that," she recalled. "You said I wouldn't enjoy myself a bit."

"And you might not. See, sun darkens these salts so much." He shook a little bottle at her. "I cannot stop the process once it begins, and then I've nothing to show but a sheet of wasted silver and blackness. Salted fresh-water slowed the process, but not enough. Will sea salt be different?"

She stifled a laugh. "I cannot say, but of course you must try it. Though whether or not I enjoy myself probably doesn't depend on the fate of your experiment."

"Philistine!" he teased. "Everyone should care. What if this is the trial that ends in success?"

When he spoke with such enthusiasm, she wanted to do unaccountable things, like trace the lines of his face. And when he looked mussed and rumpled and careless, she wanted to see him all the more undone. Cravat untied. Hair disordered. A little sweaty, as if he'd been exerting himself, and could be easily persuaded to do far more.

Her mind was a cesspool.

And he respected her, and he would not pursue.

Respect. God, it was heady stuff. George respected her, and the notion made her want to climb in his lap. Hold him close to her heart.

Or more.

"I think," she said, "I'm ready to go to bed."

He looked at the window, where sunset was only beginning to streak the blue sky with color. "Are you? I suppose you've never traveled so far in one day. It's quite usual to be—"

"George. No. I don't want to go to sleep yet." She waited a moment, until the significance of her words struck him, and his brows lifted.

"Exactly," she confirmed. "I want you to take me to bed."

Chapter Eleven

She'd thought he would be interested in the suggestion. Eager, even.

Instead, he eased around her, shut the door, and whispered, "I can't do that! You work for me."

It was rather adorable.

"But you want to?" Best to be clear about the matter.

He groaned. "Don't torture me. I've wanted nothing else since you—"

"Asked you to unbutton my clothing?"

He raked his hands through his hair. "No, ever since you put your hand over my mouth as we hid at Deverell Place. I put my tongue to your palm, and for a second I thought I'd gone insane, and then I knew I was completely sane because I'd got a taste of you."

She blinked several times. "Well. That decides it. Now you *have* to take me to bed. Wait one moment. I have— ha!" She'd found the tiny hidden pocket in her gown, one too small for a reticule but just the right size for a folded banknote. "Here. The five pounds you've paid me. I'm returning my wages. Now you've unhired me and I don't work for you anymore, and you don't have to have any ethical concerns."

George looked as if he wanted to laugh or throttle her, or perhaps both at once. "That is for work you already did. Put it back in your pocket."

She shrugged. "Then give me change for the amount I've earned and keep the rest."

Laughter won. Chuckling, he flung himself onto the foot of the bed and tugged at her hands. "Cassandra Benton. It seems as though you'd like to pay me to sleep with you, and that I'm not worth very much."

"What?" His hand had folded around hers, around the banknote. "I'm trying to accomplish the opposite. As if an amount so small as five pounds could make me yours, or you mine. I hadn't thought of there being money between us, but you did. I'm trying to remove it."

He shut his eyes. "Keep the money. If you must remove something, let it be your clothing."

Nothing could have convinced her of his desire better than his reluctance to look at her. The sight of her was a power that he could allow only in pieces.

You once said I was plain, she thought, but she did not say it. She knew he didn't see her as plain now. Probably not beautiful either, but as something she liked better. As Cass, her own and only self.

She stuffed the five pounds back in its hiding place, then locked the door and shoved a chair under the handle.

"I like a woman who's thorough," George remarked. He was watching her move about the room, eyes bright with interest.

"You'll have to help with my clothing," she reminded him. "You know I can't undo the buttons myself."

His mouth curled. "You torturer. I should like nothing more." He took her shoulders in his hands, turning her about so that her back was to him.

She faced the wall beside the door, the sunset making

dancing shadows of them on the painted surface. Her shape melded with his, their shadows larger than life. Already joined, already one, moving together.

"I never meant to tease you," she said. "Last time I really was trying to save trouble for the servants. And this time . . ." She swallowed as his hands tugged at her clothing. Surely he didn't have to rub around quite so much as he unbuttoned it. "You can do whatever you want with me."

"Can I really?" He sounded mildly pleased, as if she'd offered him extra sugar for his tea. "I could strip you bare, then?"

Her thighs clenched. "Yes. You can strip me bare."

His fingers spasmed on her arm, then continued guiding the sleeve down its length. "I could kiss every mark the seams of your clothing and stays have left on your skin?"

She shivered at the gentle rake of cloth and fingertips, then stepped out of the fallen gown. "Yes. You can kiss them until all the marks are gone."

He coughed a little, tugging now at the laces of her stays. "And . . . I could take you atop me? Watch you as you rode me?"

"Yes. To the peak."

Under his breath, he cursed. "Oh, I'll see you get to the peak."

Each knot untied, each button undone, was erotic. Like a dirty word in her ear. A hand at her breast. Knees between her thighs, spreading them.

She slid her feet along the floor, wishing for him to spread them farther apart. There seemed no end to her garments; the stays, finally, were undone, and she was still in her shift and stockings and shoes, and her hair was all pinned up.

His hands fell away from her. From behind her, his voice was quiet. "I wish the camera obscura could capture you thus. I do not think my memory will do this moment justice in the future."

"What, dressed in a strange combination of garments?" She turned to face him. The look on his face caught her by surprise in its naked wonder.

His smile was faint. "You, all the colors of the sunset, with warm light washing over you through the window. I have never seen any sight I like so well."

He sounded serious, and she wasn't quite sure how to handle him when serious. She wasn't sure how to handle *herself* when he was serious. So she kicked off her shoes, crouched to unroll her stockings, and then straightened up and clambered onto the bed with him.

"Now what?" she asked. "Do you want my shift off as well, or do you want to look at me in the sunset some more?"

"Both," he said shortly, and his hands were not gentle as he tugged the thin linen over her head. "You said I could do whatever I wanted with you. Do you still mean it?"

"I mean it," she said, kneeling on the bed and wondering where to place her hands. "I trust you."

"You're not the chattiest woman I've ever met. Yet somehow everything you say is exactly right."

"A little more of that, and you'll have me thinking you care," she said lightly.

A little more of that, and she'd begin to care herself.

She'd been in lust before. She'd been infatuated. She had admired men in fashionable clothing at the theater; when she was barely a woman, she'd stripped a handsome young man of his regimentals and given him her virginity. Eagerly, passionately.

Though she'd come to his room on an impulse, what she felt for George wasn't like that unthinking animal urge. It wasn't a burst like a firework. It was more like a candle flame. It was warm and steady and lasting, so that she hadn't even realized how much she had come to rely on it. Without it, the world around her wouldn't be the same anymore. Nothing would be as bright. Soon, she would not be able to do without it. Already she was unable to stay away, a moth to that little candlelight. Unwinking and irresistible.

She let her hands fall where they would, then turned her face up to his. "Whatever you want."

His smile was wicked and sweet and full of dark promise. "Well, you're already stripped bare. So next . . ."

He crawled up onto the bed with her, still dressed in trousers and shirtsleeves, though he'd tugged off his boots and shed his cravat and waistcoat. Gently, he pressed at her shoulders, guiding her back flat to the mattress. He bent over her then—to kiss her breast? She drew in a sharp breath, anticipating . . . but no, it was a kiss at her ribs, tender and slow. His eyelashes flicked against her skin as he kissed her like that, all along what she realized was a line her boned stays had left upon her skin.

"Every mark," he murmured. "You said I might kiss every mark on you."

"All of them." Though each of his kisses was small, there were so *many* of them, and she was beginning to wiggle into them, to wish them unending even as she longed for more.

He found the mark at her side then; she could tell by the jolt through his body, the interruption of the seductive rhythm he'd set. "This is not from your stays."

"No. That one's a scar."

"From what?" He stroked the jagged line of it; she knew it to be darker than the rest of her skin, and slightly raised and puckered. "If you want to tell me."

"Certainly. It's nothing shameful. I shot at a man who

was assaulting a woman, and he didn't like that, so he came at me with a knife."

George's head snapped up, his eyes blue pools of shock. "Cass!"

"What?"

"You could have died!"

"But I didn't. And he didn't keep hurting that woman, either. And now I'm fine." But she'd lost a great deal of her pleasure in her work as a Runner, knowing it could end her life.

She'd been fine, yes, but she hadn't quite been the same afterwards.

"You are much more than fine, I believe." George traced another scar, a faint crescent on one of her forearms. "And this? Dare I ask?"

"Oh, that one is shameful. Charles tripped and broke a cup, and I cut myself picking up the pieces."

"How symbolic," he said. "I think we should move on from the kissing of the markings, don't you?"

"Whenever you wish it." Her voice was not quite steady now that his hand, rough and broad, had begun to skate over her skin.

"Your legs are trembling. Do you wish it, too?"

By way of answer, she parted her legs, making a wide vee of them for him to settle between. Then she sank back and waited for him to join her. It could not be soon enough.

"Too subtle," he said. "I've no idea what you want."

She let her head roll to one side. "George. Are you ever serious?"

From the sounds at the foot of the bed, he was now struggling out of his remaining clothing. His shadow on the wall was purple, the sunset now warming the room with ruby light. "Yes. Sometimes. But it's terribly hard to be serious."

"I know," she said, watching his shadow move. "Because then you have to allow that something really matters to you."

She'd warned Charles against *just for now* and *I'll think of it later*. But if there could be no *later*—and for a duke's heir and an unofficial Bow Street Runner, there couldn't be—then she was going to seize the just-for-now. People like her couldn't afford to pass up chances for pleasure. If she waited for something to be perfect, she'd wait forever.

Huh. Maybe that was why Charles did the ridiculous things he did, like climbing trellises and seducing their employers. Maybe they were two sides of the same coin, as always, and where she'd grown cautious with scarcity, he'd grown reckless.

And then George climbed into bed and tucked himself behind her, and her only thoughts were of him. His warm bare skin, the faint scent of orange oil and a gunpowdery scent that meant he'd been messing with one of his picture-making powders. The hard lines of his muscles and the crisp hair over his chest and abdomen. She felt all this, sensed all this. She experienced.

"You really matter to me," he said, then kissed her neck, bared by her pinned-up hair.

"You stole my words." She was forgetting how to make words be sentences.

"Do you mean that I matter to you, too? Or that I pilfered what was a terribly good turn of phrase?"

She'd meant the second. But now that he suggested it: "Both," she said.

"One word, and she slays me," he said quietly. Still

holding her against him like a nestled spoon, he lifted his head to kiss her cheek, her brow, then her lips.

They sipped at each other, slow and yearning, letting tongues brush. His hands traced the shape of her waist, her hip, her breasts, and she ached for more. His feet tangled with hers, and then at last, his knee came between hers. Encouraging, she slid her leg over his, letting his thighs hold up her leg. She was against him, above him—and in a moment, she was around him, as he took the hint and drove forward into her wet depths.

It was slow like this, each thrust like a hill to climb and slide down. She could have lasted forever, falling under the spell of his cock, his hands plucking at her nipples, his warm breath tickling her ear. His kisses at her neck, stubble abrading the skin. She surrendered, liquid in his arms, pleasantly close to a climax, drifting ever closer.

"But you were to ride me," he said, after a few minutes of this delicious melting together. "I want to see you above me, wild and powerful. Do you want that, too?"

She loved to ride atop. Slipping from his embrace, she coaxed him flat on his back, then rose above him on her knees. The mattress was a soft cradle; his cock was a thick, hard promise, erect and flat against his abdomen. She took hold of it at the root, easing it perpendicular to his body, and he hissed his pleasure.

Scooting forward to just the right place then, she positioned herself above it. Found her entrance with his tip, then folded herself over his body and let her own weight drive him deep, deep within her until he was fully seated.

His fingers clutched at the coverlet; they'd never even pulled it back. His neck was corded, teeth gritted, eyes squeezed shut.

"Are you close?" she asked.

"Not at all. I don't even like it," he ground out.

"Then I'd better find something to do that you like." She reached a hand back to stroke his bollocks. They were high and tight, and at the touch of her fingers, he shuddered all over.

"Cass." He sounded strangled. "Just ride. Please. I want you to find your pleasure."

Ah. Well. If he put it so nicely, who was she to refuse? She eased herself up, kneeling astride him still, and kept her weight on her straightened arms. Thus could she work her hips up, letting him slide almost free, then grind down in a deep, firm stroke. He took her hips in his hands, guiding her on, helping support her weight. Sometimes his tongue found her lips, her nipples. Sometimes his hands clenched, hard, into the softness of her rear.

She found a rhythm like this, the thrust and pull, and felt the heat building within her again. It was steady like that flame she felt for him; it was inevitable that it would become a conflagration. Oh, she was shaking from it, so close, and he was touching her within and all over—and then she was a firework after all, gasping at the pleasure that burst through her, letting it rattle her from the very core of her out to her skin until she hardly knew where she was.

Dimly, she noticed George pull free from her body, roll to the side of the bed, and spend himself into a handkerchief. At once, he rolled back to her and took her in his arms. Spoons again.

"You matter to me," he said softly, and kissed the nape of her neck. It was an awkward kiss, one that surely won him a hairpin to the lip, and she adored it.

Only now did they pull back the coverlet and take down her hair. They washed what needed washing, laughing about nothing at all, then returned to bed.

He held her then, breathing in the scent of her hair, ever

more slowly until she thought he'd fallen asleep. She watched their interlaced shadows on the wall until the red sky grew purple and the shadows vanished against it.

And, wholly unexpectedly, tears came to her eyes.

The sight of Lord Deverell bleeding hadn't made her cry. She hadn't cried when Charles broke his leg, either, or the time Jenks was shot at and almost hit in the head, or when that criminal stabbed her in the side—before she used her own knife on him. She hadn't even cried, really, when Grandmama died.

She hadn't dared.

She had a heart, but it didn't beat near the surface. It was safer if she kept it hidden. And when someone needed something of her—protection, information, comfort—she could provide that. She could do whatever was needed.

But when someone offered her kindness and asked nothing in return, her eyes leaked like a watering pot, and her heart thumped for notice, and it was all too, too much.

The circumstances of an entire life were a great deal to pile up on the account of one man. It was unreasonable to expect him to balance the scale against everything else. Yet here he was, holding her, and for the moment everything was in balance. The pleasure and the responsibility of it. The power and the trust.

It had never been like this before, the way it had been with George. The bedding, the hoping, the wishing.

Which meant that it could never happen again, but that she would never stop wanting it to.

So she was unreasonable, and being unreasonable, she fell asleep in his arms.

When she awoke at dawn, it was to the sound of screaming, and George was gone.

Chapter Twelve

Not even the Duke of Richmond's well-trained servants could happen upon the Duke of Ardmore, supine and slashed by a knife, without screaming.

George was already awake when the screaming started; he'd jolted awake almost every hour as if his sleeping mind didn't trust Cass would stay with him. She had, though, sweetly in his arms. In moonlight, he saw that her brows were knitted in sleep as if she were dreaming fierce dreams.

He smiled, and looked at her, and loved it.

But he couldn't stare at her face forever. When the sun started to rise, reaching faintly pink through the window he'd never shuttered the night before, he thought about getting up and tinkering with an experiment.

No sooner had he dressed, though, than the screaming started—and no sooner had the screaming started than he was wrestling open the well-fastened door, careening out into the corridor, and slamming into the doorway of his father's bedchamber next to his.

The maid, who had carried in a lamp and prepared to lay the fire, was still shaking, her mouth an O of shock and her eyes hardly less wide.

George followed her gaze—and yes, he had to agree

the Duke of Ardmore presented a dreadful sight. His white nightshirt was liberally splashed with blood; his sheets were gory with it. He was groaning, trying to sit up in the bed and slipping in his own blood. George couldn't even tell where the wound was.

He put his hands on the maid's shoulders and looked into her eyes. "Breathe. Breathe. All right? Yes. You're all right. I need you to go for a physician. Or wake a footman and have him go. Understand? At once, all right? Leave the lamp."

She nodded, slowly at first, then with quick jerks paired with sobs. And then she was off, running. The hearth remained cold, the fire unkindled.

George shut the door behind her, praying she hadn't woken the entire inn, then strode to his father's bedside. "Father? Where are you hurt?"

The duke glared at him, grumbled something, and held out an arm.

"An *arm?*" George exclaimed. "All this blood from an arm?" He set the lamp on a small table beside the bed.

"The bastard almost cut the damned thing off!" howled the duke. "Look at it!"

George looked at it. Yes, in the crook of his father's left arm was a deep and oozing stab wound. Or was it a slash? A chop? It might be all three. It was very deep and very big, and after a moment of looking at it, he had to avert his gaze.

"That's . . . very bad. Yes. Some bastard came into your room and did this to you?" He was hunting through his father's belongings for something he could use to bind the wound. The bleeding seemed to be slowing—surely, it was?—but the sooner it was treated, the better.

Ah! A cravat would do. Perfect. He held one up, then

turned back toward his father. "Let me wrap this about your arm until the physician arrives."

"Not that one," the duke snapped. "That's my favorite cravat."

George stared at him. "Now I know you're going to be just fine." He returned the favorite cravat to its place, then picked up an identical-looking one and tied it around the horrible hatcheting of his father's arm.

"Someone was in your room?" The window was open, but it was hardly big enough for a man's shoulders. "Someone did this to you?"

"Obviously I didn't do it to myself."

George counted to three. Then he did it again. His father was hurt and probably frightened, and he could not be expected to have the mood of an angel. "What did you notice?"

"That he had a bloody big knife and was using it on me."

"So it was a man?"

For the first time, the duke seemed to take in what George was saying. "I—hmm." *Harumph.* "Didn't see well enough. Almost dark still, you know. I didn't see more than the shape of a person."

George pressed at his temples. "Someone came into your room, and slashed your arm, and left. Through the window again?"

"Must've been. And might've been trying for far more than my arm. I *said* it was dark."

"Yes." He wished for Cass. Only a room away; he could wake her when the physician arrived. She would know what to do with this evidence. She would fit it into one of her patterns.

"I know what you're thinking," said Ardmore. "That this has to do with the tontine."

George hadn't thought about the tontine. He'd thought

about his father bleeding, the maid screaming, Cass sleeping. All the problems he felt barely adequate to solve.

The cravat had soaked through, and George got another and changed the old makeshift bandage for a new one. This time, he tied it more tightly, and was satisfied when the starched white cloth didn't immediately turn red.

"I was thinking more about how to get you to stop bleeding," he replied at last. "This might have done it. I would just as soon never think of the tontine again."

"You'll be happy to think of it if I win the prize."

Again, George stared at him. Who was this man, hovering between middle and old age, who could crow about money while wearing a nightshirt and covered in his own blood? How had such a man ever created a family? Why had he bothered?

"Fine," George said. "Let's talk about the tontine. You've never thought you were in danger despite my suspicions. What do you think now?"

"That your suspicions didn't protect me. So what good were they?"

George clenched his jaw, back teeth grinding together. "I will be back shortly," he said tightly, "to see if you are all right."

And that was about all he could manage right now. After the loveliness of a night with Cass, he disliked beginning the day by being blamed for wanting to keep his father safe but not doing so.

When he returned to his own chamber, only a twist of sheets remained where Cass had slept. She'd gathered up her clothing too, leaving no sign that she'd been there.

But how had she left? Had she run naked out into the corridor? He peered out, as if she'd still be there, pale and bare. Then he remembered the communicating door between their rooms. It was bolted on his side, or had been. Now it was open just a crack.

He put his face to it. "Cass?"

"Almost ready," her reply came at once. As good as her word, she snatched the door open with one hand as her other poked a final hairpin into a simple twist. "Who is hurt? What has happened?"

Quickly, he told her, noticing as he spoke that she was wearing a plain gown he'd never seen before. "I think," he concluded, "that the duke will be all right. And how did you get yourself dressed? Doesn't that require the assistance of a small army?"

Her smile was thin and distracted. "I brought some of my own clothes from home. I've always had them in my possession, in case of need."

He was thrown for a moment by her reference to home, thinking she meant Ardmore House. But of course she didn't. That wasn't her home; it was barely even his. "Today there's need," he surmised. "Need of an investigator, not Mrs. Benedetti."

"Maybe I can manage to be both." She pressed the heels of her hands against her eyes. "God help me."

"Why should God help you?" He was merely curious. But it seemed there was no good tone in which to ask such a question, for she rounded on him.

"Because I hate the work sometimes. I like seeing people better off; I like knowing that I had some small part in that. But I get no thrill from being in danger. I feel sick when I see people hurt."

He was wordless in the face of such passion. Finally he scraped together a single sentence. "I will help you if I can."

"You can. Of course you can. Making certain your father was all right was the best help of all."

But she had reminded him, yes, how temporary their

alliance was. He had got used to leaning on her, to having her lean right back. They held each other up, and if she was gone, he felt he would topple again into wasted days and half-hearted hopes. He'd not made a difference for a long time, and she'd told him rightly: it was heady stuff, feeling as if one mattered.

Making her way into George's room, she shut the connecting door behind her and then sat on his bed again as if it were her own. "I agree with you that this has to do with the tontine. But this attacker is very bad. Two murder attempts, no successes."

"There was success with Knotwirth." George paced the room, fingers drumming his thighs. "He'd never have gone swimming in the Thames."

"But he might have fallen in?"

"He might have," George had to grant. Knotwirth had drunk as much as Lord Deverell, and without the responsibilities of a title to distract him.

"Or maybe the attacker is trying to spread fear rather than do true harm," Cass mused. "He could be targeting one person in particular, but spreading the threat around so his true target is veiled."

"Possible—but if so, who is the true target? We haven't a clue."

"We have many." Cass ticked on her fingers. "The person is not conspicuous amongst the ton. The person has access to good quality writing paper, and he or she prints well and is intelligent enough to disguise his or her handwriting."

"Because of the note left with Lord Deverell?" At her nod, George added, "His *or* her? Surely not. There weren't any women in the tontine. And besides, you just used a whole slew of masculine pronouns."

"That was for efficiency's sake. A woman could benefit

from the deaths of men in the tontine. Your mother, for example, to have a peaceful life."

"She arranges that already," George said.

"One of the other wives, then? Without a husband, Lady Deverell could take all the lovers she wants."

"*She* arranges that already," said George again. "And those two husbands are the ones who have been attacked. Killing off one's spouse is no way to make sure he wins a tontine."

"You are right." She screwed up her mouth to one side, thinking. "So that's another clue: who has motive, and who does not."

He looked longingly at his camera obscura. His special papers, his bottles of strange and wondrous chemicals. There would be no time for leisurely experiments now. "It's not much to go on, what you've said."

From behind him, her wonderful voice was tremulous. "I wish I could tell you hair color, height, preferred boot-maker, and means of capture. I'm sorry. It's dreadful work sometimes, sorting out a case."

"I'm glad for your guidance." He turned his back on the makeshift worktable. "All right. So we need to consider who else might gain from these attacks."

Cass looked pained. "This attack was against a duke with a taste for gambling he cannot seem to control, and the debts to match."

"Yes, but there's nothing for my mother to gain by murdering my father. We just said that. And anyway, she's not even here, even if she could be bothered to pick up a knife."

"Not your mother." Cass cleared her throat. "His heir might want to stop him from losing more. Hurting the dukedom that will someday pass along the male line."

George understood the words, but his mind required a

long moment to assemble them into sense. "His heir—but that's me."

"That's you."

His head snapped back. "You can't think *I'd* do this? I'm not capable of—well, physically I am, but I wouldn't—Cass!" How dare she look so calm?

And she sounded calm too, holding up a staying hand. "No, I don't think so. I never have. And if I doubted my instincts, you could never have risked an answer if you were indeed guilty."

"But you think I'm a suspect in this attack? You can vouch for me! We were together all night."

She moistened her lips, but she held his gaze. "When I woke up from the screaming, you weren't here."

"I'd only just left the room!" Good Christ! The rumpled bed might as well have been occupied by two entirely different people for all the warmth that remained to it.

"What happens next is up to your father. Lord Deverell wanted to hush up the whole matter of his stabbing and pretend he went to the country to unpickle himself a bit. What will His Grace want to do?"

"Contact Bow Street?" George sighed. "I don't know. You are very cold, Cass."

"I'm honest. I have to be. And I'd do you no favor if you first heard this from someone else."

She was right, but it still hurt. It was the sort of rightness she'd maintain with anyone she encountered on a case. This positive mandate for honesty; it was so unfamiliar in the ton. One made one's way with flippancy and manners.

He folded his arms. "What sort of someone else? Someone I haven't taken to bed?"

All right, so George just made his way with flippancy.

She raised her brows, and he felt the chastisement of it. "Someone whose motives you don't trust."

He collapsed then, sinking onto the foot of the bed at her side.

He owed her better than flippancy. She had told him once, she'd taken lovers for pleasure, companionship, protection.

Why had she added George to the list? What did he offer her?

She offered him all that. Pleasure, God yes. Companionship, none better. Protection? Call it partnership, rather. The solid delight of knowing someone relied on him and could be relied upon in return.

"I do trust your motives," he said. "I needn't ask yours, for I think I know them. You are troubled by injustice."

"Injustice is part of every corner of life. If I was troubled by injustice, I should never stop being angry. No, I'm troubled by crime. In this case, by greed on top of the greed that has been part of the tontine from its formation."

Her fists clenched.

Only now, sitting at her side, did he notice that she was wearing the emerald ring of Mrs. Benedetti. Strange that it looked as if it had always belonged to her.

George nudged her with his elbow. "But you're also here because you like me. Don't you?"

She looked at him askance—and then she smiled, slow and bright as a bloom. "I wouldn't have gone to bed with you if I didn't."

He eyed her closely, enjoying the sight of her. The determination in her heart; the simple pleasure she took in sensory indulgence. These all showed themselves on her mobile features, and he could not look away.

Must he? Not for a while, surely.

He groped for words, but they all seemed thin and tinny next to her golden goodwill. "Well. That's something."

"That's a lot. You've no idea."

"I have an idea or two," he said.

"Show me," she said. "And then let us summon the other suspects and tell them a few lies. We'll see how they react."

"Fine, but my ideas are more fun," he pointed out.

"I'm sure they will be," she agreed, and for a few minutes, they both enjoyed them, before work and worry intruded again.

"What's all this, then, Northbrook?" Lord Deverell sounded as grumpy as any man who'd missed his breakfast. "The match race will begin in a few hours. Everyone will be heading to the track."

Cass had talked George carefully through the approach to the announcement. The gathering in the private parlor of the coaching inn, so that everyone was seated almost on top of everyone else. The closed windows so the room would quickly become stuffy. Everyone was uneasy and soon to become physically uncomfortable.

It was time for a subtle interrogation.

Lord and Lady Deverell were here, and Cavender and Gerry, and a smattering of other people they picked almost at random from among Richmond's household guests.

George was to do the talking. Cass would watch the unwitting guests' reactions, keeping as silent as possible with the hope of preserving her identity as a family cousin.

"I've asked you all here," George said somberly, "because you were closest to my father."

Lady Deverell had been fanning herself. Abruptly, she stopped, her head lifting. "Were? Something has happened to His Grace?"

Cass willed herself to notice every little detail. The furrows of brows. Hair untidy in pins, cravats rumpled. How much of it was guilt? Haste? Worry? Fatigue?

Lady Deverell grasped the situation quickly. Suspiciously quickly? So it would seem, but she and her husband were also aware of—had survived—a similar attack.

"Something has happened," George confirmed. "In his sleep, my father was attacked by an unknown person. He has lost a great deal of blood and might not survive. I should like to get him back to London as soon as possible."

The bit about the duke's survival was an exaggeration. Everyone who had spoken to him that morning, from George to Cass to the physician who'd been called, had received the sharp side of his tongue and was in no doubt of his hold upon life.

"Surely he should not be moved." Gerry's hands twisted his cane. "My own medical man travels with me and could—but this is such a shock. Ardmore! I cannot credit it! Yes, do have Sullivan examine him. Perhaps it is not so dire."

"Perhaps." Polite agreement, though the doubt in George's voice was heavy.

Lord Deverell and Cavender looked curious. Rapt. Not worried. Cavender's hand drifted to his fobs. "A thief, I'd wager. Was anything taken from his rooms?"

"I hadn't thought to check," George said drily.

"A thief." Cavender nodded, satisfied with himself. "Thought I heard someone moving around outside."

Cass calculated the need for a diversionary statement here. "That could have been travelers, since this is a coaching inn."

"Travelers come and go on the ground," replied Cavender. "This person was moving about outside the windows. My room's what, two away from Ardmore? Why, I must have heard the blackguard who attacked him!"

He sounded pleased.

"A pity you didn't rouse yourself," George said. "Perhaps you could have frightened the assailant away and protected my father's life."

Cavender looked confused. "How could I? I thought it was travelers."

Cass sat back in her chair, stifling a sound of disgust.

Only Lord Deverell had remained silent thus far. Now he spoke, asking George, "Was anything left behind that oughtn't to have been there? Any belongings of the attacker? Or . . . a note? A paper, I mean. Anything dropped?"

"No note," George said. "Nothing was dropped."

This was true. There had been no note, no counting down of the number of men left in the tontine. Perhaps the attacker had lost faith in his skill. Perhaps he hadn't wanted to leave an additional clue.

Lord Deverell looked troubled. "How strange."

"Why should that be strange?" asked Gerry. "The thief was horrified to have awoken his quarry, and he fled."

"If it was a thief," said George.

"What else could it have been? Race meetings are full of thieves," said Cavender.

"Private race meetings? Hosted by dukes?" scoffed one of the other guests, a woman Cass didn't know. "More likely Ardmore was attacked for some personal reason."

"Are you *sure* there was no note?" asked Lord Deverell again.

The reason for his questioning was clear, at least to his wife and Cass and George. And damnation, but these hidden bits of knowledge were like those old excavations soldiers used to make under fortresses. The more Cass found out, the more likely it was for the ground to open beneath her feet and swallow her. How could she sort the Deverells' knowledge about the attack on the earl from their worry about Ardmore? Was their surprise because the attack had happened at all, or because it had failed?

By the time the impromptu interview was over a quarter of an hour later, they were left with more questions. As many questions as when they'd begun, and almost as many as the Duke of Richmond's honored and slightly less honored guests had posed to George.

All this time, Ardmore had remained in his room, silent. For all these people knew, near death.

He was pale and weak, but when Cass had spoken with him, he'd been well enough. And he had agreed to this gathering led by George on two conditions.

First, he would allow Cass until the end of the week—four days' time—to close the tontine case. After that, he would either consult Bow Street or would damn the whole matter to perdition, depending on what had transpired.

And second, they would return to London at once, and tell no one else the truth of what had passed in Chichester.

Chapter Thirteen

Charles looked forward to Janey's visits, though they came only every other day. By now, a few weeks into his recuperation, he had noticed a pattern.

When she arrived, she stepped into the parlor and then merely stood looking around. Not as if she were evaluating it for items to be stolen and sold—of which there were few, and not very desirable at that. She appeared instead to be settling herself. *Here I am, then; this is a nice place to be.*

After that, she sat on a tufted footstool, wiggling her feet. Her fingertips, poking always from heavy knitted fingerless gloves, stroked the brick and wooden chimney piece as if it were marble.

And Charles struggled from his bedchamber to a chair near her, joining her for the conversation about Bow Street cases. It was never long enough for his taste, and not because of his devotion to his work.

Today he made his way to the usual chair with less thumping and gracelessness than before. His broken leg was still encased in a fragile and bulky brace, but he'd better learned how to compensate for it. In fact, he had washed and shaved and dressed in an almost normal manner—save for the slit-in-half trousers he had to wear.

"I'm getting pretty good at hopping, don't you think?" he said by way of greeting. "Hullo, Janey."

She snapped him a gesture that he supposed was a greeting of her own. "Feelin' better today, eh? You'll be running in the Derby soon."

Charles laughed. "So I might. Why not aim high?"

Janey grinned. "And how's Miss Benton?" She always asked after Cass. Always with the formality of a last name, too. Charles wondered if she thought of him as Mr. Benton, or if she'd come to regard him as Charles, as he encouraged.

"She's run off to Chichester with the nobs for a few days," he answered. "Part of a case she's working."

"Coo! She'll tell us some good tales when she's back." Janey snapped her fingers. "'Fore I forget, I brought you a gift today."

"News?"

"Aye, that. But also . . ." She stood and unwound a length of cloth from about her waist. He'd thought it was a drab-colored pelisse, but when she shook it out, what he'd taken for sleeves were revealed to be legs. Trouser legs.

Handing it over, she explained, "You'll be on your feet soon and need something you haven't cut to bits."

He was strangely touched. "You brought me trousers." He rubbed the cloth between his fingers. It was good quality.

"Should be just your size." She winked. "I'm ever so good at sizing up a fellow."

His face heated. "Did you—how much do I—"

"I didn't steal them," she sniffed, plumping onto the footstool again. "And you don't need to pay for them."

"I can't take a gift. You've helped me so much."

She tipped her head. "Helpin' you's got me out of

paying a fine. So, this is my fine. Spent it on you instead of Fox."

No one ever gave him gifts except Cass, and he was all too aware that anything one of the Bentons spent came out of the pocket of the other. Not that this had ever stopped him from dipping into hers. He cast a guilty look at the washstand, where some few coins remained from the wages Cass had given him. He wished he could remember what he'd done with his own wage for that week of work with Northbrook.

"I . . ." He set the trousers aside. "Thank you. That's very—I—thank you."

Janey gave him a short little nod, her cheeks pink. "Welcome."

And then she passed along her news, beginning with the Watch off Hart Street. She had a friend who worked the streets nearby, but never Hart. "Felix wouldn't know her to look at her," Janey explained. "So she acted like she's a country girl and asked him for help."

Entrapment. It gladdened Charles's heart. "Did you have to pay her?"

Janey pursed her lips. "Bartered, like. She was doing something she oughtn't, and it got her in a scrape, and I got her out."

"You did her a favor, and she did one back."

"Ex-actly," Janey said with relish.

"But she didn't do a favor for you," Charles pointed out. "She did one for Bow Street."

Janey set a hand to her hip, though the effect was dampened by the thick swaddles of clothing she wore. "And ain't I Bow Street while you're in that bed? Or chair."

This was true, and a truth of a sort that made Charles's mind reel. "You're right," he said, and she gratified him with her lovely crooked smile.

So it was that this Mags, whom Charles had never met, caught Felix in a net. And one of the other Runners—"that nice Irish man, Mr. Lilac"—wrapped everything up.

"Admirable," Charles said. "That's really well done. Lovely work." But then he realized: "Does that hurt your business, having that case closed? The bawdy houses hereabouts can't be happy with you for ending their supply of girls."

Janey set her narrow jaw. "There's always a supply of girls. I just want them to be girls who wants the work."

He had to ask. "And what about you? Do you . . . want the work?" It had never bothered him that she sold her body, but it certainly had occupied his thoughts.

She tilted her head, thinking, then said, "I liked this better. Easier to rile a man than please him. 'Sides, I've never been in one of the houses. I work for myself." She winked.

He coughed.

"Need a handkerchief?" She pulled one of her endless supply of embroidered silks from a pocket in her skirt. Her outermost skirt, judging from the swaddled breadth of her.

"Not one of those," he admitted. "I'd feel like an arse coughing into something worth more than my dinner."

"And you would be," Janey confirmed. "Bits of lace, squares of silk—pooh." Her expression indicated she'd restrained herself from using stronger language. "What good are they? Can't eat 'em. They don't keep you warm."

"I can't say," Charles replied. "But everyone wants them. You do a good trade."

"Aye, they're easy to pinch. That is . . . I imagine as they would be. I only sell bits I finds on the ground."

Charles laughed. "Janey, please. Give me credit for more intelligence than that."

She looked merry. "I give you credit for doing your job, and so I won't admit nothing. Doin' what I oughtn't is what led me here."

"Are you sorry?" Charles thought better of the question almost at once; some things a man didn't want answered. "I've an idea. Ring for the landlady, will you?"

Mrs. Jellicoe appeared, gray-haired and stern, looking suspiciously at Janey. "You remember my associate from Bow Street," Charles said grandiosely, and the lady relaxed.

"We should like a pot of chocolate," Charles told her. "Do you know where one can be bought?"

Mrs. Jellicoe brightened. "Coffee shop the next street over sells chocolate. I could have you a pot in a trice."

"You are very good. Ah . . . Janey, look away, would you?"

He fished in his purse for one of Cass's coins. They'd hung around longer than they usually did, as he was trapped in bed and unable to spend.

Just as well. He'd no idea where his money went, usually. Wherever it went, he didn't miss the spending of it.

Mrs. Jellicoe took the coin with a nod and a curious glance at Janey, who was studying the ceiling as if erotic drawings were pasted across it.

"As if I don't know where your purse is," she scoffed, still looking at the ceiling even after the landlady had departed. "I'd 've had it off you the second I got here if I wanted to."

"Why didn't you?"

She tipped her head down, setting one of the scarves about her head to swinging. "I'm a Runner now, or close as a mort can be. I would unt steal from you."

Charles thought about this. "Thanks," he said.

Mrs. Jellicoe returned a few minutes later with a pot of

chocolate and two cups he recognized as her best. "I'll be fetching the pot back later," she said. "You enjoy, now."

She settled the dishes on a small table that was not quite within reach of Charles's chair. Once she left again, he had to rise, drag the chair and his broken leg, and then thump everything down together.

Janey watched this whole process, mystified.

Charles poured out two cups of the rich, dark liquid. "To your good health." He extended a cup to her.

She crept from her footstool, took the cup in both hands, and stared solemnly into its depths. "Why? What's this?"

"Chocolate." Charles breathed in the scent, rich and bitter and sweet at once. "It's better than a silk handkerchief. You can drink it. It'll keep you warm."

Satisfied, she returned to her seat and took a sip. After a moment, she looked up from the cup at him with something like wonder. And then she smiled, and it was worth every penny and more to place that cup in her hands. "Thanks," she said simply, an echo of his own wondering word from before.

"So. What's the surgeon say about that leg?" She waggled her brows.

Flirt when you have a broken right leg, be impotent forever. Cass had said that. She was joking—he'd known that, though a little corner of him wondered.

"He'll return to check it tomorrow. If it's healing well, perhaps I'll get a cane soon instead of this brace." He loved the idea of a cane. He'd be able to shuffle downstairs more easily; he'd be able to return to work. He couldn't pound the streets, but there was much to do in the magistrate's court itself.

God, he missed the work.

But he wouldn't see Janey anymore, at least not like

this. Sitting on the footstool as if they were a family, with chocolate on her lip and the devil in her eyes. And God, he would miss that, too.

"You'll be back at work soon," she said. "Surgeon'll know what's what."

"The thing is, Janey," Charles began delicately. "When I'm back at Bow Street, I'll have to—that is, you won't be able to be with me like . . ."

"Sure we can be together, whenever you like. You take it out, I slip it in. Simple."

Oh, the devil was in her eye now. She was laughing at him as he spluttered for words. "I wasn't talking about *that*. God. Tempting woman. But then—wait, are you offering to . . ."

"Don't you want me to?"

He shook his head, knowing that he meant yes. "What if we—no, Janey. We can't. A Runner and an informant? No one would ever confide in you again. And it's not as if I could marry you, is it?"

"Marry me!" she hooted.

Charles was silent.

Her jaw went slack. "Marry . . . me? You were thinking of it?"

He'd been thinking of her for months. Ages. He hadn't considered marriage before, but—why not? "I've been thinking of it, yes."

"I'm not the sort that marries."

"I didn't think I was either."

She still looked dumbstruck, pulling at her fingerless gloves as if she were chilled. "I work every day for my bread. I can't afford extras." She eyed Charles narrowly. "I can't afford *you*."

"Think it over," he said.

She snapped to. "Think over what? All I heard you say was that you couldn't marry me, not that I ever hinted at wanting such a thing." Her posture was tight, her voice hard. "I have to go." In a whirl of skirts, she was standing; she was already at the door.

He cursed his broken leg; he could hardly rise in time to stop her. "When will you be back?"

"When time allows. I'm a busy mort, Charles Benton. I'm a whore and cutpurse and informant and clothes seller and—"

"You're marvelous," Charles blurted. "That's you in a word."

Her mouth made an O. "I have to go," she said again. Then she darted across the room to him, took his shoulders, and tipped up her face to press a quick kiss to his lips. She was all faded flowers and mint, chocolate and fresh tobacco and yesterday's bread, the story of everywhere she'd been that day. He wanted nothing more than to accompany her wherever the day took her next.

"I really do have to go," she blurted, then rushed for the door. She paused on the threshold but did not turn and look back, and then she truly was gone.

Charles fell into his chair, heart thundering, cursing the broken leg that prevented him from following her. The broken leg that came from nothing but his own foolishness.

Yet he still tasted Janey's kiss on his lips. And he had the feeling that for the first time in a great while, he'd said and done something wise.

Chapter Fourteen

One day of the four had been lost due to travel back to London.

Another day had been tossed away at the theater, while Cass tried to chase down clues related to a Bow Street case. Not that George had minded accompanying her, because he didn't mind accompanying her anywhere. And they'd progressed on the tontine case too, sending and receiving more messages with Callum Jenks and Angelus than George had ever dashed off in one day.

Even if he and Cass didn't resolve the case in the next two days, it wouldn't be dropped. It wouldn't be over.

That wouldn't be the end of their time together.

This was the third day of the four the duke had grudgingly permitted. While His Grace remained pale and tired with his arm swathed in bandages, he was grumbling all the time about bringing the case to a close. Ordinarily, George ignored these grumbling moods, but this *was* the duke's house, and he *could* send Cass away if he wished.

How could anyone wish to? George liked knowing that she was in the house. That at any moment, she might wander into his experiment room and begin a conversation about one-could-never-guess what.

Just now, it was early afternoon, the lazy time of day between morning callers and essential errands. George was in his experiment room, and as he'd hoped, Cass had wandered in.

"Angelus sent his reply," she said. "It's all arranged for Saturday night, should we need it."

"We'll need it, I think. We keep running into walls of silence. Our shadow attacker is a lazy sort." Holding up a glass vessel containing a dusting of silver iodide, he poured in frigid water. The surface developed a pleasing skin, crackling with an icy finish.

He turned to face Cass, extending the vessel toward her. "Look at that. That's interesting, isn't it? Ice from a powder and a liquid? Surely this reaction ought to do something to help me make a picture."

She poked at it with a cautious forefinger, then smiled. "It ought to do something to help someone with some task. I can't be more specific than that."

"No, nor can I." Setting the vessel on the worktable, he capped the bottle of powdered silver iodide. "I'm acting at random with every experiment I do. There's no method to my madness, as that fellow from *Hamlet* says. Sort of."

She closed a hand over his where it still held the bottle. "You're investigating. And sometimes it seems fruitless, I know."

"Yes, exactly."

"But there's a reason for it. So—tell me about it."

"Tell you about what?" He returned the bottle to its place on one of the narrow shelves, where it abutted so many others just like it.

"Why you want to make pictures from life. Why you care about it, even when it seems fruitless."

"Oh." He pulled off his work gloves and tossed them

onto the table. "Do you really want to know? Because I might be tedious."

She trailed around the room, touching everything she could lay hands on. "Yes, I really want to know. I wish I had a talent like that. Something I really loved doing."

He watched her move, graceful and slow in a gown of rust-red that did wonderful things to the color of her hair and eyes. "Can one say one has a talent if one never accomplishes anything of note?"

She shrugged. "Why not? If you like it, and you're trying different things."

"Rather like you with investigations?"

"Not like that at all. I feel necessary sometimes. But is that a talent?"

"Right. Because you don't love it." It seemed unfair that she should have such gifts and not enjoy the use of them: her prodigious memory, her swift fists, her glib tongue. But perhaps she made up for people like George, who had no gifts and enjoyed everything.

"I like accomplishing something." She cut her gaze sideways at him. "Who is Lily? Someone you cared for very much?"

That, he had not expected. He leaned on the worktable with one hand, crossing one foot over another. "Ah, someone was gossiping in Chichester."

"No. Your sister was gossiping while I had her dresses fitted to me. I was curious, that's all."

"You held it well."

"Not so well. You mentioned her to Angelus, too. That reminded me. And then yes, someone gossiped in Chichester." Her cheeks went slightly pink.

"About Lily? And that makes you blush?"

"Lady Deverell said it was a shame I was married,

since it was nice to see you going about with a respectable lady again." She gave a crooked smile. "It was so embarrassing. If I've given the impression that I'm respectable, then I have failed completely at the role of Mrs. Benedetti."

"That's why you're embarrassed?"

"Of course," she said stiffly. "And I was embarrassed for you, since Lady Deverell implied that you went about with unrespectable ladies."

"Thanks for your concern," he said drily.

"So, who is Lily? Besides Lord Deverell's daughter, which you told Angelus."

"You really do remember every detail to do with a case." He rapped his knuckles on the rough wood surface of the table. "Well, that's who she was. She was the only child of my godfather's first marriage, and I was engaged to her when I was just twenty-one. She died of a fever."

Cass toyed with the heavy fabric of the draperies, currently open to the afternoon sun. "Did you love her?"

"I did, though I'm not sure what kind of love it was. We were expected to marry, and we were agreeable to the idea." His brow furrowed. "She was always a part of my life—do you know what that's like? So it was strange when she wasn't there anymore. Everything felt wrong.

"Maybe," he continued, "it was like awaking to find all the furniture gone in one's house. The place was familiar, but it just wasn't right, and it wasn't as comfortable. But then one gets used to it."

Cass blinked at him. "May I someday be loved enough to be compared to furniture."

"The *absence* of furniture," corrected George. "And it was only an analogy. Never mind."

She smiled a little. "Only teasing you. I do understand, I think. That is, I've never loved anyone in a romantic way. But I have lost someone dear to me." Her hand slipped into her pocket.

"Your parents?"

"I don't remember my parents. My mother was never well after she birthed Charles and me, and she died when we were only two years old. Our father always came and went from the time of their marriage, and after she died, he went and never came back."

"Blackguard."

Cass lifted one shoulder, as if she couldn't be bothered to shrug again. "He has another family now, in Devon. We used Bow Street connections to find out that much. But we never see him and don't miss him."

"You can't miss someone you never knew, can you?" But as he spoke the words, he wondered if they were true. One could notice what everyone else had. One could feel an emptiness where there ought to be love and support.

She pulled the little gold case from her pocket now, the one he'd seen pinched by that boy Jemmy. Popping the clasp, she flipped it open and held it out for his examination. "This is my grandmother."

A fine-quality miniature of a young woman regarded him from its setting. The style of the clothing and hair was old-fashioned, but the deep, frank eyes and stubborn chin were unmistakably Benton.

"She is beautiful," George said.

"Don't be silly. She looks like me." She snatched the case back and stuffed it into her pocket before George could protest. "She raised Charles and me. We both miss her very much."

"I am glad you had someone who loved you to raise you. I envy you that."

Again she took hold of the drapery fabric. "You speak as if you didn't have the same."

"I'm not sure I did. My parents are fond of me if I don't bother them too much, but they didn't raise me, really. They didn't serve as guides to the sort of person I ought to be. I had to sort that out entirely on my own, mainly using examples to the contrary."

Who had ever loved George? Until Cass spoke so warmly about her grandmother, this was not a question that had ever occurred to him. He had thought about his own love, if one could apply that word to his familial fondness for his sister and the distant dutifulness he felt for his parents. The emotion he'd felt for Lily had seemed shining and warm beside that. Yet it had faded with her death; perhaps it would always have faded.

What if there was something wrong with him, so that he couldn't inspire anyone to love him? Him, George; not the marquess or the heir.

He wanted to ask, but his throat closed on the question. If Cass said there was—If she couldn't—When he felt—

No. Those were questions that didn't bear thinking of.

"But we were meant to be talking of my experiments," he said lightly. "In a way, Lily is related to them. I don't have a single painting of her, and one quickly forgets a face without a likeness to go by. So I thought maybe I could make likenesses. But I've no talent with a brush, like all those artists my father loves. I had to think of a different way." Ruefully, he looked over the shelves of chemicals and papers. "Only I haven't succeeded yet."

"You've made little chips of ice in a glass," she said. "That's not nothing."

"True," he agreed. "That's not nothing." He peered into

the vessel that held the mixture of water and silver iodide. "Ah, it's all melted."

"So you try something else."

"So I do." She was so close to him now, and he was so far from answers. Shaking his head, he kept the conversation on his experiments. "In some way, I'll get the light of the sun to imprint the paper. I've been messing about with different sorts of salts, especially silver and iron, since they change color over time."

"Like rust or tarnish," Cass said.

"Exactly. While I try and fail with different substances, I'm trying different names for this process, too. What do you think of"—he paused dramatically—"helio-ichnographia? It uses the Greek words for 'sun-tracing.'"

"Too long."

"What about . . . techni-chartis?"

"I suppose that also means something wonderful?"

"A sort of 'art chart.'"

"Hmm." She poked at the glass vessel that now held a clear slurry, then at his discarded work gloves. "What about using English words?"

"Nonsense. No one would know what an important invention it was if I used ordinary English. It's got to have a Greek or Latin name."

"That makes sense," Cass said, sounding as if it did in fact make perfect sense to her. "What is the Greek for silver? If you're using silver salts?"

"Argyros." He rolled the word around his mouth, trying it out. "I don't know."

"Drawing, maybe? Drawing with sunlight?"

"Sun is helios, as I already said. Or there is simply light from an unspecified source. That's photos." He considered. "Light drawing . . . photos-graphé. Maybe photo-graphé for ease of pronunciation."

Cass pulled a face. "That's no better. Sorry. Maybe you should just pick a word you like and that'll be the name of the process."

"Which doesn't yet exist, and never will if I can't sort out how to get silver salts to stop darkening in helios. Or even in candlelight. What good is a picture if you can't look at it without spoiling it?"

"Poor burdened fellow. Uneasy lies the head that wears a crown." Cass sighed. "Or whatever it is courtesy marquesses slap atop their heads."

"We wear very fashionable hats," said George. "And you're no help at all."

"Did you expect I would be?"

"You always have been before."

She looked at him aslant. "You want me to help you, then? Perhaps you ought to offer me . . . motivation."

The honeyed tone of her voice caught his notice. "Oh, it's motivation you want, is it? What sort of motivation?"

"Nothing unusual." Her eyelashes fluttered.

Oh, he liked this. "How do you look so innocent and sound like a bawdy angel?"

"Do I look innocent?" She sounded surprised. "I didn't expect that. I do like that bawdy angel description, though."

Boosting herself atop the worktable, she let her feet swing as she spoke. "How about this? I'll make a suggestion. If you like it, you strip off a piece of your clothing. If you don't like it, you strip off a piece of mine."

George cleared his throat. The swing of her stockinged foot, toe barely holding the satin slipper, was transfixing him. "Which of us is meant to be motivated by this arrangement?"

"Why must it be only one of us?" Swing, swing, went her foot. When she smiled, her warm eyes crinkled at the corners. "My first suggestion is . . ." She tipped her head. "*La Belle Assemblée*."

George let out a bark of laughter. "You think I ought to name this chemical process after a lady's magazine?"

Cass shrugged. "If you don't like the idea, you know what to do." Bracing her hands on the edge of the table, she bent double, presenting him with the back of her bodice. "My buttons are at your disposal."

So that was how it was: the lady wanted to be undressed. A slow smile spread over George's features; heat began to build within him. This could become a game, and a very pleasurable one. "I don't think so. You said I might strip off a piece of your clothing, but you didn't say you'd choose which."

She snapped upright, a lock of hair falling from its pins to swing before her face. Stuffing it behind her ear, she said, "Don't you *want* to unbutton my bodice?"

"Eventually," he said. "I might."

Then he knelt before her, grateful for the carpet softening the hard floor. He took her swinging foot into his hand; instantly, she went still and taut. When he eased the slipper from her foot, letting it fall to the floor, she sucked in a breath. "What are you doing?"

"I just stripped off a piece of your clothing. Didn't you notice?" The stocking over her toes was fine as cobwebs. The nails were short and tidy, the foot narrow. He'd never thought much about feet, but he decided to have a bit of fun with hers.

He took her foot in his hands, pressing his thumbs to the arch. Her foot twitched. He did it again, stroking firmly. She moaned. "You like having your foot pressed," he observed, rather obviously.

"I've never had this done before," she said. "I just walk about and—oh, do that again. It tickles, but it feels so good."

He obliged the lady. When he did, pressing again into the tight arch of her stockinged foot, her other foot kicked. "Mmm," she said. She shoved the unshod one forward, leaning back onto the table. Letting her other foot dangle, surrendering her bared one to George's touch.

But now that she'd lain back, she'd bared quite a bit more than her foot. Her skirts were rucked up around her knees, and she was drawing them up yet higher.

"I'm not taking off any more of your clothing," George said. "Unless you want to make a suggestion for me to dislike."

"Gog Magog."

He let the other shoe fall to the floor.

Her cheeks went pink. "Call it the Cassandra process."

George paused in the act of reaching for her stocking. "Now that one, I like." Slowly, he removed his cravat.

"I ought to be doing that," Cass complained.

"Ought you? You'll have to get up from that table."

"Never mind." She let her head drop back. "I . . . I can't think of anything else."

"Triumph! I have brought the marvelous, brilliant Cassandra Benton to a state of mental fogginess."

"You can't take off any more of my clothes," she said faintly. Her eyes were fixed on his, lust-glazed and hopeful.

"My darling, I don't need to." He swept up her skirts, her petticoat, her shift, leaving her bare before him. Stockinged legs; ribbon garters; fair, freckled skin. None of the drawers favored by scandalous women; she was strictly proper. Perfectly bared to him. He traced the line of her sex with a fingertip.

She shuddered, then spread wide for him. "Do that again."

He obliged. And then he did other things, things with his fingers and tongue. Things that left Cass quaking, clutching for him, clenching tight, crying his name.

When she was sated and laughing her pleasure, he stood up. "What a beautiful sight you are. I think *that* should be called the Cassandra process."

"I like it," she said, and removed one of her stockings. "What comes next?"

"Exactly what you think," he replied, and when she reached her hands for him, he came into her and was entirely hers.

Yet they had only one more day.

One more day, Ardmore had said, and he was already making noises to George about winding up the investigation.

Still pale, still bandaged, the duke wanted Cass to leave. He wanted it all to be over, to hide from it just as he hid from the bills and letters and summons littering his desk in plain sight.

George wanted the case at an end too, but he wanted her to stay. He was beginning to think he wanted her to stay forever.

After all that talk of love and loss and experiments and investigations—and after a shattering climax that had lain waste to everything atop the worktable—George had come to the yard behind Ardmore House to shoot a few arrows. He'd last left them in the little shed, hadn't he? Where he'd found the gardener's hat that had been lost somewhere on Billingsgate Wharf.

He opened the door, looking around the tiny cluttered space. "That's odd." The archery equipment wasn't there.

As he peered forward into the dim shed, a shape slit the air beside him. It was a sound and a feeling, air moving swift and true.

With a *thup*, an arrow buried itself in the wooden wall of the shed.

"Oy!" George called out. "You might've hit me!"

Who had fired that? He twisted around, looking, looking. All the windows of the house facing him were closed. There was no one else in the yard except the cook's chickens. Was that a shape in the mews, through the back gate, or . . .

Then again came the familiar *shhh* sound, and a hard blow struck his shoulder from behind.

For a moment it was only pressure, then pain sliced like a blade. Blood welled hot and swift, soaking his shirt and coat. *His* blood. *He'd* been struck. The arrow was in his shoulder, solid as anything, and he was bleeding all around it, and if he pulled it out it'd likely be worse.

He turned his head to stare at it, unbelieving. Yet it was real. Someone had shot at his back, and now he had an arrow in his shoulder blade.

"So they were *trying* to hit me," he finally said. "Damnation."

Chapter Fifteen

The world was dark. George was floating, alone. Everything hurt, but it hurt far away and almost didn't bother him.

He blinked.

Oh. That was why the world had been dark. His eyes had been closed. Now they were open—no, they'd closed again—ah, they were back to being open. He'd try to keep them this way, but this floating feeling was strange.

With an effort, he propped his eyes open, and he saw that he was in the library of Ardmore House. A small and luxurious room, with a nice collection of books that no one read much. It wasn't often used, the duke having more fondness for cards than reading, and the duchess having more fondness for laudanum than—

"Laudanum," he murmured. "That's what this strange feeling is. I've been given laudanum." And then he said a word that he'd learned only recently, from the fishwives at Billingsgate.

The act of cursing helped to clear his head. Lifting it, beginning to sit up on the long padded bench upon which he'd been laid facedown, not only cleared his head but also brought the distant, hovering pain rolling back toward him and slamming into his body.

"Ow. Ow Ow."

"Lie back down," said the voice of Cass Benton, "and I shall pretend I didn't hear those ungentlemanly words you just said."

"The bit about the ow? Ow—I'm fine." He let himself sink back onto the padded bench, turning his head so he could see her. The world was sideways, but even so, the expression of strain on Cass's face was unmistakable.

"You're wearing one of your old dresses again," he said, recognizing as he did that this was an irrelevant statement.

Sideways Cass dragged a chair toward the bench, then dropped into it. "That's true. And you are not fine. You were shot in the shoulder with an arrow. Rest and quit trying to be a demigod."

His eyes snapped open. "What sort of demigod gets shot in the shoulder by his own arrow?"

"That's a very demigod sort of thing to have happen. Along with—"

Falling for your false cousin who's meant to be helping you solve possible murders, he thought, as she spoke words he didn't hear and fixed the bandage about his shoulder.

"How did I get into the library?" he interrupted. "I never come in here."

"You came in from the yard—"

"I remember that part. Bleeding all over and looking like a hero."

"Probably not how the maids will remember it." She smoothed his hair back from his brow. "A physician came and wanted you bled. A surgeon came and took out the arrow. The bone of your shoulder blade is broken and you'll probably have a terrible scar where the arrow pierced your skin."

"From my own arrow," George said. "Unbelievable. I *think* I remember that part. I'm to wear a sling, correct?"

"Yes, until the pain is better. Then you can begin to leave the sling off sometimes and try to move the shoulder."

"Is that the sling?" George nodded toward a contraption of cloth hanging over the back of the chair Sideways Cass was sitting in. When she agreed, he heaved himself upright—using only his uninjured arm this time, though he still had to grit his teeth against the pain of movement— and Sideways Cass became Regular Cass, and the sight of her made the pain ebb a bit and the world slow its nauseating spin.

She handed him the sling, then showed him how to settle his arm within its cradle. The process of getting it on was unpleasant and required a few more fishwife words, but once it was on, the relief was noticeable. His injured shoulder blade was practically a pillow of poultices and dressings, and the sling kept his arm tight against his body so none of the medical drama would shift about.

"Much better," he decided. "I won't be able to embrace you properly, but I'm confident I can get the job done with one arm."

She didn't smile. She didn't even look at him. Instead, she retreated to her chair, but didn't sit. She trailed her fingers over its back as if she wanted to draw it away.

"What? What's wrong?" he asked. His mouth was so dry. Was it the laudanum? He coughed, then asked for water.

"Sorry," he said after draining the glass Cass handed him. "I'm still shaking off the laudanum. One of the servants ought to have told the surgeon not to give it to me. They all know I hate the stuff."

Cass shuffled behind the chair, her fingers gripping its

back tightly. "That's what's wrong. One of the things." She bit her bottom lip. "I gave you the laudanum. In a cup of tea after the surgeon left."

His eyes flew open. "*You?*"

"I didn't want you to be in pain."

"You *know* how I feel about laudanum."

"I know," she said. "But I thought . . . just this once. While you were hurting so much."

A pulse beat in his temple. He could feel it, so strange. His body was not quite his own, and he was struggling to slip back into its familiar confines.

She looked so wan, her finger joints white from the force with which she was grasping the back of the chair. "It's all right," he decided. "I wish you hadn't, and I want you never to do it again. But I don't suppose this once will be a problem."

He wouldn't let it be a problem. He'd never let it sweep him away as it had his mother.

She still looked miserable, so he added, "I know you did it to be kind. Come now, what's this? You're meant to be comforting me."

"I didn't," Cass whispered. "I can't. I—I did it for myself."

George tried to find a more comfortable way to sit, holding his sling still as he leaned back. "I don't understand."

Cass straightened her fingers. Tucked back a strand of red hair. When she spoke again, her wonderful voice was colorless. "I've failed you again, George. This is the second failure, after Lord Deverell. I could hardly bear that one, and I wanted to leave. Now it's clear I should have done so then."

She lifted her chin, though her eyes didn't quite meet his. "You were hurt. Our ruse didn't help you. Nothing made a difference. And so . . . your cousin has to go back home."

Reaching into the pocket of her gown, she pulled out a handful of gold. George could only stare as she sorted it: the gold case that he now knew held her grandmother's miniature, and the emerald ring he'd once placed on her finger.

She held the ring out to him. And what did a man do when a woman held something out to him? He took it, wondering how gold could be so cold.

"It cannot be over like this. You have one more day, my father allowed. And even after that, we have our wonderful and elaborate plan, with Angelus and the Jenkses and—you're not even listening, are you?"

"All cases come to an end, whether they're solved or not." Her smile was tight and false. "You remember, I wanted to quit when Lord Deverell was hurt."

"And you remember that *I* remember that you cared, and that was why I wanted you to stay with the case." He tried to think of a joke, to tease her into a real smile. He'd told her once that he was never serious, but that he always meant what he said. A different man had said that, surely, because all humor now seemed drained away. "Do you care now, Cass? Is that why you want to leave me?"

"I'm not leaving you. I'm leaving the case."

"So it was always the case. It was never me at all."

She turned away as if making for the door. Done with him, with it all.

"Cass," he ventured. "It wasn't only the case for me. It was you."

"I don't know what you mean," she mumbled.

For God's sake. "Don't be a coward," he snapped. This was the right strategy, for she spun back to face him. Her gold-brown eyes all but shot sparks at him.

"*Thank* you," he said. "And what I mean is, at first I really did want help with the case. And after Lord Deverell was hurt, I really did think you were the best person to continue, because you truly cared he'd been hurt. You felt responsible."

"I always feel responsible." She cast a glance at his wounded arm, then looked away. With a sigh, she sank onto the end of the bench. Where his feet had been when he was prone and insensible.

"You're not always responsible. You weren't responsible for shooting me in the arm with one of my *own arrows,* which I still *cannot believe*—" He lifted his good hand, cutting himself off. "But let neither of us distract me. After you came to Ardmore House, and we spent more time together, and the case ground to a halt, I probably didn't need you anymore." Drawing a deep breath, he plunged. "I wanted you. I wanted you to stay, and to be with me, and—did you say something?"

She was looking at her hands. "No," she said. "No."

"Are you angry because you think you haven't helped with this case? You have. By being here, you dissuaded people from acting again."

"Not enough."

"Ah, well, maybe you're not a demigod either."

No, he still couldn't make her smile. And it was worrying him that this plan, of all plans that had ever mattered, might not go his way.

"Don't you see?" she exclaimed. "I can't be with you every second, and so I might as well not be with you at all. It's no better. You're still vulnerable."

"You speak as if I'm unable to look out for myself," he snapped. "Do you really think you're responsible for my safety? You alone? I never meant for you to bear this burden alone. Yet you would never take anything from me except what you had earned."

Warm brown eyes looked at him coldly. "I earned a place in your bed?"

"God, no. If anything, I earned a place in yours. But I'd as soon not think of that as a transaction. To me, it wasn't."

"It was an experience," she said faintly. "And its time is past."

The gorge rose in his throat. The world wanted to spin again. With an effort, he forced both reactions away. "That's me put into my place, then. If you ever let me out of it. You'd never allow anyone to help you; you might have to get off your high horse if you did."

Her mouth dropped open. Then, quick and low, she rattled back, "*If* I don't allow anyone to help me, it's because of experience. The only person I can count on is myself. Except . . . clearly I can't, because I didn't protect you."

"The world has disappointed you," he said. "But you are arrogant to reject it."

She sparked at this. "*I'm* arrogant, says the marquess who keeps a whole extra room for playing about with paper and light."

"Yes." He hated saying these things, feeling these things. But it had to be done. "It is a very great arrogance to think you can go through life alone. A duke knows that's not true; his money comes from the land and the tenants who farm it. I know that's not true, though my betrothed died and my mother is dependent on laudanum and my father cares for nothing but cards."

He sighed. "I'd hoped to convince you otherwise, to show you that other people can contribute to your life and your happiness, but I see I haven't. You don't need me. And you won't let yourself want me, will you?"

"I can't afford to."

That wasn't no. But it was far too far from yes. In his hand, the ring was warm now, and he tucked it away in his pocket.

Cass was having that feeling again. The feeling that something was wrong, something was not as it should be.

And she finally understood: it was coming from within herself.

George had thought she would fix his problems, just as Charles had always thought, too. And she was damned tired of it, of these men being disappointed in her because she hadn't sorted out all their difficulties.

She was damned tired of being disappointed in herself, too. Because she cared; she truly did. She cared for Charles, and she cared about solving problems. She cared about fulfilling the trust placed upon her.

She cared about George, with a breadth and depth that hurt her heart. She had to stop caring or it would rip her to bits.

She slipped her hand into her pocket, but the slight heft of the gold miniature case provided no comfort. *You're on your own, Cassie,* she could almost imagine Grandmama saying.

She was always on her own.

"You should know by now," she told George, "that I'm not brave. I don't love danger and adventure. I only care for the security of an income, and for rented rooms to hold the things I need to live. I don't want the responsibility you placed on me. I never wanted to be a person on whom life and death depend."

Above the whiteness of his sling, George's face was hard and dark. "So you're as lazy as you once called me.

You think keeping your wants simple is noble, but you're a woman of great intelligence and strength. Isn't it wrong for you to spend your gifts on such ordinary causes as food and shelter? Shouldn't you make a difference where you can—and isn't that why you began working with your brother in the first place?"

"You're not listening to me," she hissed. "If you'd ever worried about not being able to pay for food and shelter, you wouldn't dismiss their importance. You're trying to shame me into doing what you want. To stay and . . . I don't know."

"I am," George admitted. "But that's because it's what I think is right. I've never met anyone so capable as you, and if you don't do amazing things . . . God, Cass, who will?"

She couldn't look at him. She couldn't look away. "You. The marquess who will one day be a duke. Who lives within his means and has a curious mind. You will, George."

He looked disappointed in her. "What do you dream of, Cass?"

"Helping Charles with his work so we earn money enough for a safe bed and a good meal."

"That's not a dream. That's a routine."

Fine talk. Luxurious talk. She had to get away from here before she started to ask questions not even an investigator ought to be posing. "Dream what you want to, George, and leave me to live my life as I must."

He shrugged, then grimaced at the pain to his injury. "As you wish."

No, it wasn't as she wished. But then she realized he was agreeing with her, saying "As you wish" as if he were granting her a favor, allowing that she knew her own mind.

The temptation to smooth things over with him, to

promise to fix everything that was wrong, was almost irresistible. But she couldn't do it. She'd been Charles's conscience, Charles's hands, Charles's clerk and purse. If she always jumped in to fix what was wrong, it would be far too easy to try to become those things for George.

And if she couldn't become those things for George—since she couldn't even keep him from getting shot in his own home—then what the devil did she have to offer him? To offer *anyone?*

She stood, shaking out her skirts. Her own skirts, familiar and plain. "I must be going. You will be all right, because you're the sort of person for whom everything turns out all right."

He didn't try to stand, just slouched against the long bench. "Am I? Mother in a laudanum doze, Father under threat?"

"You're talking about other people, not yourself. Those things are true. But, George, you're all right."

She did not point out that he'd said nothing of her. It would have been just as irrelevant as his other examples, yet she would have liked knowing she was at the forefront of his thoughts. One of his top examples of a troubling creature that didn't fit neatly into the life to which he thought he was entitled.

To which he *was* entitled, by law and birth.

He tipped up his chin, fixing her with a cool gaze. "Someone shot an arrow at me, my arm is in a sling, and I'm all right?"

"Your arm is not you."

She'd once thought that if loss was the price of love, it was well worth the cost. But that was love for one's family; bedrock, inescapable love that one built each day of one's life upon. This feeling she had for George was soaring and stabbing, like a spire built on that foundation. It hurt. It trembled.

It wasn't worth the building of it, beautiful though it seemed. A topple was inevitable. And who would be the one cleaning up the mess? Who would be crushed?

It would be Cass, of course. That was what she did: she helped, she solved, she tidied, she fixed.

She'd told him once that injustice didn't trouble her, because it was too prevalent. If she once started being bothered by it, she'd never stop.

She had lied. It did bother her, a rankling like an itch. Not on her skin, but within: a feeling of wrongness that could never be eased. Injustice bothered her, and she was steeped in it, and just now she felt it would swamp her. How unjust, that she had tried her best and it had all come to nothing. How unfair that she had so little and he so much, and that she would be leaving her heart with him nonetheless.

She had been selfish, giving him the laudanum. She hadn't wanted to see him in pain—not because he couldn't bear it, because she couldn't.

And that had scared her as much as the sight of his blood.

"If my arm is not me," George replied, "this case is not you." He looked at her with those blue eyes of his. Light eyes, sky-clear and so often wicked. Eyes that held the truth, even as his mouth joked.

Not even his mouth was joking now. He was serious as she'd never seen him before.

Her hands were fists. Where had she left her gloves? "I gave it my best. You are welcome. It was not good enough. I am sorry."

"I'm not thanking you. I'm telling you how selfish you are, to think that you are the only person worthy of trust.

You lock your heart and your ideas up tightly. What have I really had of you, Cass?"

His eyes were heavy, appearing soft and sad. But it was only an illusion from injury and laudanum. A man such as George Godwin, the courtesy marquess Lord Northbrook from birth, would never need to shed a tear over what he couldn't have.

"I am leaving now," she said.

"If you leave, I won't pursue you."

She paused at the doorway. She wanted to look back over her shoulder, to see if he would entreat her.

But she wouldn't. Her valise was here, and her life was out there. Away. She had to leave before she forgot that, before she began to think it was all right to fail. Before she let him lean on her, and she leaned back. Before she began to need him so much that she couldn't stand on her own anymore.

"I know," she said, and then she left.

Chapter Sixteen

Cass walked all the way from Cavendish Square to Langley Street, a thundercloud over her head and her battered old valise bumping her knees with every step. London was a city of worlds, and she hardly noticed how many of them she passed through. From the edge of Mayfair to the outskirts of Seven Dials, they were all gray and crowded and shoving.

Every step away from George was a necessity. She'd already waited too long to take them. Still, she wasn't prepared for the familiar sight of her lodging house when her feet finished carrying her there. She wasn't ready to go upstairs to the set of rooms she shared with Charles.

And she *definitely* wasn't expecting, when she swung the door open, to be greeted by the sight of her brother kissing a dark-haired young woman she did not at once recognize.

Whatever surprised sound popped from her lips, it was enough to alert the couple. Charles lifted his head. "Oh, hullo, Cass," he said smoothly, as if she'd just stepped out of their lodgings for a few minutes to fetch a newspaper.

"Hullo, yourself." She entered the room fully, booting the door closed behind her. "Don't let me spoil your fun."

The woman, clad in a dark blue gown, turned in Charles's arms, revealing a light brown skin of great loveliness. "Miss Benton. I didn't know as you were gettin' back today." She flashed a cheeky grin of charmingly crooked teeth.

The grin clicked like a gear into memory. "Janey! I didn't know you at first."

"Aye, I'm dressed different." This was true. Janey was wearing enough clothes for only one person. She was in a pretty dress of blue serge, with her hair pulled back in a simple twist.

"That, and . . . I didn't see your face when I walked in."

"That, too." Janey blushed. "This is my work dress. I'm working now."

"For Charles?" Cass tossed her valise into her bedchamber, then leaned on the frame of the doorway and regarded the other two with confusion.

"No! For Fox. Had a problem with cutpurses at the theater, he did." Janey looked pious. "Said I'd put a stop to it."

"I tried to work on that matter a few days ago." Cass felt a step behind. True, she hadn't caught anyone picking pockets, but she hadn't expected Janey to step into the breach.

"Be going there tonight," Janey said. "Been a couple other nights, too. No problems while I'm keepin' a eye on things. Fox is right happy. He's going to give me your brother's pay for the week. We're partners, like." This, for some reason, brought another dusky blush to Janey's cheeks.

"Ah. So you're making sure Charles keeps his job."

Finally, Charles spoke, looking a little abashed. "Look here, Cass. You might as well know—I've asked Janey to marry me."

He couldn't have surprised Cass more if he'd cut a hole in the floor for her to drop through. "And . . ." she fumbled. "And she said yes?"

"'Aye,'" replied Janey, "is what I said, really."

"Took her long enough." Charles wrapped his arms around the young woman's slim figure from behind, resting his chin atop her head. "Had to ask her, what? Three times?"

"I wanted you to be sure," answered Janey.

"I—huh." The whole encounter felt unreal. Cass's gaze roved the room. Same furniture; same walls. Same crack in the ceiling plaster right by the parlor fireplace. She couldn't have been gone *that* long, yet everything was different.

"Miss Benton? You all right?" Janey asked.

Cass shook herself. Manners, manners. "I'm fine." She managed a smile. "Very happy for you both. And please, you must call me Cass. When do you post the banns?"

"Soon as ever we can. This Sunday we start." Janey looked from Cass to Charles, her expression uncertain. "For now I'd best leave."

"Don't go yet. There's plenty of time. It's hardly evening." Charles extended a hand. Only now did Cass realize that he was standing, which meant something had altered about his leg. It was wrapped in a contraption of hard plaster, with a cut-out space for the knee. Below the foot was a wooden block like a small patten built into the dressing.

"Look at you, up and about." She managed another smile. She was doing well with those. "Why, you can stand and walk."

"I'm getting around fine now that I've developed a new sort of brace."

"You did it yourself?"

"The surgeon did the plastering. But I came up with this bit of wood so I can step." He folded his arms. "You needn't be so surprised. I am a resourceful fellow."

"Yes, I know it. Well, I'm moving back in, so you needn't be too resourceful if you don't wish."

"Oh. All right." He didn't sound relieved. He sounded surprised, as if this were a possibility that had never occurred to him, and he wasn't pleased about it.

Janey must have seen something strange on Cass's face. "Really got to go. I want to be gettin' to the theater when Jemmy does."

"Jemmy?" Cass was surprised. "That boy from Billingsgate?"

"Aye, taken 'im under my wing, I have. He needed practice keepin' a eye out for thieves. Whether he wants to be one or not."

"Maybe he'll work for Bow Street one day," Cass mused.

Janey tugged at Charles's arm, pulling his head down to hers, and whispered in his ear.

"It's fiiiiine," replied Charles, not at all quietly. "She won't mind."

Janey whispered something else, and Charles nodded. "All right, then—I'll see you after the theaters close?" When she agreed, he kissed his betrothed upon the lips.

"I'll be seeing you later, then," Janey said. "Welcome home, Miss . . . Cass." She ducked her head and sidled out the door. Mystified, Cass waggled her fingers by way of farewell.

When the door closed, she rounded on Charles. "What's all this? I saw you only a few days ago, and now you're *engaged?* And you can *walk?*"

"And I'm going back to work." He beamed. "I'll be back at Bow Street on Monday, doing what I can in the courtroom."

Cass ground her teeth together. Somehow, she had to anchor herself.

"I thought you'd be happy for me, Cassie. I never thought you were small-minded."

"No. Don't do that. Don't toss blame at me. Go sit in that chair and tell me what's been happening, and don't call me small-minded when what I am really feeling . . ." She trailed off. Was what? Was that all her hopes had dwindled away, but she'd known she could at least resume her old life? Only, that too was gone? Charles walking and Janey helping him, and the two of them to marry?

". . . when what I'm feeling is happy for you," she finished. Because it was easier than saying all the rest. "Though Janey's far too good for you."

"Always has been," Charles confirmed. "Always will be. And I won't forget it."

He sat not in the parlor's best chair, but on the little footstool. His plaster-bound leg stretched out at a stern angle, taking up seemingly half the room. "Do you know, I was sitting in that chair—that very chair right there— and I asked her to marry me? Only I bungled it badly. Didn't say what was on my mind, only some stupid words that didn't come near the point. And there I was, injured, and she left me."

"What a monster," Cass said faintly. "To walk out on an injured man."

"Well, she did kiss me first." Charles's ears went red at the tips. "So I thought—you know, that it might turn out all right. And it did!"

Cass said nothing. She slipped from the doorway of her own little room to put Grandmama's miniature back on the mantel.

This was what Grandmama had always wanted for them: a home, and the ability to rely on each other. Wasn't it?

"Janey'll have an easier life than if she's an informant, and if she still wants to sell clothes and cut purses, I don't mind." Charles paused, thinking. "Guess I'd rather she didn't, ah . . . sell herself anymore. Hope she won't if she likes being married to me."

"Start sentences with pronouns," Cass snapped.

Charles blinked at her mildly. "You're in a bad mood."

"There's that magical twin connection of ours." She stomped across to the chair Charles had been regarding with such fond memories—the Proposal-Chair, she'd now think of it—and fell into it with a huff. "So, you're getting married. And you're going to keep working for Bow Street."

"Of course," he said. "Fox is like family."

"I know," Cass groaned. She felt as if a candle inside her had been snuffed, and she couldn't bear to think of the work awaiting them at Bow Street. Now she understood why Fox always looked so tired: a city was a heavy weight to carry.

She'd never realized how lonely it was to carry a city, or a job. She'd thought herself independent. But was she arrogant to think so? Had George been right?

"And that means," Charles was saying, "that she knows me well enough to know I can't do it on my own—or not yet. So Janey can work with me whenever she likes."

Cass's mouth dropped open.

Charles, of course, misunderstood. "There's no shame in taking help, as long as I give it in return when I can."

There it was. The difference between accepting grace and living in selfishness. But where was Cass in all these plans? Discarded? Forgotten?

"What about me?" she asked. "What am I to do?"

Charles blinked. "Why, whatever you like."

He said it so simply, as if there was no question about it. Of *course* she must do what she liked. And for the second time that day, she had no idea what that might be.

George had asked first. He had ruined her for a life

without dreams, just by asking the question: *What do you dream of, Cass?*

She'd dreamed of things going back to the way they were before she met him. When everything was fine. But nothing was the same now—not here, and not at Bow Street, and certainly not within her. And now she realized that *fine* wasn't enough, and never had been. And surviving wasn't enough; existing wasn't enough. Being safe and warm and not going hungry—none of that was enough.

Not even being needed or feeling that she'd helped make London safer was enough. Just because she took pride in her work didn't mean it was the work she wanted to do. It was hard work—not in the doing, but in the imprint it left on her soul.

Why had she thought she could return to that?

But what else could she have done?

"Fox really does need a woman at Bow Street," she said slowly. "There are some cases a woman sees to the heart of in an instant. Like that business with the stolen china cups."

Cass had known at once that the actress's sister was the one with the light fingers, even though the actress's maid came in for all the blame. But you'd only to listen to the older sister's yowlings and palpitations to know she was covering for herself. She wasn't half the performer her sibling was, though Charles had been taken in by the long-lashed eyes and heaving bosom.

"I've asked you never to mention those china cups again," Charles said with a long-suffering expression. "And Janey wants to work with Bow Street. She's come to like it there while she's been helping Fox, and certainly no one knows it better from the other side of the bench."

Cass had to laugh at this. "It was only supposed to be her atonement for one minor offense. Now she's taking you on for life, and Bow Street, too?"

Charles bristled. "I'm not all that bad a catch, Cass. I've nice rooms and a good income. And I look all right enough. I wash, and I shave, and all that."

I, I, I. Perhaps he'd made a good case to Janey. But Cass's concerns remained.

He didn't say Cass *couldn't* live there anymore. But he was making a home and she wasn't at the heart of it anymore. They'd always been a pair, the Benton twins, and now he would cleave to someone else.

She *was* happy for him. She just hadn't expected how alone she'd feel. Was this what most people felt like—the ones who didn't have twins? She'd been counting on Charles, at least, to need her around. Not that she particularly enjoyed it, but the annoyance was familiar. If one of them was going to change, it ought to be her. If one of them was to move on, it should be the one who put out more effort.

"What won't I mind?" Cass remembered suddenly. "Janey said something in your ear, and you said it would be fine."

"Oh, that." He waved a hand. "If she lives here once she and I are married."

"She asked if I'd mind you living with her? Your wife?" Cass had to laugh. "I think she was telling you that *she'd* mind you living with your spinster sister."

"Not at all. She loves you. Or she will, once she gets to know you like I do." His brows knit. "Strike that. Maybe she'd better not get to know you any better."

"If I had anything in my pockets, I'd throw it at you. Tell me exactly what she said."

Charles adopted an expression of great patience. "She said she didn't know if these lodgings would work once she and I were married, and I said it'd be fi—oh, I see what you mean. She wasn't asking about moving in. She wondered if there'd be space enough."

"The two bedchambers share a wall," Cass pointed out.

At the same time, she and Charles shuddered. "That's not going to work," he said.

Finally, he seemed to take in fully the fact of her return. "Why are you here? Did you solve that tontine case?"

"It's over," she replied crisply.

"That's not what I asked you."

"I . . . left."

Charles's mouth dropped open. "You *left?* Without solving a case? With wages owing you?"

"It sounds bad when you put it like that," she mumbled, lacing her fingers together. "But it really wasn't. I hadn't solved it, and I wasn't going to solve it, and the Duke of Ardmore was going to put a halt to the case tomorrow anyway, and then Lord Northbrook was shot with an arrow, and—"

"Wait. *What?*" Charles was gaping. "You accuse me of holding back information, and here you've got a marquess injured and a duke in a temper with you?"

"Not with *me*," she huffed. "With everything. But yes, that's it. In essence."

As briefly as she could, while leaving out the passionate bits, she described the events of the past few days. Charles whistled when she concluded.

"So there's a case, for sure, and the duke doesn't want it pursued? You didn't think he might change his mind when his heir turned up with an arrow in his back?"

"I . . . no, I didn't think of that." She should have thought of that. But she hadn't been able to think about anything except George, wounded, and about getting the devil away from there before her heart was hurt just as badly.

"But," she excused, "we did come up with a plan. George—Lord Northbrook and I. And Angelus. And Callum and Isabel Jenks. And we can put it into practice this weekend."

Charles had stuck on the first part of what she'd said. "Calling him George, are you?"

"Don't leer. That's disgusting."

"So you only respect him professionally, and you called him by his Christian name because . . . ?"

"Stop it," she said. "Just stop, Charles. He was shot with an arrow today, and it seems like it was half a lifetime ago, yet I know I'll never be able to forget it."

Charles's eyes, mirrors of her own, went soft. "Cassie." He leaned over, patted the floor. "Come sit by me."

"I'm not a puppy," she grumbled, yet she went. She folded herself up on the floor, leaning against the footstool, her head against his side. Perhaps they'd leaned on each other like this before birth.

Perhaps leaning on someone, just a bit, wasn't so bad.

Charles patted her on the head, almost idly. "So you got fond of him, and he got hurt, and you left. Does that make sense?"

"No. But it's what happened." She squeezed shut her eyes. She'd cried over George once, for his sweet closeness and the passion that touched her heart. She wouldn't cry again now that those things were gone. "I didn't quit the case. I just quit him."

"You wanted to have him, then?"

"It doesn't matter what I wanted. He told me no one had ever loved him, and he was fine with that."

"Seems a strange thing not to be bothered by," Charles mused.

"And anyway, he never asked me. For anything. And he told me if I left, he wouldn't follow."

"So he's a proud fellow. Can't say I'm surprised. But you didn't answer me. You didn't say whether you wanted him."

She waved an impatient hand. "It doesn't *matter*. He said he didn't need me. And I'm proud, too."

Charles's hand paused in its idle stroking of her hair. "Ah. Right. Sorry. Men are simple creatures, and if he was sure he wanted you, he'd have said so."

"He did say he wanted me," she whispered.

Charles smacked her on the head.

"Ow!" Crablike, she scuttled back from him on her hands and feet. "What was that about?"

A grin spread over Charles's face. "Cass, I never thought to say this. But you have been remarkably stupid."

"What? What do you mean?"

"I mean, if he said he doesn't need you, but he does want you, then there's no reason for him to be with you but . . . you. He won't make you do favors for him, and he won't pinch your wages, and he won't fall off a trellis unless it's your window he's climbing to."

"Let us never say the word *trellis* again."

"Fine. But it's true. As I said, men are simple creatures. He was honest with you."

"And I left him," she said numbly. "After he'd told me he thought no one had ever loved him."

"Bad timing, that."

"It wasn't *right* after. But yes, bad timing." She settled into a less crablike position, still huddled on the floor. "Maybe there's something wrong with me. Is there?"

"There's no question about that." Charles held up his hands. "Sorry. I'm your brother. I couldn't let that one pass."

And he was happy, and Janey was happy. When had Cass last been happy, reveling in it?

At Chichester for a night; at the Harroughs' ball in George's arms.

She swallowed, hard, and tried to smile. She would sort out some way of being that happy again on her own. No man in her bed, no one's arms around her. George had reminded her how she wanted to feel, but she could not rely on him to make her feel that way. She could only rely on herself.

There she went, not trusting again. Yet experience had taught her it was the safest way to be. That wanting something was a sign to stop, to lock up that urge and focus anew on the shoulds of life.

But there was a difference between being dependent and being part of a team, just as there was a difference between selfish pride and grace. Charles had sorted that out long before she had. He'd done his work and skived off; he hadn't let it take over his life.

And George was worthy of trust. Creditors knew he'd pay his bills. His friend had staked a restaurant on George's good word and goodwill. He'd brought Charles home with a broken leg and paid the surgeon.

He'd slid a gold ring onto Cass's finger and told her he wouldn't touch her unless she wanted him to. And even now, she wanted him to, and she missed the clasp of warm gold on her hand.

"You told me," she said slowly, "that I could do whatever I wanted. That Janey would work at Bow Street with you."

"Right." Charles looked puzzled.

"Here's what I don't want: I don't want to live with you and Janey after you're married. And I don't want to work at Bow Street anymore. I don't want to keep doing your job, living your life."

"I never wanted that for you." Surprise made Charles appear startled, boyish. "Is that really how you feel?"

"It is. I've been following you about, tidying behind you for all our lives."

Charles rolled his eyes. "I never asked you to clean up my messes, Cass. I'd get around to them eventually."

"That would carry a lot more weight if you didn't have a broken leg from the last case we worked together. And when would you clean up your messes, as you called them? When you got blood poisoning from the fall? When you'd overspent your income and we'd been warned we'd be out on the street the next day unless we paid the rent?"

From the mantel, Grandmama seemed to frown. Which of them she was frowning at, Cass couldn't tell.

"You worry too much," Charles scoffed.

"And you, not enough. If you care about people, you want to give them what they need. I didn't need *things* from you; I needed security. I'd rather have old clothes and money in the bank than empty but new pockets."

God, it felt good to say this. Or not good, exactly, but like the peeling away of something bad. Like armor that had grown too tight, had begun to hurt her. She flung it all away.

And Charles tipped his head, thinking. Listening. Finally, he said, "What do you think Janey needs?"

Good heavens, he was besotted. "I think you should ask her," Cass said carefully. "Just as you should tell her what you need. And you should both do your best to give it."

"Hmm." He scratched his head, then nodded.

"You were happy for me to solve your problems, Charles. You never told me to stop."

Now he looked ashamed. "You'd have to search far and long to find a man who wouldn't let someone else do his work for him. But why did you, Cass?"

She'd done it for so long, she had almost forgotten why. Or that there *was* a why, and that it wasn't simply the way things had to be. "Because I worried. I worried about money and wanted to be sure we had enough. And I worried about your safety and wanted to protect you."

"You did it for us."

"Yes, in a way. But I also wanted credit. I wanted everyone to know that I was doing a man's work and making it my own. There are so few ways for a woman to matter." She sounded wistful. She hated that she sounded wistful.

She stood, shaking out her skirts. They were rumpled and dirty from when she trekked through London, then sat in a puddle on the floor.

Charles watched this elaborate process, then looked ruefully at his broken leg. "You matter to me, Cassie. I'd never have amounted to anything if it weren't for you. But now I think I can go on my own."

"With Janey's help," Cass said crisply.

"With Janey's help," he granted. "There's no shame in taking help, as long as I don't also take it for granted."

"No," she said. "Don't take it for granted. Any of it."

She shouldn't have taken George's kindness for granted; she shouldn't have taken for granted that he would fail her. That he couldn't mean what he said, and that he cared only for the case, and that it was best if she left before this became all too plain.

Instead, she expected a pattern: that he would be like the other men in her life. Her father, who had left. Charles, who loved her but took advantage of her, and Fox, whose kindness came with so many burdens.

But George was none of them. He was just himself, and she missed him like she missed the sight of flowers in the middle of winter. She missed him like the sun during a thunderstorm. It was an aching way of missing, wanting something beautiful outside of its proper time and place.

And who decided the proper time and place for George, for her life? She alone.

God. She loved him. She loved him like flowers loved the sun.

No, she couldn't be with him every second—just as she'd told him. But like Janey at the theater; like her friend Mags, keeping watch on the Watch: each moment held the possibility of goodness. Nothing was perfect, but a moment together, a moment spared, wasn't nothing.

In fact, it was everything.

Of course her heart hurt; its armor was being broken open. And there were so many possibilities, weren't there? So many, after all.

There were other ways to help, to matter, besides working with Charles. Maybe she would find someone who wanted help starting a restaurant. Maybe she would take a case or two for Fox, as a private consultant, and be paid for her efforts at last. Maybe she'd help an artist build a camera obscura.

Maybe she'd build one herself, and look at the world in a different way.

She had five pounds in her pocket. She was a woman of resources. Including people who cared about her and wanted to help her.

"I'll take Mrs. Jellicoe's attic room," she told Charles. "You and Janey must have this space as soon as you're wed."

"Ah, Cassie." Charles struggled to his feet, waving off her outstretched hand—then folded her in a cracking hug. "It was the worst luck of your life to be born my twin, and the best luck of mine to be yours."

Just for a moment, she settled her head on his shoulder. Then she patted him on the back and extricated herself. "That is one of the best insights you've had since you fell out of Lady Deverell's window and broke your leg. Injury seems to be good for you."

Charles rolled his eyes. "Back to the tontine case? I didn't fall out of her window. I never made it to her window. I told you, the trellis broke."

This again. "I *asked* you not to say that horrid word anymore. And I thought it broke on your way back down from the window. She said you'd been with her."

"I'd been with her all right—"

"Spare me."

"—but not that night. I'd used the tr—ah, the t-word before. Lady D liked me to use it. She climbed down it sometimes, too. Thought it romantic, I expect."

Bells of memory jangled, unmistakable. "Wait. You're saying you weren't with Lady Deverell the night you broke your leg. Which was also the night her husband was stabbed."

"Right." Charles lurched to the mantel and seized it for balance.

"And that the trellis broke as you were climbing up, not down."

"I thought we weren't saying that word anymore?"

Cass speared him with a Look.

"Yes," Charles replied. "I just said all of that."

"So you never made it up to the window."

"Correct."

Memories jarred with this new information, then began to resolve into harmony. If something didn't make sense, she should know better than to toss it aside. And Lady Deverell's cringing assertion that all she'd done was kiss the footman on that eventful night had never made sense. Her ladyship should have professed innocence.

Unless she wasn't innocent, and a small confession was her shield against a much larger wrongdoing.

"What are you thinking?" Charles said.

That maybe she'd already found the pattern. That it had been there, all along, hidden by an earl's much younger wife's secrets and kisses, and by an unfortunate accident that might have been nothing of the sort.

Cass seized Charles's cheeks in her hand and planted a smacking kiss on the end of his nose. "I'm thinking," she said, "that you might just have solved the tontine case. And that I need to see that trellis before another day is gone."

As she passed the mantel before careening from the room, Grandmama smiled at her.

Chapter Seventeen

In the morning, George awoke in his own bed with a powerful headache, a pain in his shoulder, and the teasing feeling that there was something he didn't want to think about.

The emerald ring on the table by his bed was eager to remind him.

First, that this was the day the Duke of Ardmore—at his duke-iest—had decided must mark the end of the tontine case. Second, that Cass had left the day before.

Third, that he'd all but flung his heart at her trying to make her stay, and she hadn't done so. She'd left anyway.

He was used to his plans going as he wished them to, but he never *had* made a plan for Cassandra Benton. He'd made a plan for the case, but Cass? She'd just . . . happened. She had happened to him like rain happens: you cannot predict it, and you cannot do without it, and it seems it will always be there. Until it's not, and everything goes dry and bright and one's head pounds horribly.

Right, that was the laudanum from yesterday. It was a stubborn bastard. Once it got into your system, it didn't leave lightly.

Of course, the same description also applied to Cass.

He drank off a glass of water, rang for coffee, and with the help of a manservant, struggled into some semblance of dress. The bandages on his injured shoulder made it impossible for him to squeeze into a coat, but while at home, he could get by with shirtsleeves, a waistcoat, and that wonderful sling that made the broken bones of his shoulder sit still and stop aching.

After draining a cup of bitter, strong coffee and slipping the emerald ring into his pocket, he made his way up to his experiment room. Wasn't that what he'd used to do when he was completely at leisure, before his suspicions about his father's accident-prone peers turned into a case? What had he done with his time? Already, it was difficult to remember the Northbrook who had flippantly called Cass plain and hadn't known her at all. That man had deserved to be shot in the shoulder.

Here on the giant worktable she'd sat, and he'd stripped off her shoes and very little else—and still brought her to pleasure. There was no sign now that she'd been here at all, save for a paper he'd slipped into the camera obscura before they left the room. Once again, he'd pointed the lens out the window, at the opposing structures of Cavendish Square.

Drawing the draperies, he lit the amber-shaded lamps, then lifted the lid of the camera obscura and drew out the paper he'd treated. What image would show itself?

Nothing. It was a blank. A waste of paper and silver salts.

All the expensive oil paintings that hung around Ardmore House sneered, taunting him that he would never be able to fasten an image as long-dead artists had been doing for centuries. They painted joy and lust and wrath and sloth and every sin and leaping feeling, and he couldn't even get the image of a damned window to imprint on paper.

His fingers contracted into a fist, crumpling the paper; then he tossed it aside.

A whole room for playing about with paper and chemicals, and he'd little to show for it. Really, nothing. Cass had been right; it was a sign of wealth and privilege to have such spaces for doing nothing.

George wished he could make her need him. She needed work, of course; money, yes. But she could have worked for anyone. Applied her gifts to any case. Worn a ring for any role. Danced and planned with any man.

Taken anyone to bed, if he caught her fancy. George could have been anyone, anyone at all.

He wanted to kick something. To curse, to lash out.

To be better. Irresistible, so that a woman with red hair and a clever mind would not be able to do without him.

But it was too quiet for kicking things, and he'd no desire to injure his toes as well as his shoulder. He tried out a curse, but it just reminded him of the fishwives of Billingsgate.

Cass had made it look easy, leaving him. And he was fooling himself to hope that this was one of those difficult things that hurt her heart.

He turned the larger camera obscura sideways, so it would look upon the table where Cass had sat. He wished she'd left behind some sign that she'd been here, but there was nothing. As if she had never stayed in the house at all. As if Mrs. Benedetti had never existed, even in imagination.

Still he aimed the camera obscura. Within it, all would be turned and flipped about. Cass Benton tended to have that effect on a person.

And was that enough, to be able to look at things differently? Did it matter if George could never get anything to stay?

Wasn't it better than if it had never existed at all?

The answer shouldn't be yes; that went against all sense. But he thought that it was, all the same.

Shutting his eyes, he pulled in a breath as deeply as he could. It was a breath of old metal and worn wood, of the faint scent of oranges and dusty draperies. It was his space, his room, and his ribs were tight and his lungs were full and his heart was heavy.

He let the breath go, then took another. Again, then again. Each breath was the same, yet a bit different. The same room, the same air, but something changed within.

He opened his eyes. Picked up the used sheet of paper, smoothing the side he'd crumpled. Crossing to his shelves, he retrieved another sheet of paper, then considered the little bottles of chemicals. In the resinous light of the lamps, the glass vials held their secrets close. He could hardly tell one from the other. His eyes were blurred.

He had tried every combination he could think of—but only of a few things. Sunlight. Paper. Silver salts. Iron oxides.

Cass was adamant that patterns revealed the truth, if one could only spot them. And the truth was, he was in a pattern of endless tinkering. Changing small things, not accomplishing anything real. Maybe not even expecting to.

To hell with all that.

Maybe he should work with plates of something else. Glass? No, it would break. Tin, maybe? Something that would neither break nor rust nor tarnish. Something that would stay forever, fixed.

He would order plates of tin and zinc. They would cost the earth, but he'd no use for scrabbling at the problem. Trying things he thought would probably not work, but that had the virtue of being easy or convenient.

To hell with all of that. To hell with fragile glass, with rusting iron or tarnishing bronze or green-patinaed copper or dull dark brass. To the devil with silver; it wanted to turn black no matter what he tried. He'd stick the image on there with glue, with gum paste, with bitumen. He'd leave the camera obscura alone for hours of sunlight, getting every ray, and force the image into the plate.

He would make a new pattern, and it would be the pattern he wanted to see. And he would persist until it was complete.

When he'd finished in the experiment room, he remembered that he still had the emerald ring in his pocket. As he was already on his way downstairs, he veered aside to the duchess's rooms and rapped at the door.

Gatiss didn't answer at once, which surprised him. The lady's maid almost never left the duchess unattended. But even lady's maids had bodily needs, he supposed; she was likely in the washroom or the kitchens.

He didn't care to return, so he eased open the bedchamber door and stepped gingerly across the room. There was a writing desk, neat and never used; he'd leave the ring there.

"George," came the dusty voice from the bed. "You have hurt your arm."

The duchess was awake, as awake as she ever got. Awake enough to notice the sling he wore.

George ceased his silent creeping and faced the canopied bed. "Good morning, Mother. Someone else hurt my arm. My shoulder, really."

This seemed an inadequate explanation. He wasn't in the habit of coming in every morning simply to wish her good morning—though now that he thought of it, he probably should be.

The draperies were drawn back, and summery sunlight

made the grand room appear warm and cheerful. Her Grace looked rather nice today, clothed in a morning gown and with her hair dressed neatly. If she had been standing, and her eyes had remained open for more than a few seconds at a time, she would have looked almost like her old self.

"I'm returning your ring," he explained. "The emerald one you lent me. Is Gatiss in the dressing room? I can hand it back to her at once."

"She's at dinner," murmured the duchess.

"Dinner?" George replied doubtfully. "It's very early for dinner. Is she having a late breakfast?"

"Maybe." Which meant that Gatiss could be anywhere, and back anytime.

"I'll leave the ring on the writing desk," he said. No other servants would enter the chamber before the lady's maid returned, so it would be safe enough. Now that it wasn't on Cass's hand anymore, he was done with it. He didn't want to look at it.

The duchess made a noise that could have been agreement. It could also have been a protest. It could, for that matter, have been the first bars of a song she'd sung to him when he was a baby.

It meant nothing.

With a clack that rang loud and solid through the silent room, he set the ring onto the desk and turned his back on it.

"She will be back," said the duchess faintly, "before my next dose. Gatiss never misses a dose."

"Of course she doesn't, because you've told her you cannot live without it."

When the duchess turned her head to regard him, he saw a vague suggestion of the mother who had once looked at him with reproach. "I cannot. It eases the days. They are all the same, but I hardly notice."

By now, he supposed this was true. What had begun
the decline of her health, he wasn't certain. It might have
been nothing more than a strained back or a twisted ankle.
But the injury had stilled her, stripping the usual activi-
ties from her day. And the empty place had to be filled
somehow.

George knew that. He'd filled so many spaces with late
nights and strong drink. When he'd stopped, seeing his
mother's health slipping away, he hadn't known what to do
with the gaps in his life. He'd thought maybe nothing
would ever come to fill them.

He had drifted, tethered only by the first of his unsuccessful experiments at capturing images with chemicals
and light. His father's request to return to Ardmore House
had been something to do. Someone needing him. It was
always nice at first when someone needed you, until you
found you could make no difference to them at all.

"You are a duchess," he said now. "You have power to
make your days whatever you wish."

"I thought so once. But this is easier."

He couldn't control what she did all the time, especially
if being present to the world—or even alive in it—was
against her own inclination. He knew that, and yet he'd
given up his own lodging and redirected his life to try
to help.

He wasn't sorry. He *had* helped—though himself more
than his mother. No one could deny he was better off, financially and physically, than he'd been when he'd been
playing the role of Corinthian and rake.

And the duchess was still alive. That was about all he
could say to the good. It was helping that had gone its
course. Now it felt more like control, and . . . did a grown

woman, a duchess, deserve to be spied upon and chided? Even for the sake of her loved ones?

It wasn't an easy question. But George rather felt the answer was no. If his father was allowed to ruin their finances with gambling, his mother must be allowed to ruin her health with laudanum.

He didn't have to be a part of their destruction, though. Not anymore.

"You never fought for us," George said, not really expecting a reply. "Your husband and children. You surrendered to laudanum."

The moment of clarity in her eyes faded, and they closed again. Blue eyes, veiled. "It was the cards. Your father. If I never fought back, I could never be beaten."

"Rubbish," said George. "If you never fight back, you are beaten from the start."

Why did George himself not fight back more against his father's will? Why did he accept impoverishment and ignorance, wasted days and years, as inevitable?

So he thought about what could come next. What he truly wanted and had the power to get, beyond the case and the damned tontine. He'd thrown himself into Cass's plan, because it was something to do. Some reason not to feel so damned useless, like a man biding his time and hating that he was doing so. God willing, he'd outlive his father and become the next Ardmore—but he couldn't wait until that day to make more of himself than a consumer of fabric and tea and Antoine's delicious cream sauces.

And the kisses of a woman beautiful in and out.

He didn't want to. It wasn't fair to his father, and it certainly wasn't fair to himself. Even if he never won Cass's heart, he'd become a better sort of man. The process was worth the effort, just like shooting arrows into the target in the yard.

Aloud, he decided, "I'm going to solve the tontine case. And then I will return to my own lodgings." The sentences were the impulse of a moment, but they were right. They *felt* right. He'd make them true.

His mother smiled faintly. "What will you do until then? Try another experiment with your camera?"

"A camera obscura, Mother. Camera is merely the word for a room, not for a device."

"You knew what I meant."

"Yes, yes." And, he decided, the conciseness of it was nice. "A camera," he tried out. "I will carry out more experiments with my camera."

There was much he would have liked to record, to pin on paper with the camera's light. Not just Lily's face, stolen away by time, but his mother's when she was young and fresh and active. When she cared; before years and worry and laudanum—remorseless all—had turned her into a shell.

Then he added a fuller answer. "I will write a letter to Father's steward in Berkshire. It's time I learn how the estates are being managed, since Father takes no notice. And it's time I do what I can to make them function better."

But first he would leave Ardmore House. Take rooms in a hotel; he could have them this very night. Given a few more days, or weeks if need be, he could find suitable bachelor quarters for the long term.

He looked at the ring, emerald and gold, on her desk, then looked away. "I won't be staying here any longer. You'll have to survive on your own."

But she was already drifting away again, there but

absent all at once, and he knew she was exactly where she wanted to be.

When he exited the room, he almost ran into the lady's maid. "Beg pardon, my lord. Were you visiting Her Grace?" Gatiss sounded breathless. One hand pressed her side as if against a stitch; the other clutched a familiar glass bottle bearing a chemist's label.

George explained where he'd left the ring. "The duchess knew you'd be back shortly. In time for her dose."

"That's where I was—getting more laudanum." Gatiss held up the bottle. "I was that sure there was another bottle in the dressing room, but it was empty." The placid-faced servant's brow knit. "If you'll forgive my saying so, my lord?"

"Of course."

"It's my opinion your mother is taking more laudanum than she ought."

George almost laughed at the obviousness of this statement. "Yes, Gatiss, I quite agree." But really, there was nothing funny about it.

"I'm sorry for it," he added. "I wish I knew how to make her stop. But I've never had the least success, because she doesn't really wish to stop."

"Ah, well. Her Grace has been doing as she wished longer than either of us has known her." Yet Gatiss looked troubled.

"I promise you this," George decided. "When I remove from this household again, I'll come back and visit her. Real visits, not just brief calls to drink tea and pay my respects. Do you think once a week would do her good?"

"Whenever you like, my lord. Her Grace doesn't always know what day it is, or what time of day."

"Well do I know it." It seemed unfeeling to schedule time with one's own parent. But it would be more unfeeling never to come at all, or to forget that she'd once been more than what she'd let herself become.

And it would be unfeeling, too, not to toss out a rope—of time, of remembrance, of occupation. If the duchess were lonely or bored, he could help with that, or at least try.

But he wouldn't give up pieces of his own life in exchange. Not anymore.

Next, then, he descended to the first floor and knocked at the door of the duke's study. Instead of the barking that would have once succeeded his knock, growls followed. When the duke grunted—the human equivalent of a growl—George entered. He didn't bother greeting the painting of card players this time. Froggy was always there. He'd never finish playing his hand.

From the floor, the great hounds regarded George balefully. Crouching, George looked them in the eye. "She taught me all the tricks. I know how to handle you now." One of the dogs growled, so George turned to the other and scratched it behind the ears with his good hand until its yellow eyes blinked slowly and its doggy tongue lolled.

"Did you come in to play with them?" Ardmore barked. "I need to take them out to the yard."

George straightened, regarding his father across the wide, cluttered desk. "Miss Benton could have taught them to use chamber pots."

"She was good with Gog and Magog," granted the duke. "But it's just as well that she left. This whole idea was foolishness, that someone in the tontine was coordinating attacks on—"

"You say this as I stand before you with my arm in a sling, my shoulder bone broken."

One of the dogs—George still couldn't tell Gog from

Magog—gave a hearty sneeze. "*Thank* you," George replied. "Father. You cannot deny the truth."

Behind his desk, the duke picked up a letter, squinted at it, then shook his head. "Could've been coincidence. Could've been chance."

"And the slashing of your arm? Even now, you move it stiffly."

"A thief."

George smacked his hand on the surface of the desk, sending papers flying and falling and scattering. "It was *not*. All these things are connected. Why can you not admit the truth?"

"Because I don't know what to do!" the duke roared, shoving back his chair into the painting of the card players and sending it rocking. Two canine heads lifted, bristling. The duke gave them a command to calm, then added more quietly to George, "If there's a plot, it's among men I've known my whole life. And I don't know how to tell which or how to stop them."

"Miss Benton does."

"If she did, she'd have done it."

"She did do it. She will," George replied. Of this, he felt sure. Cass wouldn't let the case go unsolved, because then it would never leave her. And then she'd never be able, truly, to leave George and Ardmore House behind.

He trusted in her stubbornness more than in her feelings for him.

Just for a moment, some emotion must have shown on his face, for his father's eyes sharpened. "You've fallen in love with the lady, haven't you?"

"You called her a lady," George replied. "It's about time."

"She was," granted the duke. "Is. Though I never saw the need for her presence in this house."

"Neither did she, in the end."

"You haven't answered me." Ardmore leaned close, closer. He never smiled, but he looked as if he were considering the notion. "Did you fall in love with Cassandra Benton?"

Did he? Had he? It was . . . something. It was the feeling of wanting to be with her; not wanting to be without her. Not remembering what he'd been like before he met her; not sure how he'd been able to stand it.

She'd changed him. And better yet, she'd made him want to change.

And if he never saw her again, he would never stop missing her.

He'd been foolish not to spot the pattern before. But it was a new one to him, and he'd been wrapped up in the feel of it without seeing it for what it was.

"Yes," he said quietly. "I love her."

"And what are you going to do about it?"

George arched a brow, gesturing with his free hand to the cluttered top of the desk. "Really? You're going to lecture me about doing things?"

Ardmore stood, then shuffled around the side of his desk. "Heirs are more trouble than they're worth."

And that was the end of their familial moment. "Indeed. Shameful how they want to inherit something of value, isn't it?"

The promise of a smile vanished. "Get your hands out of my purse."

"I'm not talking about money. I'm talking about *value*." George fumbled for words, not quite knowing what he meant. The idea teased him. "Maybe they're the same thing."

The duke looked old and tired. Like the sort of man

who'd gambled away his life forty years before, thinking the reckoning would never come, or that he would never have to bear it. "And maybe they're not."

It was an olive branch, a white flag, a dove. George grasped it. "Father. You can trust me. Let me help you."

The duke looked at the piles of correspondence unanswered, bills unpaid. "I can't afford to. I can't take the chance. There's so much here, if you . . ."

He trailed off. George understood, or thought he did. Every day brought another wave of responsibilities and expenses, and once the duke had fallen behind, he could not catch up alone.

"You can trust me," George said again. "You've never let me prove myself, and several years ago it was wise you didn't try. But now—I could help you."

The duke pulled out his watch. "I haven't time to teach you anything now. I must take the dogs to the yard, then I'm due."

"At a gambling den?"

Ardmore stiffened. "It's not for you to question my actions."

"Which means yes." George sighed.

"It's the only place I get any peace," grunted the duke. "Only place I have things as I like them."

If George had been able to move his right shoulder, he would have pressed his temples. "A place where someone is literally dipping into your purse, and you bring home vowels. That's what you like."

The duke swept his hand across the desk, scattering papers and spilling ink and shoving everything to the floor. Gog and Magog leapt to their feet, yelping.

"It's the only time I get away from all this!" shouted the duke. Breathing hard, he stared at the ruin of letters and writing tools. "It's the only time I get to be myself, not Ardmore."

"If you don't feel you're Ardmore after all this time, then no wonder you want to get away," George said quietly.

"I wasn't supposed to be. I wasn't raised to it. But my older brother took sick, and . . . that was that. My father was a selfish sort, chasing women instead of running his dukedom. He hired good servants, good stewards." The duke kicked at a pile of fallen papers. "In that, I've copied his example."

But he was still chasing, George realized. Chasing what he wished for. A duke ought to be the one running the race, and at his own pace.

But he kept that thought inside, saying only, "I see you have never had an example of someone who could do what they say, and no less. Take what they ought, and no more."

"Nor have you," said Ardmore, looking at his litter of possessions with a lost expression.

His grandfather had chased oblivion in women; his father, in cards. George had joked before that he needed his own defining flaw, a vice that dominated his life. It didn't seem funny now.

"Go, then," he told his father. "I will tidy this."

"That's what servants are for," snapped Ardmore. "Know your place."

"I do. This is it. This *should* be it."

Blue eyes met their match. George held his father's gaze. At last, with one of his expressive grunts, with a nod of agreement, the duke turned away.

"Come," he summoned the dogs. And with a thump of boots and a click of canine toenails, they left.

Then George discharged his purpose, crouching on the floor to flip through the letters littering it. Most of them hadn't even been opened.

The duke was like a man in a skiff on the ocean. Every day brought a new wave, and he was almost drowning, and he was afraid to take a hand from the rudder in case his reaching fingers found no help.

George would give him that help without making him reach out for it.

It was easy enough to find the latest communications from the steward in Berkshire, from the old caretaker at the hunting box in Scotland, and from the smaller estate in Northumberland.

He'd take them and read them and learn from them, and he'd begin writing replies. With his father's blessing if he could get it; if he couldn't, he'd simply write to the men on his own. Not with orders, but with questions. And not from here, but from wherever he chose to live instead.

But he rather thought he could get his father's blessing. Who would do more work than absolutely required? Besides Cass, he thought. Cass would, and maybe she'd had an influence on George.

And the restaurant, he thought. That had been enjoyable. Maybe he'd find someone else with a talent that needed funding to grow. What would Cass say? *Find the pattern.*

As if summoned by this thought, a note came to hand. It had been scattered along with everything else from atop the desk, spattered with ink from a tossed inkpot.

Unmistakably, the writing was Cass's. And it bore no postmark, so it had been delivered by hand, which meant that it must have arrived today.

It was directed to both George and his father. It was short, and it was polite—and it was full of hope.

We can solve this. Indeed, I believe we already have. Proceed with the plan: Saturday at nine o'clock in the evening. George knows the place.

Cass

Well. Wasn't that an interesting development? George crumpled the note in his hand, smiling.

Find the pattern. Try everything.

Complete the case.

Maybe that was the answer to winning Cass, too. Not that George was a gambler by nature—but some stakes were irresistible.

Chapter Eighteen

At last, it was Saturday evening. Nine o'clock.

Cass had given Angelus the text to be included on the note: "an exclusive gathering by invitation only." The invitation didn't say what the gathering was for.

Angelus had offered the use of one of his gambling establishments for the evening. If the people invited assumed they would be given a chance to wager in elite company, so be it. The stakes would indeed be high.

Cass had arrived early to make certain of all the details, though her host only looked at her with pitying tolerance and informed her that his servants had everything in hand. She was fizzing with anticipation, though, and checking and rechecking helped her pass the time and settle her nerves.

This gambling hall had the look of a stately home, a stone mansion in the heart of London. Once it had belonged to a marquess. With debt it had changed hands, and now it belonged to a man of no background at all. The grounds around it were slight compared to the wealthy's country estates, but for a city property, it was lavish indeed to have one's own patch of green. A stone staircase stretched up from the street to the building itself, another barrier between Angelus and the rest of the world. As Cass had climbed the steps, she felt herself crossing from one world to another: from Miss Benton to Mrs. Benedetti, from who she'd been before to the person she'd become.

But really, she was always Cass, and always had been and would be.

Now everything was ready. In the grand, turreted mansion, every window blazed with light. It was a beacon, beckoning in the fortunate invited.

Or so they thought themselves.

Inside, the entrance hall stretched wide and yawned high above. It was a restful space, almost sleepy in its rich, muted colors and welcoming furnishings. *Go on, then— stay a while.* While an army of discreet servants welcomed guests, taking wraps and greatcoats and hats and sticks, Cass stood at Angelus's side to observe everyone as they entered. Conscious always of effect, their host was garbed in his usual black and silver, and a chandelier threw down flame light that made him all glitter and shadow.

At his side, Cass was all bright color, and her presence there drew puzzled gazes. *Isn't that the Ardmore bastard? The old duke's daughter . . . ?*

She should have worn her best gown, the green cotton print that had never seen wear while she played the part of Mrs. Benedetti. But she couldn't forget the blue silk of her first ball at George's side, the first gown altered for her. The gown George had undone so reluctantly and so eagerly at once.

It was much too fine for tonight, and it had been left behind at Ardmore House. But Selina, careless of her belongings as someone who had possessions beyond number, said Cass might take whatever she liked once the case was complete.

Maybe Cass should have taken some and turned them

over to Janey to sell. There wouldn't be another five pounds next week. Instead, she'd taken nothing—but Selina had sent something over all the same. It had arrived at Mrs. Jellicoe's lodging house that afternoon, with a note written on expensive, scented paper.

My lady's maid still had your measurements, you tricky creature. I look forward to seeing you tonight.

This gown was a compromise: a little of the ton, a little of plain Cass. It was of beautiful fabric, orange as a sunset, and that was all there was to it. No ornamentation, no embroidery, and certainly no ruffles. It laced up the back, but Janey—always around now, and ever-welcome—had helped Cass into it and could help her out of it again until she was able to have it altered to fasten in the front.

She would like having a sister. She had let her heart grow too small, protecting it. Being everything she thought she had to be. Now she wanted to be herself, the worried and loving and eager parts all together.

If she didn't do Charles's work, or Fox's work anymore, what would she do? A part of her would miss the feeling of purpose. The gratitude, too—when it came. Best of all, the feeling of right being done. Injustice lessened. Talents put to use. She liked that bit of it.

She'd just close this case first. This one last case. Because Cass Benton took pride in her work, whether her heart was in it or not.

On a related note, George had not yet arrived. But he'd be here; she was sure of that. Whether he could coax his father to attend as well . . . she rather thought he would. Ardmore would not be able to resist a chance to gamble with his greatest creditor.

There was plenty to look upon as she waited. First had come the widow of Gregory Knotwirth, the opium eater whose body had been fished from the Thames after a long disappearance. Mrs. Knotwirth was a thin woman of about sixty years, much the age her late husband had been. She was carefully correct in gray edged with black, a woman who had just put off full mourning as according to custom. The strain about her eyes, the wobble in her voice as she greeted Cass and Angelus, indicated that she had not put off her loss along with her blacks.

John Gerry came next, crabbed and leaning on a cane that Angelus complimented effusively. As the two men compared ebony walking-sticks, Cass noted the arrival of James Cavender, a veritable tulip in fashions that even young men would have shied from. He greeted Gerry with both pleasure and puzzlement, then chased both away by accepting a glass of champagne in his left hand and brandy in his right.

Lionel Braithwaite arrived; then Lord and Lady Deverell. Lady Isabel and Callum Jenks. Augustus Fox, rumpled and stout and tired. A dignified elderly man Cass didn't recognize, whom Angelus identified as the elder brother of Francis Lightfoot, who had poisoned himself in despair when his son died. Selina, resplendent in gold satin and waving a cheerful greeting from the side of her middle-aged husband, Lord Wexley, a serious-looking fellow who regarded his wife with adoration.

A very old woman, her hair dressed high in curls of powder-white, entered on the arm of a youth barely old enough to shave. Angelus stepped forward to meet her, his strides covering the ground of three of her own. "Lady Pollard. So glad you were able to join my gathering."

In her papery, wrinkled face, the faded eyes were alert and sharp. "You said my Thomas would want me here."

She clutched at the arm of the young man next to her, stooped back swaying. "This is his grandson, named for him. Thomas Whiting."

And Cass's heart broke a little. This was the mother, then, and the grandson, of the man who had died in what might have been a hunting accident. Every person touched lives, and every loss was deeply felt. One could not know by how many.

She hoped everyone in the entrance hall noticed the arrival of Lady Pollard, who had lost her younger son and lived on. And she hoped the sight struck them to their hearts.

A few others arrived then, people unconnected with the tontine at all—but who held sway in society, and who would Talk About Things. And be listened to. Lady Teasdale, dignified and shrewd; Mrs. Gadolin, young and eager, whose tongue never stopped running. One or the other of the patronesses of Almack's; Cass had never yet learned which was which.

The entrance hall was getting rather full now, the buzz of conversation slightly strained. Should they move along? They had not been directed to. Where would their host lead them? When would the gaming begin?

Everyone here had clearly thought they'd be part of a much larger group, and they weren't sure what to think. Without a group of one's peers to follow, what was the right thing to do?

Last of all, if Cass was recalling the invitation list correctly—and she always did—came the Duke of Ardmore and his son and heir. George Godwin, Lord Northbrook, who had squeezed his injured shoulder into a beautiful coat, and who wore a sling on his right arm. Whom she had dosed with laudanum and left so that she wouldn't have to see the pain in his eyes or feel it within herself.

How wrong she'd been.

She shut her eyes and tried not to think of all that. They belonged in different worlds and he'd no need of her anymore. She should be grateful she'd come to know him; he'd led her to expect more of her life than work and worry.

But she wasn't grateful right now, even as she looked upon him again. She *was* worried. She had that sense of dread that something was not as it ought to be, the same sense she'd felt when Lord Deverell's study remained shut while his wife screamed about Charles's fall.

From a trellis that had never been broken, but had been cut. And mended, with the arrogant certainty that no one would ever check.

Cass overheard a thread of conversation between Angelus and Lady Isabel, something about paintings he had acquired from her. George supposed the late Morrow, Isabel's first husband, had sold to the crime lord as well as to the Duke of Ardmore. The duke, too, had sold to Angelus—or rather bartered, in exchange for forgiveness of some of his debts.

As she listened, a familiar form—scented faintly of oranges—came to stand at her side. She breathed in, smiling, but did not know what to say.

But he did. He always did. "A new gown?" said the voice she loved in her ear. "You are lovely."

She was lovely, he said. Not the gown. Her throat caught before she replied. "It is indeed new. It was a gift from your sister."

"Ah, I hoped you had bought it for your own enjoyment. But to accept a gift, given with good wishes and liking, is very pleasant, too. I hope it brings you great joy to wear it."

She turned to look up at him. Did he look different? Had she hurt him? No, he offered the same quirk of the eyebrow, the same curve of the lip as always. His eyes, though, were fixed upon hers, as if he could not look enough. "I wondered if I would see you tonight."

All that nervousness she thought she had dispelled returned in a quick swoop. "I've too much pride to leave a job undone. And I'm not going to let another woman take credit for my work."

"Lady Isabel Jenks?" George looked confused.

"No." Cass grinned. "Mrs. Benedetti."

"Ah." He returned her grin. "She is to be returned to the ether whence she came, then, having served her purpose."

"She's already gone," Cass confirmed. "The problem is that there were two patterns. That's why we didn't spot them at first. We were trying to fit them together, but they were two separate things, and—"

Just then, Angelus seemed to tire of keeping his guests penned in the entrance hall. With the end of his walking stick, he struck the marble floor. Hard, once, then when the buzz of conversation did not immediately cease, again. Ebony rang on stone, and in the sudden silence, it echoed.

"Follow me into the drawing room," he called out. "We will have food and drink. You must make yourselves comfortable."

And so they did, proceeding into a room that resembled an ordinary drawing room as little as the Prince Regent resembled Cass. Yes, this room was draped in red velvet and cloth of gold, and adorned with paintings that looked old and costly. But there were no tables. No chaises. No sofas or tables or any type of furniture other than chairs. Twenty-four of them, identical, arranged in a circle. On each one was a name card.

Murmuring, people sidled into place. Some chose to

accept beverages from the servants who passed behind them; some took dainties on tiny plates, which were swept away by those same capable servants as soon as the food had been consumed.

Last of all to take his seat was Angelus. Theatrically, he then raised his hands. Those sitting beside him leaned away, as if he had created a stage with the lift of a finger. And then his voice sounded, and the unraveling of the evening began.

"You all know me by reputation, if not by sight," he started. "I counted on your eagerness to meet the elusive Angelus in person, and to join in the most exclusive of games. We will not be gambling tonight—my apologies, Ardmore; I know you are disappointed—but we will be playing a very exciting game instead. It is called tontine, and it is forty years long."

Cass watched the familiar faces: Deverell, Ardmore, Gerry, Cavender, Braithwaite. They were good, very good. Even now, none showed anything but puzzlement. For the sake of those in attendance who did not know, Angelus explained the terms of the tontine's formation so long ago; the original members; the recent deaths.

"As the holder and investor of these funds, I was naturally interested when two enterprising people informed me that they suspected criminal interference. One of them"—he nodded to George—"was Lord Northbrook, whom you all know. The other was a Bow Street Runner named Cassandra Benton."

Augustus Fox lifted his head sharply. Cass met his gaze, wondering if he'd protest that she wasn't formally a Bow Street Runner. She'd *told* Angelus that she wasn't, that women couldn't be.

"A private investigator," she corrected. "Hired by Lord Northbrook to protect the Duke of Ardmore."

Fox's heavy brows lifted. "And a Bow Street Runner in nearly every sense of the word," he added. "I should know, as I'm the magistrate over that court."

Cass became the focus of every gaze. This was notoriety at last, and she did not mind it as she'd thought she might. It was honest, and the freshness of truth buoyed her like air in her lungs. She smiled and gave a little waggle of her fingers to the remainder of the circle. "Hullo, everyone."

"But that is Mrs. Benedetti," squeaked Mrs. Gadolin. "She's the . . . the natural daughter of the old duke. Isn't she? I had tea with her! What will my dear Gadolin say?"

"And so scandalous—I saw her knock at the door of White's!" said the pinch-faced patroness of Almack's.

"You only saw that if you were watching," pointed out Lady Teasdale.

"And Miss Benton's birth, while no concern of yours, was decidedly within wedlock," interjected George.

This did not stop the clamor.

"Is she a duke's daughter or isn't she?"

"An investigator? With no connection to the duke? But . . ."

"I saw Northbrook dancing with her at the Harroughs' ball. Do you suppose . . ."

"I cannot credit it. I invited her into my home!"

At last, the Duke of Ardmore bestirred himself to speak. "So did I."

Lady Isabel, too, said it, "So did I."

And then so did Selina, adding, "And I would do it again. At any time."

The other women fell silent, looking at Cass, then each other, then Cass again.

At last, she realized why: because they were worried.

She had underestimated the women of the ton, just as she had herself. She had thought they made no difference, but they were the backbone of society. They were the hands of the city, the conscience of Parliament, the womb of the world. They were divided into so many pieces that she'd not seen their worth. It was easy to overlook it, especially when the men who ran the government and made the laws were convinced they did it on their own.

They didn't. These matrons mattered in countless ways, large and small. A woman who gave pleasure to her friends by throwing a truly splendid tea had made a difference to them. If she paid her servants a good wage, she made a difference. If she carried water in for her charwoman to spare the elderly woman's aching back, she had made a difference.

If she invited a Bow Street Runner into her house, she made a difference. But she might worry about what sort of difference it would be. Would it be the sort that would strip away her own consequence?

No, Cass wanted to tell them. *It's all right. You will only make your hearts bigger.*

George was sneaking looks at her. She made herself meet his eye. She wouldn't pretend she was unaware, and she wouldn't dodge from his gaze as if she feared him. He was part of the job, and she would tie it all up neatly and put it behind her.

Her knees shook, and she was relieved she was sitting down.

"I am reluctant to take any credit." George spoke up. "Anyone could have done what I did. My own role was nothing compared to Miss Benton's, though I wish I could say otherwise."

Her mouth dropped open.

"Also," he added, "she is descended from gentlefolk. We all care about a person's accomplishments, but we are in the habit of caring about antecedents, too. There you have it, then. Miss Benton deserves your respect."

Damn the man. He was tossing about that R-word again. There was nothing so dangerous as words that started with R.

"Thank you," she said, feeling the words wholly inadequate. "And thank you all for being here today. This evening. Ah—tonight."

"You've no flair for the dramatic at all." Angelus sighed. "Tell the good people why they're here, Miss Benton."

"Right." Cass cleared her throat. Wiggled on her seat. Lifted her chin and spoke the matter simply. "We've sorted out which of you is a murderer."

Chapter Nineteen

"Don't just *tell* them," said Angelus. "Make it amusing."

George laughed. From across the tight little circle, his father glared.

It wasn't funny, really. But he was in the same room as Cass again, and even though the tontine case was about to be wrapped up and knotted and stowed away, now everyone here knew who she really was and what she'd done. Under her own name.

That made him happy, a sort of happiness that twisted him all up inside.

"Oh," said Cass. "All right. Um—well, when Lord Northbrook hired me to investigate what we began to call the tontine case, he first had me keep watch on Lord Deverell. The man was his godfather and he had a great fondness for him. At the same time, he vowed to watch over the safety of his own father."

"Some job he did," bit off Cavender. "Since the duke almost died."

"I doubt that very much," said the dry little voice of Gerry. His knobbly fingers worked the head of his cane, twisting it. "Ardmore was never in such danger as you professed, was he, dear boy?"

Angelus frowned. "You're quite spoiling the story. Don't interrupt Miss Benton."

Cass blinked at this. Unused to having elderly men chastised on her behalf, probably. "Right. So . . . Lord Northbrook was suspicious of the deaths of Mr. Whiting, Mr. Knotwirth, and Mr. Lightfoot." With every name, she nodded to that man's loved one. "If you all will forgive me—each of those deaths took advantage of a characteristic the victim was known to possess. So Lord Northbrook and I assumed that if further crimes were to be carried out, they would follow the same pattern. We soon learned that we were wrong."

She described her placement in Lord Deverell's household. "I *knew* I recognized you!" exclaimed Lady Deverell.

Then came the familiar events: the fall of the footman—unidentified in Cass's retelling—from the trellis. The attack on Lord Deverell, discovered soon after. The note implying he would die of his injuries.

"But he didn't," said George, recognizing this to be unnecessary since Lord Deverell, very much alive, was seated only a few chairs away from him. "And he chose to hide the fact of his attack. Which allowed Miss Benton, as Mrs. Benedetti, to infiltrate the ton and determine whether the rest of you were concerned about your safety, or curious about the fate of your old compatriot."

Angelus looked pleased. "Infiltrate. A good word."

"Enough of this," said Mrs. Knotwirth in a tone as sharp and brittle as broken glass. "Who killed my husband?"

"And my son," added Lady Pollard.

"My brother." Francis Lightfoot's elder brother sat taut as a bowstring, waiting.

"I didn't know that at first," explained Cass. "And even now, it's only a guess. But I know who stabbed Lord Deverell. Because I know who slashed the Duke of Ardmore, and who shot Lord Northbrook with an arrow. Those acts made an entirely new pattern, and the culprit was clear."

"Well?" Deverell folded his arms, his face flushed red with drink or strain—or both. "Who was it, then? Name the blackguard at once. We've a magistrate here to see him settled."

Cass looked at George for a moment. He nodded. Then her clear brown gaze held Lord Deverell's. "It was you."

George had never been in battle, but he imagined this was what happened when a bomb exploded: the detonation, then a ringing silence, then a rain of chaos as dust fell and began to settle. Thus it was when Cass accused Lord Deverell before his peers and friends and the greatest gossips of the ton. And a magistrate from Bow Street, for good measure. Complete quiet followed for at least fifteen seconds; then no one could say enough at once.

Lord Deverell shook his head. George could read the movement of his lips: *Madness. The girl's mad.*

"That's not possible," said the Duke of Ardmore over the sudden clamor. "Deverell could not have fit through the window of the coaching inn to slash my arm."

"He had help, of course, from his wife." Cass looked as cool and unbothered as if she were drinking champagne at a ball.

Another silence, as if all talk were smothered by a blanket.

"It took me too long to realize it," Cass said. "Even after the, ah, footman communicated that Lady Deverell sometimes climbed down the trellis outside her bedchamber. Even then, I wasn't certain until I saw the trellis at Deverell Place had been cut and mended."

"That doesn't prove anything except that I care about maintaining our property," sniffed Lady Deverell. She looked waxy and hard in the warm, gleaming room, like a candle unlit. "These accusations are a scandal, and I intend to see them answered in court."

"You want to go to court?" Fox looked interested. "I'd be happy to hear the case at Bow Street. But maybe you'd like to hear the rest of Miss Benton's evidence first."

As Lady Deverell gaped, a feeling of satisfaction stole through George. Look at how they all listened to Cass; look at how Fox believed in her skill and judgment.

Cass continued. "Who knew that this footman liked to climb trellises? Who would have guessed that tampering with a trellis would remove the footman from his post indefinitely?"

Lord Deverell waved this off, then slid a finger into his cravat to tug it from his perspiring neck. "Someone would have had to know that the footman was a Bow Street Runner. And we didn't know that until after I was attacked."

"Someone would have had to know only that the footman could be used as an excuse," Cass replied. "It was very well planned. You have a fondness for injuring people, and not, perhaps, caring whether they would be killed. Fortunately the footman will be all right as soon as his broken leg is mended, and he will be back to his true post at Bow Street."

Lord Deverell was sweating profusely now. "I tell you I had nothing to do with that! I was in my study alone, and—asleep."

"It was very well planned," Cass repeated. "In fact, I suspect Lord Deverell planned the whole thing. Beginning a few years ago, with the deaths of Mr. Whiting, Mr. Lightfoot, and Mr. Knotwirth."

"Ridiculous." The earl moistened his lips with his

tongue. "Madness. These are wild accusations. I had nothing at all to do with the death of Lightfoot."

Too late, he realized what he had said. Too late for denial; too late for his wife's composure. She spun from her chair, making a desperate dash for the door—only to be blocked by the same excellent servants who had given her the food and drink she had been so happy to consume shortly before.

"That's not what I meant," tried Deverell. "Of course I had nothing to do with their deaths. Any deaths. Any attacks—any . . ." He trailed off, looking alarmingly red. As footmen came to flank his chair, someone pressed a glass of water into his hand. He took a sip, then dashed it to the floor.

Angelus watched this as if an observer at a play. "Be kind to the carpets. They are very expensive. Ah—Miss Benton? Lord Northbrook? Perhaps you'd like to fill in the remaining gaps in our tale. It is so edifying."

"It all comes back to money, I suppose," said Lady Isabel. "So many cases do."

And indeed this one did. Delicately, Cass communicated that it must have become clear to Lord and Lady Deverell about two years before that there would be no more children of their marriage. "His lordship had a daughter of his first wife and two of his present lady, but he has no heir. He must have become worried about money, that he'd leave his family with nothing."

"And there sat a fortune in the unworthy hands of a crime lord," Angelus intoned. "It was easier to eliminate a few of your friends than ask me to unwind the tontine, wasn't it, Deverell? Though you got to that point eventually."

"A fifth share now is better than the whole thing in the

future," blustered Deverell as beefy footmen held him down in his seat. "That's all I admit to. Wanting to unwind the damned tontine."

This was not convincing. Ardmore leaned forward, his eyes ice. "You stabbed me!" The words seemed to astound him as soon as they left his mouth. "You . . . had me stabbed? *You?*"

"*And* had your son shot," George pointed out.

"Only with an arrow," tossed back Ardmore.

"Lady Deverell slashed your arm, Your Grace," said Cass to the duke. "If she could manage the trellis at her house, she could manage the climb outside the inn. And she could have fit through the small windows."

Now the duke's nostrils were flaring. He looked like one of his hounds, bristling and growling. "You sent your wife to kill me?"

Deverell cringed back, now using the silent footmen as shelter. "No, not that. Never that. I was horrified when I heard you were near death."

"I think," Cass said, "he needed you to perceive danger connected with the tontine. He needed you to want to dissolve it. That was the reason for the failed attacks upon both you and your son—and himself."

"What about me?" Gerry said in his dry little voice. "I'd have had to agree. And Cavender, and Braithwaite."

Cass regarded him gravely. "I am very sorry, sir, to say that I think you might soon have suffered a fall if you did not agree. It would appear an accident."

"It would fit the pattern," George mused. "The first pattern. The original pattern."

Cass nodded. "Anyone who didn't agree would be—I don't know how to put it."

"No need to be delicate now," said Braithwaite. It

was odd to see him without a touch of humor on his big square face. "They'd have killed us off. A man we've known since boyhood, and he and his wife would have killed us for money."

"People do," said Callum Jenks. "They so often do. And it is never right."

Augustus Fox cleared his throat. "There's no proof here. Nothing but coincidence and likelihood and inference. I believe it all, but there's nothing here the law can act upon." He heaved himself to his feet. "If you don't mind, sir"—this he addressed to Angelus—"I'll have a bit of a walk. Let you all sort this out. When I return, you can let me know what you'd like me to do—if there's anything I can do, as magistrate."

And George understood: the stern old fellow was giving them a chance to end this situation as they saw fit. Because justice and the law weren't always the same, and the law could do little to a peer, even if he were caught with blood on his hands.

Once the servants at the door had stepped aside, letting Fox exit, Lady Deverell crept back to her place in the circle of chairs.

"None of us here represent the law," said Angelus. "Not officially. A lady of society need never be tried or imprisoned. But should there not be some punishment?"

"The victims' families would have to prosecute," spoke up old Lady Pollard. The evening's events seemed to have diminished her. "I do not wish to spend my final days fighting with criminals."

"Perhaps," suggested Braithwaite, "Deverell's share of the tontine could be split and distributed to the victims' families."

"That is like putting a price on a life," protested Mrs. Knotwirth.

"It is," said Angelus, "and that is the whole purpose of a tontine. It is a damnable arrangement. I recommend you dissolve it at once, especially since you all arranged it as twenty-year-olds. You hadn't the right to sign a binding contract. If I'd chosen to embezzle your funds in the intervening years, you'd have had no recourse." His smile was vulpine.

"Fine with me," Cavender said. "Split the money evenly and be done with it."

"What about the shares of the members who've died?" George asked.

"I'm not a moral compass," said Angelus. "You must find one of those yourself."

"And their punishment?" Lady Teasdale, powerful and blunt, pointed a finger at Lord and Lady Deverell. "How much of this are we to allow to circulate outside of this room?"

"I should think word will get out," Cass said. "It always does. Lord and Lady Deverell might want to live abroad from this time forward."

"A good shunning, that's the answer." Cavender sounded cheerful. "The law can't touch you, but no one else will either."

"The punishment will fall on our daughters," cried Lady Deverell. "It should fall on ourselves alone."

George cut a glance at his father. "Children often suffer because of their parents' actions. I regret that yours will be no different."

Angelus stood, making a graceful, sweeping gesture with his arms. "Have the magistrate brought back in," he called to no one in particular. Instantly, three servants left the room to do his bidding.

Cass, too, jumped to her feet. "It was George who solved this," she blurted. "I mean—Lord Northbrook. He saw the pattern and arranged everything. My investigation. This gathering. He . . . saved his father's life, and his own."

George could no more have made sense of her words than if she were speaking French. He'd never been an outstanding student. Couldn't be bothered to try hard, because what was the point? He'd be a duke one day no matter what.

His wasn't the only puzzled face as he looked around the circle. "I didn't do anything," he replied. "I hired you."

Cass shook her head so earnestly that a lock of fiery hair fell from its pins. "That's something, isn't it? You didn't know what to do, so you hired an expert." She pulled a face. "Sort of an expert. You wouldn't expect to cook your own food; you hire an expert. You saw there was a danger. No one else saw that, and if you'd done nothing, more people might have died.

"And besides," she added, "you did a great deal more than hire me. You housed me and planned with me and gave me the resources and protection of your name."

A flame that had gone out within George when she'd left Ardmore House flared into existence again. Sparked. Glowed. Grew. "I thought you considered me lazy."

"No! You just don't spend your time as other people do. But that's not a fault; that's a choice and a skill."

She looked around the circle, only now appearing to notice the curious stares of everyone present. "So," she stammered, lacing her fingers together, "that's all I wanted to say."

She dropped into her chair and slouched against the back.

And George . . . George smiled.

He'd been wrong about so much.

He'd helped to build his own cage and hadn't even realized it. He'd been content with what he thought was due him, when he hadn't thought of what he could *do*. Until chance, and Cass, and the thread of a pattern snagged his notice.

And in the end? There was a reason, a purpose to it all. Life itself. And the truth, and knowing it, and seeing wrongs righted.

Cass was holding his gaze, and her eyes were more beautiful than amber. Warmer and brighter than the ring he'd slid onto her finger without knowing why it mattered, very much, that he carry out that part of the charade himself.

It really had mattered, in the end.

Well. How about that.

When Fox returned to the drawing room, the rest was all coda. Angelus informed him that Lord and Lady Deverell were planning an extended trip to the Continent for their health. "I think they ought to leave within the week, don't you all?" he asked the room at large.

Mrs. Knotwirth marched from her seat to glare in the faces of the earl and countess. "A week? I'll give them forty-eight hours."

"A woman of spirit," Angelus approved. "Forty-eight hours it is. Oh—and while I have you all gathered, might I make it known that I would prefer no one accept vowels from the Duke of Ardmore anymore? Consider it . . . more than a suggestion." Again, that vulpine smile.

Everyone was starting to stand, and mill, and whisper, and prepare to leave. This didn't prevent the duke from jumping to his feet and snapping, "You can't treat me like a child whose purse you can take away."

Angelus lifted black brows. "I can, for you've no more sense than a child. Even with a fifth share of the tontine paid to you, you'll have tens of thousands in debt. And you owe most of it to me."

"He's right," said George. "And you will leave it to me. It might take me most of a lifetime to discharge all your debts."

"Not much of a legacy to leave your son," Angelus said. "Well, you must do as you like."

"He does, always. No one has a hold over him," replied George. "No one can touch his influence or take his title."

The duke was too dignified to say *I'm right here,* but his eyes burned them.

"Father. If there were something you cared about—" George shrugged, hoping the gesture communicated both *I wish there were* and *Damn you* at once.

Ardmore was silent.

"That's that." George turned away. "Thank you, Mr. Gabriel. It has been most satisfying to work with you on this case."

Angelus nodded. "Ah, and here is Miss Benton, who skulks about and listens at doorways. Have you arranged a meeting time?"

Cass slipped to George's side, ticking on her fingers. "Gerry and Cavender will return at noon tomorrow. Braithwaite will be here no more than a half hour later. Your Grace, perhaps you can join them as well? It will be time to dissolve the tontine."

"Of course I'll be here," grumbled the duke. "And . . ." He shuffled his feet, looking decidedly uncomfortable. "I should like to see it split eight ways, if the others agree.

Some for Knotwirth's widow and Whiting's mother and Lightfoot's brother."

"And the eighth share?" Angelus sounded skeptical.

"Those girls of Deverell's," said the duke gruffly. "They're just children. Not sure if they've got a dowry, but when they return to England . . ."

Something softened in their host's manner. "If the others agree, I will see it done. And even if the others do *not* agree, I will see the girls dowered. Though I am rather good at getting people to agree with me."

"That will make all the difference to Deverell's daughters." Cass's gloved fingers, unadorned by jewelry, laced before her. "Scandal without money is insurmountable. Scandal plus money means notoriety. They might do very well once the time comes for them to marry, some years from now."

"I'm glad," George said to his father, "that you will not allow those children to suffer for the wrongs of their parents."

That seemed about all there was to say to him, and George turned away again. Cass joined Augustus Fox, drawing the older man into a conversation.

"Wait. Angelus." The duke spoke up as if the words were ripped from him, unwilling. Yet his voice came.

"Ye-es?" Their host's response was slow.

"Would you care to buy any more of my paintings? To decrease my debt?"

Slowly, George turned back to regard his father. The duke gave a curt nod. It meant . . . something. Apology, maybe? Maybe. Maybe that was what it was.

George nodded back. There. Maybe the duke would take that as forgiveness. Maybe he'd assume George had a crick in his neck. It was all the same to him. He wouldn't believe Ardmore was ready to change until his behavior altered—and stayed that way.

Cass was saying something that had the magistrate nodding his heavy head, then looking grave. To George's surprise, Fox took her in his arms and gave her a tight squeeze, then a pat on the head. It looked more than anything like a father bidding a beloved daughter farewell.

"Everything all right there?" George asked when Cass again made her way to his side.

"Yes. I think so." Cass looked back at Fox, biting her lip. Her eyes were a little teary. "I told him I wasn't planning to work with Charles anymore, but that Janey would. And I told him he ought to pay her, even if it meant taking part of Charles's salary away from him and giving it to his wife—soon-to-be wife—instead."

Interesting. "And how did he take the matter?"

She gave a little laugh. "He hugged me. In all the years I've known him, he's never done that. He hugged me and said he'd see it done, and if I ever wanted to come back, he'd find a place for me."

"And how did *you* take the matter?"

"Very well, as you might expect. Could anyone mind hearing that? He listened to me. He implied he'd miss my work. It is . . ." As she considered, a smile lit her face. "It is beautiful to hear."

"What you said about me was beautiful to hear, too. It wasn't necessary for you to say it."

"I did make a spectacle of myself, didn't I? But you made a great deal of difference. I hope you realize it."

"Yes, I do. It's odd. But I rather do." He smiled. "Now. Because of you. Thank you."

She shook off his thanks. "You've done it yourself, you know. And I'm not only talking about this plan to save your father. You invested in the restaurant; you bought supplies for photographia."

"Helio-ichnographia," he corrected.

"Whatever you want to call it. George, you're your own man. You're not like your father. You spend your money on helping other people get ahead, and on learning."

Surely there could be no more beautiful sound than Cass Benton, professing her faith in him in that wonderful voice of hers. "You make me sound marvelous."

She went pink. He loved it when she went pink. "That's because you are."

"Such faith in me?"

"Yes," she said. "I have it. And now you do too, don't you?"

"I do, though it took me a bit of time. I had to sort out who I was apart from my title and my father's son."

"You are so many things." She smiled, but the expression fell at once. "And I am no longer a Bow Street Runner, nor am I Mrs. Benedetti."

George tried to hold out his right hand to her, remembering the sling only too late. He settled for the left, taking her fingertips in his. "Who you are is enough for me, which means it ought to be enough for anyone."

She rolled her eyes. "So much confidence! If only one could bottle it."

"I don't mean that my opinion is more worthwhile than anyone else's—though I shouldn't care to disagree if you said so." He grinned. "I only mean this: who should care more about the woman I love than I do?"

She gaped. "I thought you weren't going to pursue me."

"I'm not. I'm standing right here with you. Side by side. Will you allow it?"

"Yes. Oh, yes." Her eyes were wide and starry.

A weight lifted from his heart; a sweet fullness settled

within it instead. It felt like certainty. Like home. "I wonder if you might like to be Lady Northbrook? I've already given you a ring, you know."

She tilted her head, all impishness. "That was a fake proposal for a fake person."

"Not altogether. I could never have slipped it on your finger in that way if a piece of me hadn't already belonged to you."

"Ah. Patterns." Cass tapped her temple. "You just said you loved me. But really, you've been besotted with me ever since you first called me plain, haven't you?"

"Fascinated, yes. Intrigued by, undoubtedly. *Besotted* is such a watery sort of word. It sounds as though all the feeling is on my side, like I'm soaked in it. When really, it all comes from you. Wonderful you."

"You really do love me," Cass said. "That's quite wonderful."

"Couldn't you tell that from the pattern of my words? I dropped enough clues."

"Oh, yes. But sometimes one craves a confession, even if the solution is perfectly obvious."

"All right, we'll do it properly." Holding her hand for balance, he sank with some difficulty—a man wasn't used to having his arm pinioned like this—to one knee. "I love you, you brilliant woman. If you'll have me, I'll love you my whole life long. And I'll try to keep up with your determined mind and I will sometimes be serious."

She beamed at him, heedless of the attention they were gathering. "Will you undo my buttons?"

"Now? Gladly."

She laughed, pulling him to his feet. "I love you, too. And I'll have you, and happily."

George put two fingers to his mouth and let out a piercing whistle. "Attention, please, everyone! I am about to kiss Miss Benton, as she has just agreed to be my wife."

"The scandal sheets will be full tomorrow," commented Isabel.

"I know it," said George. "Everyone will be shocked that the Duke of Ardmore is selling some of his paintings." And then he lowered his head to Cass's and found her lips, and neither of them cared about anything else.

Epilogue

One Year Later

"Three more applications today, my lady." The maid dipped her head, handing over the papers.

Cass thanked her, settling the applications atop the desk in her study and shuffling through them quickly. This one wanted a bit of capital to open a dress shop in a village on the outskirts of London; that one wanted help paying off a surgeon's bills. The third asked for references to teach French to a nobleman's children. The rest of the application was in French; Cass laughed and set it aside to show to George later.

The one with the dress shop, she'd look into herself. Perhaps Janey would like to research the application about the surgeon's bill; she scribbled a note to remind her to ask her sister-in-law when Janey and Charles came to dine the next day.

Over the years, Cass had seen that simply giving money to Charles never did him a bit of good. He had no use in mind for it, and so it dribbled away. But to give money to someone with a need, or a talent? What a difference that made to someone like George's friend, Antoine

Fournier. Or to Janey, who with a sliver of a Bow Street salary had now hired three other women to sell clothing for her.

With her pin money, then—which seemed a ridiculously generous amount—Cass gave out small loans and donations. Women had simply to apply to the marchioness, and someone researched the merit of each application. Janey helped with some; so did her friend Mags. So too did Lady Isabel Jenks, when her attention could be pulled from her baby daughter. Each woman had a particular set of skills.

And each was paid, always. Even Lady Isabel, wealthier by far than Cass and George, who took the money with a bemused smile and probably popped it right into the poor-box at church.

Other applications, Cass researched herself, her Bow Street knowledge drawing her into parts of London that the ordinary marchioness would never penetrate.

But Cass was no ordinary marchioness.

The sort of marchioness she was—one with a courtesy title, as George had once explained—did not have much with which to occupy herself unless she so chose.

And she did.

The fallout from the revelation of Cass's true identity ought to have been dire. Had she merely tricked people, it surely would have been. But knowing she was part of a case, one that struck to the heart of the ton and saved lives and involved Angelus and adultery and murder and a fortune? She was more notorious than ever, and this time for her own sake.

It was rather like the tonnishness that had cloaked Callum Jenks in respectability when he saved Lord Wexley—and oh yes, now people recalled that Miss Benton had been part of that rescue as well. And she *was* the great-granddaughter of a gentleman, wasn't she? So her blood had a tinge of blue.

Besides this, she hosted the most wonderful teas at a restaurant called Antony's—the same place, in fact, where she and her marquess had held their wedding breakfast. The power of a perfectly made quiche or hand-pie was strong; the enticement of perfectly brewed teas and little sugary cakes was irresistible.

"You shall be a marvelous society hostess," said George after the first, not-entirely-not-awkward of these gatherings. "You are so wonderfully yourself, and people will love you for it."

"You confuse me with yourself. People love *you*."

"Yes, well, that's only because I'm a little of everything. Enough to make people feel comfortable but not inferior."

Cass had laughed. "Nonsense. People love you because you are delightful to be around. You have a happy heart."

"I do when I'm around you."

"Silver tongue," she teased. "Well, I can play the part of a marchioness."

"No part. Just you." He kissed her hand. "You will make the title yours, and not the other way around."

For himself, Lord Northbrook was hardly as tonnish as he'd used to be. Though he'd never been much fun at the gambling tables, he'd at least been out in company at all hours, dressed in the latest and best. He'd dropped out of the pinkest company the year before, with the proper excuse of his mother's health. But now he was as likely to be found at Antony's as he was at Ardmore House— perhaps no wonder, as he'd moved to his own house as soon as the tontine was dissolved. Unnecessary, since there was ever so much more space in Ardmore House now that the duke had sold all his oil paintings . . . though rumor had it he was already collecting more.

Cass set aside the three new applications. From the corner of her desk, Grandmama smiled at her.

This had been Cass's wedding gift from Charles, who explained, "I didn't spend all your money. I had a copy made of Grandmama's painting. This is the original."

"So you used my own money to buy me a gift."

"I used your gift to me to get a gift for you," Charles corrected.

"So glib," Cass said, shaking her head. "Thank you. I wouldn't have taken the miniature from you."

"I know. And I wouldn't have asked you to go without it. She loved you that much, Cassie." He turned very red. "I love you too, you know."

"I know that, you oaf. And I love you, too."

Yes, she and Charles got along quite well now that neither of them relied upon the other. At least once a week, he and Janey came to dine at the small house Cass and George rented in Piccadilly. They kept Cass informed of all the most interesting cases going at Bow Street, and sometimes she offered ideas. They'd become interested in George's experiment room too, so he always showed him his latest assays in helio . . . whatever it was. The process had a different name every week.

Pushing back her chair, she decided to check on the fate of George's latest experiment. His room was next to her own study, on the second floor of their little house, so she had only to slip from behind her desk and rap at the door.

"One moment," came the reply. "Let me put away my plate before you open the door."

Ah. He was working in the dim amber light, then. When he bade her enter, she drank in the sight of him. She loved him at work like this, all preoccupied and rumpled. "What plate were you working with? One of glass?"

He turned to face her, smiling. He had a smudge of bitumen on one cheek. "Yes, and I think I've got the image to hold. It's not at all clear, but if I let it sit in the camera longer, perhaps it'll become so."

"And we'll be able to see . . . ?"

He laughed. "Nothing very exciting. The line of the roof visible through this window."

"An image from life," Cass marveled. "That would be very exciting indeed."

"If it works," George cautioned. "I might be imagining it. It's very faint yet; it might only be the way I've spread the bitumen."

"Even so. It's wonderful. You'll hit upon the answer someday."

George nodded. "Even if it never comes to anything, I enjoy the process of trying."

"That's what life is." She smiled. "A process of trying."

"Getting philosophical with me?" Her handsome husband looked wolfishly at her. "You know how that excites me, darling Cass. Close the door, will you?"

And Lord Northbrook carried out the process of bringing his lady to pleasure an unprecedented number of times in one afternoon. The experiment was enjoyable for both.

Books by Bestselling Author
Fern Michaels

___The Jury	0-8217-7878-1	$6.99US/$9.99CAN
___Sweet Revenge	0-8217-7879-X	$6.99US/$9.99CAN
___Lethal Justice	0-8217-7880-3	$6.99US/$9.99CAN
___Free Fall	0-8217-7881-1	$6.99US/$9.99CAN
___Fool Me Once	0-8217-8071-9	$7.99US/$10.99CAN
___Vegas Rich	0-8217-8112-X	$7.99US/$10.99CAN
___Hide and Seek	1-4201-0184-6	$6.99US/$9.99CAN
___Hokus Pokus	1-4201-0185-4	$6.99US/$9.99CAN
___Fast Track	1-4201-0186-2	$6.99US/$9.99CAN
___Collateral Damage	1-4201-0187-0	$6.99US/$9.99CAN
___Final Justice	1-4201-0188-9	$6.99US/$9.99CAN
___Up Close and Personal	0-8217-7956-7	$7.99US/$9.99CAN
___Under the Radar	1-4201-0683-X	$6.99US/$9.99CAN
___Razor Sharp	1-4201-0684-8	$7.99US/$10.99CAN
___Yesterday	1-4201-1494-8	$5.99US/$6.99CAN
___Vanishing Act	1-4201-0685-6	$7.99US/$10.99CAN
___Sara's Song	1-4201-1493-X	$5.99US/$6.99CAN
___Deadly Deals	1-4201-0686-4	$7.99US/$10.99CAN
___Game Over	1-4201-0687-2	$7.99US/$10.99CAN
___Sins of Omission	1-4201-1153-1	$7.99US/$10.99CAN
___Sins of the Flesh	1-4201-1154-X	$7.99US/$10.99CAN
___Cross Roads	1-4201-1192-2	$7.99US/$10.99CAN

Available Wherever Books Are Sold!
Check out our website at www.kensingtonbooks.com

More from Bestselling Author
JANET DAILEY